C000112269

JANE EYROTICA

**Charlotte Brontë
and
Karena Rose**

pıatkus

PIATKUS

First published in the United States in 2012 by Skyhorse Publishing
This paperback edition published in 2012 by Piatkus

Copyright © 2012 Karena Rose

The moral right of the author has been asserted.

*All characters and events in this publication, other than those
clearly in the public domain, are fictitious and any resemblance
to real persons, living or dead, is purely coincidental.*

All rights reserved.
No part of this publication may be reproduced, stored in a
retrieval system, or transmitted, in any form or by any means, without
the prior permission in writing of the publisher, nor be otherwise circulated
in any form of binding or cover other than that in which it is published
and without a similar condition including this condition being
imposed on the subsequent purchaser.

A CIP catalogue record for this book
is available from the British Library.

ISBN 978-0-7499-5942-5

Printed and bound in Great Britain by
Clays Ltd, St Ives plc

Papers used by Piatkus are from well-managed forests
and other responsible sources.

MIX
Paper from
responsible sources
FSC
www.fsc.org FSC® C104740

Piatkus
An imprint of
Little, Brown Book Group
100 Victoria Embankment
London EC4Y 0DY

An Hachette UK Company
www.hachette.co.uk

www.piatkus.co.uk

Table of Contents

CHAPTER I 1

CHAPTER II 9

CHAPTER III 15

CHAPTER IV 23

CHAPTER V... 33

CHAPTER VI 43

CHAPTER VII 49

CHAPTER VIII 57

CHAPTER IX 65

CHAPTER X... 75

CHAPTER XI 83

CHAPTER XII 97

CHAPTER XIII 107

CHAPTER XIV 115

CHAPTER XV... 121

CHAPTER XVI 133

CHAPTER XVII 139

CHAPTER XVIII 151

CHAPTER XIX 159

CHAPTER XX... 167

CHAPTER XXI 179

CHAPTER XXII 191

CHAPTER XXIII 197

CHAPTER XXIV 207

CHAPTER XXV 217

CHAPTER XXVI 223

CHAPTER XXVII 233

CHAPTER XXVIII.. 241

CHAPTER XXIX 251

CHAPTER XXX 257
CHAPTER XXXI 265
CHAPTER XXXII 269
CHAPTER XXXIII 273
CHAPTER XXXIV 279

CHAPTER I

There was no possibility of meeting John Reed that day. I had been wandering in the leafless shrubbery of the grounds an hour that morning, trying to lose Bessie, my younger cousin's nursemaid, but to no avail. John and I would have to see each other later.

A cold winter wind began to blow, bringing with it clouds so sombre and rain so penetrating, that further out-door exercise was now out of the question. Bessie called at me to turn back, and I abandoned my search for John and joined her and my younger cousins in walking back to the house. John and I had agreed to meet beside the willow trees this afternoon, but something had clearly waylaid him.

I was glad of it since it was a chilly afternoon and I did not relish the thought of lying under the wet willow tree with him for a further hour, always conscious that at any moment we might be discovered, our cheeks burning with the knowledge that we were doing something wrong yet unable to stop ourselves. Instead, I returned to the house, my heart saddened by the chidings from the nurse Bessie, and humbled by the consciousness of my physical inferiority to the beautiful Eliza and Georgiana Reed, my younger cousins.

The said Eliza and Georgiana clustered around their mama in the drawing-room as soon as we returned. She lay luxuriously on a sofa by the fireside with her darlings about her (for the time being neither of them quarrelling nor crying), and looked perfectly happy. Me, she had dispensed from joining the group saying, "She regretted to be under the necessity of keeping me at a distance; but until she heard from Bessie that I was endeavouring in good earnest to acquire a more sociable and childlike disposition—she really must exclude me from privileges intended only for good, pretty, little children."

"What does Bessie say I have done?" I asked, wondering if it was my trying to wander off on our walk that had angered the nursemaid.

"Jane, I don't like cavillers or questioners," returned Mrs. Reed. "Be seated somewhere and until you can speak pleasantly, remain silent."

I pursed my lips and left the room, knowing where I would go; where I stole to whenever I had a rare, free moment to myself.

A breakfast-room adjoined the drawing-room and I slipped in there. It contained a bookcase and, checking that I was not watched, I snatched a favoured volume from the shelf. I mounted onto the window-seat, my heart thudding in my chest and my fingers shaking in anticipation. Gathering up my feet, I sat cross-legged and drew the red curtain around me, its silken material slippery in my hot, wet grasp.

Folds of scarlet drapery shut in my view to my right; cascading undulations of fiery red that mirrored the tingling rush of heat I could feel pumping through my body. To my left, the clear glass offered a pale blank of mist and cloud; a scene of wet lawn and storm-beat shrub with ceaseless rain sweeping away wildly before a long and lamentable blast. I shivered. The droplets of rain trickled down the pane and I turned and pressed my damp back against its shocking coolness, gasping.

With eager, trembling fingers I leafed through my book,

the familiar pages sliding softly against my thumb like a caress until I reached my desired place. There I gasped again.

A pair of deep, dark eyes burnt into mine.

I pressed my back harder against the chilling glass pane and felt a rush of heat sweep through me. I had seen the portrait many times since discovering it a few months ago in a worn copy of collected paintings. I had slowly been making my way through the contents of the bookcase in the drawing-room, devouring each book as I went when I came across it. The corner of this particular unnamed portrait had been turned down, and it had caught my attention immediately.

Those eyes. They smoldered into mine, penetrating deep into my soul and laying bare my naked core. Upon first seeing them, I had felt a jolt of pleasure beneath my petticoat; a tingling throb that I wished I felt when I looked upon John Reed, but he did not compare.

Slowly my finger traced the figure's strong jaw-line, rubbing the smooth, crisp page. I did not even know his name. I imagined by his rich, black clothing and jeweled adornments that he must be wealthy and the way that he stood reclining against a paneled wall with his broad shoulders hunched made him appear arrogant and dangerous. The sweep of rough stubble across his chin and his unruly dark hair assured me that he would not be taken in by the neat, constrained prettiness of Eliza or Georgiana. His spirit desired a kindred wild, screaming soul.

A scarlet blush scorched my cheeks and a throb tore through my stomach. I put my hand to my chest, imagining it was his, and traced the delicate curve of my collarbone, leaving a burning trail across my skin. I tilted my head back, letting my mouth drop open as I pictured his full lips sweeping feather-light kisses over my neck. I moved my hand down lower, caressing the bodice of my dress, feeling myself swell in my stays.

Suddenly the breakfast-room door flew open and I jumped, snatching my hand away.

"Jane!" cried the voice of John Reed.

He paused, finding the room apparently empty.

"Jane?" he continued. "Where are you? Mother thought she saw you come in here. I am sorry I did not meet you at the willow trees but something came up. I am free now."

Relieved I had drawn the curtains, I fervently wished that he would not discover my hiding-place for I was still upset that we had not met under the willow trees. With my book balanced on my knee, those dark eyes still boring into me, I waited, pleading he would go away. I suspected that one of the serving maids was what had 'come up'. Master Reed had an unquenchable appetite and he was a fool if he thought I did not know about the others that laid down with him. He said that he loved me, but surely he would not seek solace in others if he did.

He was about to leave when Eliza suddenly burst into the room. "Are you looking for Jane?" she asked coyly. She had caught him once with his hand knotted in my hair and though she was young; but ten years old, she suspected something. "Jane is in the window-seat, to be sure, Jack," she said.

And I came out immediately, for I trembled at the idea of being dragged forth by the said Jack. He had a temper and if he knew I had ignored his whispered pleas, he would not be happy. I closed my book and tried to hide my secret lover in the folds of my dress.

"What do you want?" I asked.

"Say, 'What do you want, Master Reed?'" was the answer. He told me that he treated me harshly in front of his sisters to ensure secrecy, but I knew enough of his controlling ways to realise that this was not entirely so. I wished that he would always treat me as he did when we were alone and he was tenderly pressing his lips against every freckle across my chest.

"I want you to come here," he added, seating himself in an arm-chair. He intimated by a gesture that I was to approach and stand before him.

John Reed was a schoolboy of eighteen years old; two years older than I, for I was but sixteen, although treated as if I were much younger by Bessie and the rest of the household. He ought now to have been at school, but his mama had taken him home for a month or two, "on account of his delicate health." Mr. Miles, the master, affirmed that he would do very well if he had fewer cakes and sweetmeats sent him from home; but the mother's heart turned from an opinion so harsh, and inclined rather to the more refined idea that John's sallowness was owing to over-application and, perhaps, to pining after home.

Habitually obedient to John, I came up to his chair and he spent some three minutes staring at me and running his eye up and down my body as he was aware how I hated it. This was punishment for disobeying him just now and not showing myself when he called me.

I mused on the slightly ugly appearance of him compared to my dark-eyed lover. When he kissed me, I tried to forget it, but it was hard not to notice the slack nature of his jaw and the hardness of his eyes. My dark-eyed lover's dashing, rugged countenance slipped into my mind and I imagined that it was he standing in front of me instead, appraising my slight but lithe figure and the independence of my look.

"What were you doing behind the curtain?" he asked.

"I was reading."

"Show the book."

I felt a roaring in my ears and suddenly my knees trembled. I thought he noticed the change in my manner for a smile came across his face. He liked to unnerve me in front of his sisters and when we were alone. I think he liked to feel that he controlled me. Gently, I took the book out from the folds of my dress and he snatched it from me. Unfortunately, the page of my dark-eyed lover with the corner turned down piqued his interest and he turned to it first. Abruptly a jealous look gleamed in his eye, for he guessed I had been looking at that page and why.

"You have no business to take our books; you are a dependent," he growled. "Now, I'll teach you to rummage my bookshelves, for they are mine; all the house belongs to me, or will do in a few years. Go and stand by the door, out of the way of the mirror and the windows."

I did so, not at first aware what was his intention; but when I saw him lift and poise the book and stand in act to hurl it, I instinctively started aside with a cry of alarm. Not soon enough, however since the volume was flung and it hit me. I fell, striking my head against the door and cutting it. The cut bled, the pain was sharp and I jumped up, all terror gone. I could not believe that he had treated me thus, this was further than an act purely to hide our love from his sisters.

"Wicked and cruel boy!" I said.

"What! What!" he cried. "Did she say that to me? Did you hear her, Eliza and Georgiana? Won't I tell mama? But first—"

He ran headlong at me and I felt him grasp my hair and my shoulder. I shut my eyes and imagined it was my dark-eyed lover, clutching me as I had often dreamed he would late at night when everyone else was asleep. I felt a drop or two of blood from my head trickle down my neck, and I imagined him kissing them away with his full, smooth lips. He tugged a lock of my hair fiercely behind my head and I yelped. I became limp, allowing him to take me.

Plunged from my imagined embrace, a pair of strong hands dragged me backwards and I heard the words, "Dear!

What a fury to fly at Master John!"

"Did ever anybody see such a picture of passion!"

Eliza and Georgiana had alerted their mother and a servant.

Still reeling from my fantasy, I stood panting and looking up into the eyes of Mrs. Reed.

"What has—" she began, before her gaze fell on the book, discarded on the floor.

Her eyebrows raised just enough for me to realise who had turned the corner of my dark-eyed lover. Her cheeks flushed and she glared at me, her grip on my shoulder tightening and the nails sinking deep into my skin.

"Take her away to the red-room, and lock her in there," she commanded.

Four hands were immediately laid upon me, and I was borne upstairs.

CHAPTER II

I resisted all the way which was a new thing for me, and a circumstance which greatly strengthened the bad opinion Bessie and Miss Abbot were disposed to entertain of me.

"For shame! For shame!" cried the lady's-maid, Miss Abbot. "What shocking conduct, Miss Eyre, to strike a young gentleman, your benefactress's son! Your young master."

"Master! How is he my master? Am I a servant?"

"No, you are less than a servant, for you do nothing for your keep. There, sit down, and think over your wickedness."

They had got me by this time into the red room and had thrust me upon a stool.

There Bessie and Miss Abbot stood with folded arms, looking darkly and doubtfully on my face, as incredulous of my sanity.

"She never did so before," said Bessie at last.

"But it was always in her," was the reply. "I've told Missis often my opinion about the child, and Missis agrees with me. She's an underhand little thing."

Bessie answered not; but ere long, addressing me, she said, "You ought to be aware, Miss, that you are under obligations to Mrs. Reed. She keeps you and if she were to turn you off, you would have to go to the poorhouse."

I had nothing to say to these words since they were not new to me. My very first recollections of existence included hints of the same kind.

"What we tell you is for your good," added Bessie, in no harsh voice, "If you become passionate and rude Missis will send you away, I am sure."

"Come, we will leave her," said Miss Abbot. "Say your prayers, Miss Eyre, when you are by yourself. If you don't repent, something bad might be permitted to come down the chimney and fetch you away."

They went, shutting the door and locking it behind them.

The red-room was a square chamber, very seldom slept in. A bed supported on massive pillars of mahogany and hung with curtains of deep red damask, stood out like a tabernacle in the centre. The two large windows, with their blinds always drawn down, were half shrouded in festoons and falls of similar drapery. The carpet was red, the table at the foot of the bed was covered with a red cloth and the walls were a soft fawn colour with a blush of pink in it.

The room was chill because it seldom had a fire. It was silent because it was remote from the nursery, and solemn because it was known to be so seldom entered. The house-maid alone came here on Saturdays to wipe the mirrors. Mrs. Reed herself, at far intervals, visited it to review the contents of a certain secret drawer in the wardrobe, which I could only guess from the events of this afternoon held more portraits similar to that of my dark-eyed lover. Perhaps she too craved the warm touch of a tender hand as I so dearly did, her husband having passed away. In those last words lay the secret of the red-room—the spell which kept it so lonely in spite of its grandeur.

Mr. Reed had been dead nine years and it was in this chamber he breathed his last. Here he lay in state and since that day, a sense of dreary consecration has guarded the room from frequent intrusion.

My seat, to which Bessie and the bitter Miss Abbot had left me riveted, was a low ottoman near the marble chimney-piece. I was not quite sure whether they had locked the door and when I dared move, I got up and went to see.

Alas yes! No jail was ever more secure. Returning, I had to cross before the looking-glass and my fascinated glance involuntarily explored the depth it revealed. All looked colder and darker in that visionary, and the strange little figure there gazing at me with a white face and arms had the effect of a real spirit. I returned to my stool.

My head still ached and bled with the blow and fall I had received, and I touched it gently, wincing. I still could barely believe that John had treated me so. He was quick-tempered and aggressive but I did not know that he was cruel, perhaps jealousy had made him so.

"Unjust!—unjust!" said my reason, for Mrs. Reed had not chided him for his violence. His cruelty was borne in her.

Daylight had begun to forsake the red-room. It was past four o'clock and the beclouded afternoon was tending to drear twilight. I heard the rain still beating continuously on the staircase window, and the wind howling in the grove behind the hall. I grew by degrees cold as a stone, and then my courage sank.

My thoughts wandered to Mr. Reed once more and dwelling on his death, gathered dread. I could not remember him, but I knew that he was my own uncle—my mother's brother—that he had taken me as a parentless infant to his house, and that in his last moments he had required a promise of Mrs. Reed that she would rear me as one of her own children. A singular notion dawned upon me. I doubted not—never doubted—that if Mr. Reed had been alive, he would have treated me kindly. As I sat looking at the white bed and overshadowed walls—occasionally also turning a fascinated eye towards the dimly gleaning mirror—I began to recall what I had heard of dead men, troubled in their graves by the violation of their last wishes, revisiting the earth to punish the perjured and avenge the oppressed. I thought of Mr. Reed's spirit, harassed by the wrongs of his sister's child, which might quit its abode and rise before me in this chamber.

I wiped my tears and hushed my sobs, fearful lest any sign of violent grief might waken a preternatural voice to comfort me, or elicit from the gloom some haloed face, bending over me with strange pity.

At this moment a light gleamed on the wall. Was it, I asked myself, a ray from the moon penetrating some aperture in the blind? No, moonlight was still, and this stirred. While I gazed, it glided up to the ceiling and quivered over my head. Prepared as my mind was for horror, shaken as my nerves were by agitation, I thought the swift darting beam was a herald of some coming vision from another world. My heart beat thick, my head grew hot and a sound filled my ears, which I deemed the rushing of wings. Something seemed near me, I was oppressed and suffocated. Endurance broke down and I rushed to the door and shook the lock in desperate effort. Steps came running along the outer passage, the key turned and Bessie and Abbot entered.

"Take me out! Let me go into the nursery!" was my cry.

"What for? Are you hurt? Have you seen something?" demanded Bessie.

"Oh! I saw a light, and I thought a ghost would come." I had now got hold of Bessie's hand, and she did not snatch it from me.

"She has screamed out on purpose," declared Abbot, in some disgust. "And what a scream! If she had been in great pain one would have excused it, but she only wanted to bring us all here. I know her naughty tricks."

"What is all this?" demanded another voice, and Mrs. Reed came along the corridor, her cap flying wide, her gown rustling stormily. "Abbot and Bessie, I believe I gave orders that Jane Eyre should be left in the red-room till I came to her myself."

"Miss Jane screamed so loud, ma'am," pleaded Bessie.

"O aunt! Have pity! Forgive me!" I squealed, beside myself. "I cannot endure it—let me be punished some other way! I shall be killed if—"

"Silence! This violence is all most repulsive!"

I was a precocious actress in her eyes. She sincerely looked on me as a compound of virulent passions, mean spirit, and dangerous duplicity.

Bessie and Abbot having retreated, Mrs. Reed, impatient of my now frantic anguish and wild sobs, abruptly thrust me back and locked me in. I heard her sweeping away.

I screamed and unconsciousness took me.

CHAPTER III

The next thing I remember is waking up with a feeling as if some one was handling me; lifting me up and supporting me in a sitting posture. It was more tenderly than I had ever been raised or upheld before, even by John in our love making. I rested my head against a pillow or an arm, and felt easy.

In five minutes more, the cloud of bewilderment that had at first engulfed me dissolved and I knew quite well that I was in my own bed. It was night and a candle burnt on the table with Bessie standing at the bed-foot with a basin in her hand. A gentleman sat in a chair near my pillow, leaning over me.

Turning from Bessie (though her presence was far less obnoxious to me than that of Abbot, for instance, would have been), I scrutinised the face of the gentleman. I knew Mr. Lloyd, an apothecary, sometimes called in by Mrs. Reed when the servants were ailing. For herself and the children she employed a physician.

"Well, who am I?" he asked.

I pronounced his name, offering him at the same time my hand and he took it, smiling. "We shall do very well by-and-by," he said.

Then he laid me down, and addressing Bessie, charged her to be very careful that I was not disturbed during the night. Having given some further directions, and intimates

that he should call again the next day, he departed. I felt so
sheltered and befriended while he sat in the chair near my pillow that I did not want him to go. As he closed the door after
him, all the room darkened and my heart again sank.

"Do you feel as if you should sleep, Miss?" asked Bessie, rather
softly.

"I will try."

"Then I think I shall go to bed, for it is past twelve o'clock;
but you may call me if you want anything in the night."

Wonderful civility this! It emboldened me to ask a question.

"Bessie, what is the matter with me? Am I ill?"

"You fell sick, I suppose, in the red-room with crying.
You'll be better soon, no doubt."

Bessie went into the housemaid's apartment, which was
near, and I heard her say, "Sarah, come and sleep with me
in the nursery; I daren't for my life be alone with that poor
child to-night. She might die; it's such a strange thing she
should have that fit. I wonder if she saw anything. Missis
was rather too hard."

Sarah came back with her and they both went to bed. They
were whispering together for half-an-hour before they fell asleep. I caught scraps of their conversation, from which I was
able only too distinctly to infer the main subject discussed.

"Something passed her, all dressed in white and
vanished"—"A great black dog behind him"—"Three loud
raps on the chamber door"—"A light in the churchyard just
over his grave," &c.

At last both slept and the fire and the candle went out.
I endeavored to go to sleep as well, but I was too caught up
in terror to settle and not even the gentle breathing of Eliza
and Georgiana asleep in their own beds in the nursery could
calm me.

Suddenly, the nursery door slid open and I was about to
scream when I heard the familiar voice of John.

"Jane?"

I did not answer, hoping he would go. I had not forgiven him for hitting me thus, nor would I ever. I had suddenly realised in the red-room that John did not love me. It was a cold and hard shock and I still had the cut across my forehead to prove it. I should not have believed him when he said he did, knowing as I did the selfish nature of his mother and sisters, and it was some relief to me that I realised that I did not sincerely love him either. I desperately sought tender affection having been starved of it my whole existence and I had found a false kind for a time in John Reed, but I was fooled no longer.

"Jane, I am sorry about the book. I did not mean to hurt you, I was only pretending in front of Eliza and Georgiana. You know that."

I knew far more than that so I stayed silent.

But he was not to be so easily put off. John crept across the nursery and right up to my bed. He visited me often in the midnight hours and we were both lucky that his sisters were such heavy sleepers. Our first meeting had been at night like this some six months ago, when John had spent his week home from school pursuing me. I was naïve and hungry for affection and I had fallen right into his arms.

"Jane, you know I love you," he said, gently stroking a lock of my hair.

I retained the act of sleep no longer. He did not love me, I knew, but I wanted someone to, and I gently licked my lips, as I knew he liked.

A glazed look passed across his face and he bent over me, leaning down on the bed. Gently he pressed himself to me, the sheets between us, and his erection pushed against my stomach. My own groin throbbed with returned yearning.

"Oh, Jane," he breathed into my ear, tickling the tiny hairs across my neck.

A rush of delight surged through my body and I tilted my head back, gasping softly and closing my eyes. It was then in my mind that I saw my dark-eyed lover and it was him that I felt slide under the sheets with me, not John. It was he that moaned my name again, "Oh, Jane."

Hot lips found mine and kissed them gently at first, then harder and faster. He thrust his tongue into my mouth and we tasted the sweetness of each other. Meanwhile, his hand skimmed down my body, cupping my small breasts at first and then reaching down further between my legs. There he gently rubbed me in tantalising circles, while ripples of pleasure shocked my body. I bit down firmly on my lip to stop myself from crying out and my hips jerked with wanting.

He stopped rubbing me and teasingly began running his fingers up and down my stomach, between my navel and my legs, every now and then pinching the delicately soft skin.

"I want you," he said, hitching up my nightdress further and hurriedly undoing his own clothing.

Again, it was my dark-eyed lover that I felt move on top of me and gently slide between my legs. I caught my breath as he entered me, sending a thrilling twinge bolting up my body. Then slowly he drew himself in and out of me, filling and leaving me. The sensation built a pounding rhythm in the depths of my stomach, but suddenly, he stopped.

He pulled out of me and came, sighing.

"Good-night, Jane," he said, and I was left unsatisfied as I always was and now in the full knowledge that I was equally unloved as well.

The next day, by noon, I was up and dressed, and sat wrapped in a shawl by the nursery hearth. I felt physically weak and broken down, but my worse ailment was an unutterable wretchedness of mind; a wretchedness which kept drawing from me silent tears. No sooner had I wiped one salt drop from my cheek then another followed. Yet, I thought, I ought to have been happy, for none of the Reeds were there, they were all gone out in the carriage with their mama. But I was ashamed of myself for relenting to John last night when I should have stayed strong in my will, and still suffering from my fit in the red-room.

Bessie brought me a tart on a brightly painted china plate, but I could not eat it and had to put it aside. She next asked if I would have a book. The word "book" acted as a transient stimulus, and I begged her to fetch *Gulliver's Travels* from the library. I did briefly entertain the thought of asking for my volume of portraits but I did not want further questions that I knew Bessie would ask. Anyway, *Gulliver's Travels* I had again and again perused with delight and I felt it might balm my agitated soul. Yet, when this cherished object was placed in my hand, all was eerie and dreary. I put it on the table beside the untasted tart.

In the course of the morning Mr. Lloyd came again.

"What, already up!" said he, as he entered the nursery. "Well, nurse, how is she?"

Bessie answered that I was doing very well.

"Then she ought to look more cheerful. Miss Jane you have been crying, can you tell me what about? Have you any pain?"

"No, sir."

"Oh! I daresay she is crying because she could not go out with Missis in the carriage," interposed Bessie.

"Surely not! Why, she is too old for such pettishness."

I thought so too and my self-esteem being wounded by the false charge, I answered promptly, "I never cried for such a thing in my life. I hate going out in the carriage. I cry because I am miserable."

The good apothecary appeared a little puzzled. He fixed his eyes on me very steadily. They were small and grey; not very bright, but I dare say I should think them shrewd now. He had a hard-featured yet good-natured looking face. Having considered me at leisure, he said, "What made you ill yesterday?"

"She had a fall," said Bessie, again putting in her word.

"Fall! Why, that is like a baby again! Can't she manage to walk at her age? She must be twelve years old."

"I was knocked down," was the blunt explanation, jerked out of me by another pang of mortified pride; "And I am sixteen. But the knock did not make me ill," I added.

"Sixteen! Then you are too old for a nursery," he said, looking around.

I knew it and Mrs. Reed knew it, but it was yet another means of punishing me. She enjoyed treating me like a child and my small, under-grown appearance lended itself to such abuse.

A loud bell rang for the servants' dinner and he knew what it was. "That's for you, nurse," said he, "you can go down and I'll give Miss Jane a lecture till you come back."

Bessie would rather have stayed, but she was obliged to go because punctuality at meals was rigidly enforced at Gateshead Hall.

"The fall did not make you ill, but what did, then?" pursued Mr. Lloyd when we were alone.

"I am unhappy, very unhappy, for other things."

"What other things? Can you tell me some of them?"

How much I wished to reply fully to this question! How difficult it was to frame any answer! Fearful of losing this first and only opportunity of relieving my grief by imparting it, after a disturbed pause, I contrived to frame a meagre, though true response.

"For one thing, I have no father or mother, brothers or sisters."

"You have a kind aunt and cousins."

Again I paused, but then bunglingly enounced, "But John Reed knocked me down, and my aunt shut me up in the red-room."

"But don't you think Gateshead Hall a very beautiful

house?" asked Mr. Lloyd. "Are you not very thankful to have such a fine place to live at?"

"If I had anywhere else to go, I should be glad to leave it, but I can never get away from Gateshead till I am a woman."

"Perhaps you may—who knows? Have you any relations besides Mrs. Reed?"

"I think not, sir."

"Would you like to go to school?"

Again I reflected. I scarcely knew what school was. Bessie sometimes spoke of it as a place where young ladies sat in the stocks, wore backboards, and were expected to be exceedingly genteel and precise. John Reed hated his school, and abused his master; but John Reed's tastes were no rule for mine, and if Bessie's accounts of school-discipline (gathered from the young ladies of a family where she had lived before coming to Gateshead) were somewhat appalling, her details of certain accomplishments attained by these same young ladies were equally attractive. She boasted of beautiful paintings of landscapes and flowers by them executed, of songs they could sing, pieces they could play, of purses they could net, of French books they could translate; till my spirit was moved to emulation as I listened. Besides, school would be a complete change.

"I should indeed like to go to school," was the audible conclusion of my musings.

"Well, well! Who knows what may happen?" said Mr. Lloyd, as he got up. "The child ought to have change of air and scene," he added, speaking to himself, "nerves not in a good state."

Bessie now returned and at the same moment, the carriage was heard rolling up the gravel-walk.

"Is that your mistress, nurse?" asked Mr. Lloyd. "I should like to speak to her before I go."

Bessie invited him to walk into the breakfast-room, and led the way out. In the interview which followed between him and Mrs. Reed, I presume that the apothecary ventured to recommend my being sent to school. The recommendation was no doubt readily enough adopted; for as Abbot said, in discussing the subject with Bessie when both sat sewing in the nursery one night, after I was in bed, and, as they thought, asleep, "Missis was, she dared say, glad enough to get rid of such a tiresome, ill-conditioned child, who always looked as if she were watching everybody, and scheming plots underhand."

On that same occasion I learned, for the first time, from Miss Abbot's communications to Bessie, that my father had been a poor clergyman, that my mother had married him against the wishes of her friends, who considered the match beneath her, and that my grandfather Reed was so irritated at her disobedience, he cut her off without a shilling. After my mother and father had been married a year, the latter caught the typhus fever while visiting among the poor of a large manufacturing town where his curacy was situated, and where that disease was then prevalent. My mother took the infection from him, and both died within a month of each other.

Bessie, when she heard this narrative, sighed and said, "Poor Miss Jane is to be pitied, too, Abbot."

"Yes," responded Abbot; "if she were a nice, pretty child, one might compassionate her forlornness; but one really cannot care for such a little toad as that."

"Not a great deal, to be sure," agreed Bessie, "at any rate, a beauty like Miss Georgiana would be more moving in the same condition."

"Yes, I doat on Miss Georgiana!" cried the fervent Abbot. "Little darling!—with her long curls and her blue eyes, and such a sweet colour as she has, just as if she were painted!—Bessie, I could fancy a Welsh rabbit for supper."

"So could I—with a roast onion. Come, we'll go down." They went.

CHAPTER IV

I gathered a change seemed near and I desired and awaited it in silence. However, days and weeks passed and I had regained my normal state of health, but no new allusion was made to the subject over which I brooded. Mrs. Reed surveyed me at times with a severe eye, but seldom addressed me. Since my illness, she had drawn a more marked line of separation than ever between me and her own children; appointing me a small closet to sleep in by myself, condemning me to take my meals alone, and pass all my time in the nursery. Not a hint, however, did she drop about sending me to school. Still I felt an instinctive certainty that she would not long endure me under the same roof with her; for her glance when turned on me, expressed an insuperable and rooted aversion.

My first night alone in my sorry closet, I was visited by John again, as I suspected I might be.

"Jane," he whispered, slipping through the door.

"No," I said sharply, sitting up in bed.

He halted, his eyes searching mine in the darkness. At the thought of his tender caresses, my insides melted slightly and my skin begged to be touched, but I refrained firmly. I would not be taken in by my own longing and I would not allow John to use me any more.

A deep frown creased his ugly brow, for ugly he was and I now saw it. He had the large, bulging face of his mother and a wide girth.

"Go to one of the serving girls and do not come back here again," I said.

I thought he might hit me, his temper certainly looked roused and his lip curled, but he turned from me abruptly and left the room. From them on he never looked at me.

The next day I heard him complain of my presence in his house to his mother.

"Don't talk to me about her, John," said Mrs. Reed. "I told you not to go near her, she is not worthy of notice."

Here, leaning over the banister, I cried out suddenly, "He is not fit to associate with me!"

Mrs. Reed was rather a stout woman but, on hearing this strange and audacious declaration, she ran nimbly up the stair, swept me like a whirlwind into the nursery, and crushing me down on the floor, dared me in an emphatic voice to rise from that place, or utter one syllable during the remainder of the day.

"What would Uncle Reed say to you, if he were alive?" was my reply to such treatment.

"What?" said Mrs. Reed under her breath. Her usually cold composed grey eyes became troubled with a look like fear and she took her hand from my arm, and gazed at me as if she really did not know whether I were child or fiend.

"My Uncle Reed is in heaven, and can see all you do and think. So can papa and mama, they know how you shut me up all day long, and how you wish me dead."

Mrs. Reed soon rallied her spirits. She shook me most soundly, she boxed both my ears, and then left me without a word.

November, December, and half of January passed away. Christmas and the New Year had been celebrated at Gateshead with the usual festive cheer. Presents had been interchanged and dinners and evening parties given. From every enjoyment I was, of course, excluded. My share of the gaiety consisted in witnessing Eliza and Georgiana descend to the drawing-room, dressed out in thin muslin frocks and scarlet sashes, with hair

elaborately ringletted. Afterwards I would listen to the sounds
of the piano or the harp played below, to the jingling of glass
and china as refreshments were handed, and to the broken hum
of conversation as the drawing-room door opened and closed.
When tired of this occupation, I would retire from the stair-
head to the solitary and silent nursery. There, though somewhat
sad, I was not miserable. I would sit with my legs curled under
me, thinking of my dark-eyed lover, for I had no one else that
I could imagine who would wish to be near me. If Bessie had
but been kind and companionable, I should have deemed it a
treat to spend the evenings quietly with her, but Bessie, as soon
as she had dressed her young ladies, used to take herself off to the
lively regions of the kitchen and housekeeper's room, generally
bearing the candle along with her. I then sat with my doll on
my knee till the fire got low, glancing round occasionally to
make sure that nothing worse than myself haunted the shadowy
room. When the embers sank to a dull red, I undressed hastily,
tugging at knots and strings as I best might, and sought shelter
from cold and darkness in my bed. To this bed I always took my
doll; human beings must love something. It was at those times
that I would conjure the image of my dark-eyed, dark-haired lover most keenly. I had not seen his portrait since I was banished
to the nursery, but I still remembered every detail of his face.
The wild fire in his eyes was what I loved best and what kept me
company in those dark hours. I imagined them burning into
mine with the passion I so desperately craved.

Sometimes Bessie would come up to seek her thimble
or her scissors, or perhaps to bring me something by way
of supper, and then she would sit on the bed while I ate it.
When I had finished, she would tuck the clothes round me,
kiss me and say, "Good night, Miss Jane." When thus gentle,
Bessie seemed to me the best, prettiest, kindest being in the
world, and I wished most intensely that she would always
be so pleasant and amiable. I remember her as a slim young
woman, with black hair, dark eyes, very nice features, and a

good, clear complexion, but she had a capricious and hasty temper. Still, such as she was, I preferred her to any one else at Gateshead Hall.

It was on the 15th of January, at about nine o'clock in the morning that my waiting was finally over. Bessie was gone down to breakfast and Eliza was putting on her bonnet and warm garden-coat to go and feed her poultry. Georgiana sat on a high stool, dressing her hair at the glass, and I was making the beds, having received strict orders from Bessie to get it arranged before she returned (for Bessie now frequently employed me as a sort of under-nurserymaid).

Having spread the quilts, I went to the window-seat to put in order some picture-books and doll's house furniture scattered there. An abrupt command from Georgiana to let her playthings alone (for the tiny chairs and mirrors, the fairy plates and cups, were her property) stopped my proceedings and then, for lack of other occupation, I fell to breathing on the frost-flowers with which the window was fretted, and thus clearing a space in the glass through which I might look out on the grounds.

Just as I had dissolved so much of the silver-white foliage veiling the panes to look out, I saw the gates thrown open and a carriage roll through. I watched it ascending the drive with indifference since carriages often came to Gateshead, but none ever brought visitors in whom I was interested.

Suddenly, Bessie came running upstairs into the nursery. "Miss Jane, take off your pinafore. What are you doing there? Have you washed your hands and face this morning?"

"No, Bessie. I have only just finished dusting."

"Troublesome, careless child! What are you doing now?"

I was spared the trouble of answering, for Bessie seemed in too great a hurry to listen to explanations. She hauled me to the washstand, inflicted a merciless, but happily brief scrub on my face and hands with soap and water, and then hurrying me to the top of the stairs, bid me go down directly into the breakfast-room.

I would have asked who wanted me, but Bessie was already gone so I slowly descended. For nearly three months I had never been called to Mrs. Reed's presence. The breakfast, dining, and drawing-rooms had become for me awful regions, on which it dismayed me to intrude.

I now stood in the empty hall and before me was the breakfast-room door. I stopped, intimidated and trembling. I feared to return to the nursery, and feared to go forward to the parlour. Ten minutes I stood in agitated hesitation. The vehement ringing of the breakfast-room bell decided me that I must enter.

"Who could want me?" I asked inwardly, as with both hands I turned the stiff door-handle, which, for a second or two, resisted my efforts. The handle turned, the door unclosed, and passing through and curtseying low, I looked up at a man.

Mrs. Reed occupied her usual seat by the fireside and she made a signal to me to approach. I did so, and she introduced me to the stony stranger with the words, "This is the little girl respecting whom I applied to you."

He turned his head slowly towards where I stood, and having examined me with two inquisitive-looking grey eyes which twinkled under a pair of bushy brows, said solemnly, and in a bass voice, "Your name, little girl?"

"Jane Eyre, sir."

In uttering these words I looked up. He seemed to me a tall gentleman, but then I was very little. His features were large, and they and all the lines of his frame were equally harsh and prim.

"Well, Jane Eyre, and are you a good child?"

Mrs. Reed answered for me by an expressive shake of the head, adding, "Perhaps the less said on that subject the better, Mr. Brocklehurst."

"Sorry indeed to hear it! She and I must have some talk." Bending from the perpendicular, he installed his person in the arm-chair opposite Mrs. Reed's. "Come here," he said.

I stepped across the rug and he placed me square and straight before him. What a face he had, now that it was almost on a level with mine! What a great nose! And what a mouth! And what large prominent teeth!

"No sight so sad as that of a naughty child," he began, "Do you know where the wicked go after death?"

"They go to hell," was my ready and orthodox answer.

"And what is hell?"

"A pit full of fire."

"And should you like to fall into that pit, and to be burning there for ever?"

"No, sir."

"What must you do to avoid it?"

I deliberated a moment. "I must keep in good health, and not die."

At this point Mrs. Reed interposed, telling me to sit down, and then she proceeded to carry on the conversation herself.

"Mr. Brocklehurst, I believe I intimated in the letter which I wrote to you three weeks ago that this little girl has not quite the character and disposition I could wish. Should you admit her into Lowood school, I should be glad if the teachers were requested to keep a strict eye on her, and to guard against her worst fault, a tendency to deceit."

This untruth uttered before a stranger cut me to the heart more than it could had she said it to me alone. I dimly perceived that she was already obliterating hope from the new phase of existence which she destined me to enter. I felt that she was sowing aversion and unkindness along my future path. I saw myself transformed under Mr. Brocklehurst's eye into an artful, noxious child, and what could I do to remedy the injury?

"Deceit is a sad fault in a child," said Mr. Brocklehurst, "she shall be watched, Mrs. Reed. I will speak to Miss Temple and the teachers."

"I should wish her to be brought up in a manner suiting her prospects, to be made useful and to be kept humble. As for the vacations, she will spend them always at Lowood."

"Your decisions are perfectly judicious, madam," returned Mr. Brocklehurst.

"I may then depend upon this child being received as a pupil at Lowood?"

"Madam, you may."

"I will send her as soon as possible, Mr. Brocklehurst. For, I assure you, I feel anxious to be relieved of a responsibility that was becoming too irksome."

"No doubt, no doubt, madam; and now I wish you good morning. I shall send Miss Temple notice that she is to expect a new girl, so that there will be no difficulty about receiving her. Good-bye." With these words, Mr. Brocklehurst departed.

Mrs. Reed and I were left alone and some minutes passed in silence. She was sewing and I was watching her. The whole tenor of the past conversation was recent, raw, and stinging in my mind. I had felt every word as acutely as I had heard it plainly, and a passion of resentment fermented now within me.

Mrs. Reed looked up from her work, her eyes settled on mine and her fingers at the same time suspended their nimble movements. "Go out of the room and return to the nursery," was her mandate.

I got up and I went to the door, but I came back again. I walked to the window, across the room, then close up to her. Speak, I must. I had been trodden on severely, and now I must turn. I gathered my energies and launched them.

"I am not deceitful. If I were, I should say I loved you, but I declare I do not love you. I dislike you the worst of anybody in the world except John Reed. This book about the liar you may give to your girls, Georgiana and Eliza, for it is they who tell lies."

Mrs. Reed's eyes of ice continued to dwell freezingly on mine.

"What more have you to say?" she asked.

Shaking from head to foot, thrilled with ungovernable excitement, I continued, "I am glad you are no relation of mine. I will never call you aunt again as long as I live. I will never come to see you when I am grown up. And if any one asks me how I liked you, and how you treated me, I will say the very thought of you makes me sick, and that you treated me with miserable cruelty."

"How dare you affirm that, Jane Eyre?"

"How dare I, Mrs. Reed? How dare I? Because it is the truth. You think I have no feelings, and that I can do without one bit of love or kindness; but I cannot live so. You have no pity. I shall remember how you thrust me back into the red-room, and locked me up there to my dying day. Though I was in agony, though I cried out, while suffocating with distress, you showed no mercy. And that punishment you made me suffer because your wicked boy struck me—knocked me down for nothing. People think you a good woman, but you are bad and hard-hearted. You are deceitful!"

Ere I had finished this reply, my soul began to expand, to exult, with the strangest sense of freedom and triumph I had ever felt. Mrs. Reed looked frightened; her work had slipped from her knee and she was rocking herself to and fro.

"Jane, you are under a mistake, what is the matter with you? Why do you tremble so violently? Would you like to drink some water?"

"No, Mrs. Reed."

"Jane you are too passionate. Now, return to the nursery—there's a dear—and lie down a little."

"I am not your dear, I cannot lie down! Send me to school soon, Mrs. Reed, for I hate to live here."

"I will indeed send her to school soon," murmured Mrs. Reed sotto voce, and gathering up her work, she abruptly quitted the apartment.

I was left there alone—winner of the field. It was the hardest battle I had fought, and the first victory I had gained. I stood awhile on the rug where Mr. Brocklehurst had stood, and I enjoyed my conqueror's solitude.

I knew immediately what my reward would be. With a buzzing rush of excitement coursing through me, I ran into the breakfast-room. My fingers itched and my chest fluttered at the thought of being reunited with those dear dark features. I almost could not find the volume of portraits for Mrs. Reed had moved it; tucked it away in a corner. I dragged it out with growing anticipation and leafed hurriedly through the pages, but I frowned. The page was gone; ripped out from the bind. Mrs. Reed had taken it from me or perhaps it was John.

In some way I was not surprised at this added unjust punishment. In some way I had expected the portrait to be gone. I closed the book and placed it back on the shelf, before sinking to the floor in a state of melancholic sadness. At least they could not steal his image from my mind that was ingrained.

All at once I heard a clear voice call, "Miss Jane! Where are you? Come to lunch!"

It was Bessie, but I did not stir and her light step came tripping into the room.

"You naughty little thing!" she said. "Why don't you come when you are called?"

Bessie's presence roused me and I put my two arms round her and said, "Come, Bessie! Don't scold."

The action was more frank and fearless than any I was habituated to indulge in and somehow it pleased her.

"You are a strange child, Miss Jane," she said, as she looked down at me, "a little roving, solitary thing. You are going to school, I suppose?" I nodded.

"And won't you be sorry to leave poor Bessie?"

"What does Bessie care for me? She is always scolding me."

"Because you're such a frightened, shy little thing. You should be bolder."

"What! To get more knocks?"

"Nonsense! But you are rather put upon, that's certain. Now, come in, and I've some good news for you."

"I don't think you have, Bessie."

"Child! What do you mean? What sorrowful eyes you fix on me! Missis and the young ladies and Master John are going out to tea this afternoon, and you shall have tea with me. I'll ask cook to bake you a little cake, and then you shall help me to look over your drawers, for I am soon to pack your trunk. Missis intends you to leave Gateshead in a day or two."

"Bessie, you must promise not to scold me any more till I go."

"I will, but mind you are a very good girl, and don't be afraid of me. Don't start when I chance to speak rather sharply; it's so provoking."

"I don't think I shall ever be afraid of you again, Bessie, because I have got used to you, and I shall soon have another set of people to dread."

"And so you're glad to leave me?"

"Not at all, Bessie. Indeed, just now I'm rather sorry."

"Just now! How coolly my little lady says it! I dare say now if I were to ask you for a kiss you wouldn't give it me."

"I'll kiss you, bend your head down."

Bessie stooped, we mutually embraced, and I followed her into the house quite comforted. That afternoon lapsed in peace and harmony, and in the evening Bessie told me some of her most enchanting stories, and sang me some of her sweetest songs. Even for me life had its gleams of sunshine.

CHAPTER V

Five o'clock had hardly struck on the morning of the 19th of January, when Bessie brought a candle into my closet and found me already up and nearly dressed. I had risen half-an-hour before her entrance, and washed my face and dressed. I was to leave Gateshead that day by a coach which passed the lodge gates at six a.m. Bessie was the only person yet risen and she had lit a fire in the nursery, where she now proceeded to make my breakfast. Few can eat when excited with the thoughts of a journey and nor could I. Bessie, having pressed me in vain to take a few spoonfuls of the boiled milk and bread she had prepared for me, wrapped up some biscuits in a paper and put them into my bag. She helped me on with my pelisse and bonnet and we left the nursery. As we passed Mrs. Reed's bedroom, she said, "Will you go in and bid Missis good-bye?"

"No, she came to me last night and said I need not disturb her in the morning. She told me to remember that she had always been my best friend, and to speak of her and be grateful to her accordingly."

"What did you say, Miss?"

"Nothing. I covered my face with the bedclothes, and turned from her to the wall."

"That was wrong, Miss Jane."

"It was quite right, Bessie. Your Missis has not been my friend, she has been my foe."

"O Miss Jane! Don't say so!"

"Good-bye Gateshead!" cried I, as we passed through the hall and went out at the front door.

The moon was set, and it was very dark. Raw and chill was the winter morning and my teeth chattered as I hastened down the drive. There was a light in the porter's lodge and when we reached it, we found the porter's wife just kindling her fire. My trunk, which had been carried down the evening before, stood corded at the door. The distant roll of wheels announced the coming coach and I went to the door and watched its lamps approach rapidly through the gloom. "Is she going by herself?" asked the porter's wife.

"Yes."

"And how far is it?"

"Fifty miles."

"What a long way! I wonder Mrs. Reed is not afraid to trust her so far alone."

The coach drew up and the guard and coachman loudly urged haste. My trunk was hoisted up and I was taken from Bessie's neck, to which I clung with kisses.

"Be sure and take good care of her," cried she to the guard, as he lifted me into the inside. "Ay, ay!" was the answer.

The door was slapped to and a voice exclaimed "All right."

Thus was I severed from Bessie and Gateshead and thus whirled away into unknown.

I remember but little of the journey. I only know that the day seemed to me of a preternatural length, and that we appeared to travel over hundreds of miles of road. We passed through several towns, and in a very large one the coach stopped, the horses were taken out, and the passengers alighted to dine. I was carried into an inn, where the guard wanted me to have some dinner, but as I had no appetite, he left me in an immense room with a fireplace at each end. After a long while the guard returned and once more I was stowed away in the coach and we rattled away.

The afternoon came on wet and somewhat misty. As it waned into dusk, I began to feel that we were getting very far indeed from Gateshead since we ceased to pass through towns. The country changed and great grey hills heaved up round the horizon. As twilight deepened, we descended a valley, dark with wood, and long after night had overclouded the prospect, I heard a wild wind rushing amongst trees.

Lulled by the sound, I at last dropped asleep. I had not long slumbered when the sudden cessation of motion awoke me and the coach-door was opened. A person like a servant was standing at it. I saw her face and dress by the light of the lamps.

"Is there a little girl called Jane Eyre here?" she asked.

I answered "Yes," and was then lifted out. My trunk was handed down, and the coach instantly drove away.

Gathering my faculties, I looked about me. Rain, wind, and darkness filled the air; nevertheless, I could see a house or houses—for the building spread far—with many windows and lights burning in some. I followed my guide up a broad pebbly path, splashing wet, and we were admitted at a door. Then the servant led me through a passage into a room with a fire, where she left me alone.

I stood, warming my numbed fingers over the blaze when an individual carrying a light entered, followed by another close behind. The first was a tall lady with dark hair, dark eyes, a large forehead, and a grave countenance.

"She had better be put to bed soon," said she. "She looks tired. Are you tired?" she asked, placing her hand on my shoulder.

"A little, ma'am."

"And hungry too, no doubt. Let her have some supper before she goes to bed, Miss Miller. Is this the first time you have left your parents to come to school, my girl?"

I explained to her that I had no parents. She inquired how long they had been dead, then how old I was, what was my name, whether I could read, write, and sew a little, and then she touched my cheek gently with her forefinger saying, "I hope you will be good." Then she dismissed me along with Miss Miller.

Led by her, I passed from compartment to compartment and from passage to passage of a large and irregular building. We emerged at last into a wide, long room, with two great deal tables on which burnt a pair of candles, and seated all round on benches, a congregation of girls of every age, from nine or ten to twenty. Seen by the dim light of the dips, their number to me appeared countless, though not in reality exceeding eighty. They were uniformly dressed in brown stuff frocks of quaint fashion, and long holland pinafores. It was the hour of study and they were engaged in conning over tomorrow's task.

Miss Miller signed to me to sit on a bench near the door, then walking up to the top of the long room she cried out, "Monitors, collect the lesson-books and put them away!"

Four tall girls arose from different tables, and going round, gathered the books and removed them. Miss Miller again gave the word of command, "Monitors, fetch the supper-trays!"

The tall girls went out and returned presently, each bearing a tray with portions of something, a pitcher of water and a mug. All was then handed around but when it came to my turn, I drank, for I was thirsty, but did not touch the food since excitement and fatigue had rendered me incapable of eating.

The meal over, prayers were read by Miss Miller, and the classes filed off, two and two, upstairs. Overpowered by this time with weariness, I scarcely noticed what sort of a place the bedroom was, except that, like the schoolroom, it was very long. Tonight I was to be Miss Miller's bed-fellow and she helped me to undress. In ten minutes the single light was extinguished, and there was silence. I remember briefly telling myself with relief that I now never needed to fear that I would ever receive a midnight visit from John Reed; that temptation at least was far behind me. After that, I fell asleep.

The night passed rapidly. I was too tired even to dream. I only once awoke to hear the wind rave in furious gusts, and the rain fall in torrents, and to be sensible that Miss Miller had taken her place by my side. When I again unclosed my eyes, a loud bell was ringing and the girls were up and dressing. I too rose reluctantly since it was bitter cold, and I dressed as well as I could for shivering, and washed when there was a basin at liberty. Again the bell rang. All formed in file, two and two, and in that order descended the stairs and entered the cold and dimly lit schoolroom. Here prayers were read by Miss Miller and afterwards she called out, "Form classes!"

Business now began. The day's Collect was repeated, then certain texts of Scripture were said, and to these succeeded a protracted reading of chapters in the Bible, which lasted an hour. By the time that exercise was terminated, day had fully dawned. The indefatigable bell rang again and the classes were marshalled and marched into another room to breakfast. How glad I was to behold a prospect of getting something to eat! I was now nearly sick from inanition, having taken so little the day before.

The refectory was a great, low-ceiled, gloomy room. On two long tables smoked basins of something hot, which to my dismay, sent forth an odour far from inviting. I saw a universal manifestation of discontent when the fumes of the repast met the nostrils of those destined to swallow it. The tall girls of the first class whispered, "Disgusting! The por-ridge is burnt again!"

"Silence!" yelled a voice.

Ravenous and now very faint, I devoured a spoonful or two of my portion without thinking of its taste, but the first edge of hunger blunted, I perceived I had got in hand a nauseous mess. Burnt porridge is almost as bad as rotten potatoes and the spoons were moved slowly. I saw each girl taste her food and try to swallow it, but in most cases the effort was soon relinquished. Breakfast was over, and none had breakfasted.

A quarter of an hour passed before lessons again began, during which the schoolroom was in a glorious tumult for in that space of time it seemed to be permitted to talk loud and more freely. The whole conversation ran on the breakfast, which one and all abused roundly. Miss Miller was now the only teacher in the room and a group of great girls standing about her spoke with serious and sullen gestures. I heard the name of Mr. Brocklehurst pronounced by some lips, at which Miss Miller shook her head disapprovingly, but she made no great effort to cheek the general wrath and doubtless she shared in it.

A clock in the schoolroom struck nine and Miss Miller left her circle. Standing in the middle of the room, she cried, "Silence! To your seats!"

Discipline prevailed and in five minutes the confused throng was resolved into order and comparative silence. The upper teachers now punctually resumed their posts but still, all seemed to wait. I gazed around the room, confused, but suddenly, the whole school rose simultaneously, as if moved by a common spring.

What was the matter? I had heard no order given and I was puzzled. Ere I had gathered my wits, the classes were again seated, but as all eyes were now turned to one point, mine followed the general direction and encountered the personage who had received me last night. She stood at the bottom of the long room surveying the two rows of girls silently and gravely.

"Monitor of the first class, fetch the globes!"

While the direction was being executed, the lady moved slowly up the room. Seen now, in broad daylight, she looked tall, fair, and shapely. This I later learnt, was Miss Temple— Maria Temple, as I afterwards saw the name written in a prayer-book intrusted to me to carry to church. The superintendent of Lowood (for such was this lady) having taken her seat before a pair of globes placed on one of the tables, summoned the first class round her, and commenced giving a lesson on geography. Writing and arithmetic succeeded, and music lessons were given by Miss Temple to some of the elder girls. The duration of each lesson was measured by the clock, which at last struck twelve. The superintendent rose

"I have a word to address to the pupils," said she.

The tumult of cessation from lessons was already breaking forth, but it sank at her voice. She went on, "You had this morning a breakfast which you could not eat and you must be hungry—I have ordered that a lunch of bread and cheese shall be served to all."

The teachers looked at her with a sort of surprise.

"It is to be done on my responsibility," she added, in an explanatory tone to them, and immediately afterwards left the room.

The bread and cheese was presently brought in and distributed, to the high delight and refreshment of the whole school. The order was now given "To the garden!" Each put on a coarse straw bonnet and a cloak of grey frieze. I was similarly equipped, and, following the stream, I made my way into the open air.

The garden was a wide inclosure, surrounded with walls so high as to exclude every glimpse of prospect. A middle space divided into scores of little beds were assigned as gardens for the pupils to cultivate, and each bed had an owner.

When full of flowers they would doubtless look pretty, but now, at the latter end of January, all was wintry blight and brown decay. I shuddered as I stood and looked round me, while the other girls ran about and played. After a while, I noticed a hollow cough behind me.

The sound made me turn my head and I saw a girl sitting on a stone bench nearby. She was bent over a book, on the perusal of which she seemed intent and from where I stood I could see the title—"Rasselas." In turning a leaf she happened to look up, and I said to her directly, "Is your book interesting?" I had already formed the intention of asking her to lend it to me some day.

"I like it," she answered, after a pause of a second or two, during which she examined me.

"What is it about?" I continued. I hardly know where I found the hardihood thus to open a conversation with a stranger, but I think her occupation touched a chord of sympathy somewhere; for I too liked reading. I had spoken to no one here thus far and I was craving human company.

"You may look at it," replied the girl, offering me the book.

I did so and a brief examination convinced me that the contents looked dull to my trifling taste. I returned it to her and she received it quietly. She was about to relapse into her former studious mood, when again I ventured to disturb her.

"Can you tell me what the writing on that stone over the door means? What is Lowood Institution?"

"This house where you are come to live."

"And why do they call it Institution? Is it in any way different from other schools?"

"It is partly a charity-school. You and I, and all the rest of us are charity-children. I suppose you are an orphan, are not either your father or your mother dead?"

"Both died before I can remember."

"Well, all the girls here have lost either one or both parents, and this is called an institution for educating orphans."

"Does this house belong to that tall lady who said we were to have some bread and cheese?"

"To Miss Temple? Oh, no! I wish it did. She has to answer to Mr. Brocklehurst for all she does. Mr. Brocklehurst buys all our food and all our clothes."

"Does he live here?"

"No—two miles off, at a large hall."

"Is he a good man?"

"He is a clergyman, and is said to do a great deal of good."

"Did you say that tall lady was called Miss Temple?"

"Yes."

"Do you like the other teachers here?"

"Well enough."

"But Miss Temple is the best—isn't she?"

"Miss Temple is very good and very clever. She is above the rest because she knows far more than they do."

"Have you been long here?"

"Two years."

"Are you an orphan?"

"My mother is dead."

"Are you happy here?"

"You ask rather too many questions. I have given you answers enough for the present, now I want to read."

CHAPTER VI

The next day commenced as before, getting up and dressing by rushlight, but this morning we were obliged to dispense with the ceremony of washing because the water in the pitchers was frozen. A change had taken place in the weather the preceding evening and a keen north-east wind, whistling through the crevices of our bedroom windows all night long, had made us shiver in our beds and turned the contents of the ewers to ice.

In the course of the day I was enrolled a member of the fourth class and regular tasks and occupations were assigned me. Hitherto, I had only been a spectator of the proceedings at Lowood, but I was now to become an actor therein. Being little accustomed to learn by heart, the lessons appeared to me both long and difficult. I was glad when at about three o'clock in the afternoon, Miss Smith put into my hands a border of muslin two yards long, together with needle, thimble, &c., and sent me to sit in a quiet corner of the schoolroom with directions to hem the same.

At that hour most of the others were sewing likewise, but one class still stood around Miss Scatcherd's chair reading. As all was quiet, the subject of their lessons could be heard, together with the manner in which each girl acquitted herself. It was English history and among the readers I observed my acquaintance of the day before. At the commencement of the lesson, her place had been at the top of the class, but for some error of pronunciation or some inattention to stops, she was suddenly sent to the very bottom. Even in that obscure position, Miss Scatcherd continued to make her an object of constant notice. She was continually addressing to her such phrases as the following: "Burns" (such it seems was her name: the girls here were all called by their surnames, as boys are elsewhere), "Burns, you are standing on the side of your shoe; turn your toes out immediately."—"Burns, you poke your chin most unpleasantly; draw it in."—"Burns, I insist on your holding your head up; I will not have you before me in that attitude," &c.

A chapter having been read through twice, the books were closed and the girls examined. The lesson had comprised part of the reign of Charles I., and there were sundry questions about tonnage, poundage, and ship-money. Most of them appeared unable to answer, but every little difficulty was solved instantly when it reached Burns. Her memory seemed to have retained the substance of the whole lesson and she was ready with answers on every point. I kept expecting that Miss Scatcherd would praise her attention, but instead of that she suddenly cried out, "You dirty, disagreeable girl! You never cleaned your nails this morning!"

Burns made no answer and I wondered at her silence.

Miss Scatcherd delivered an order which I did not catch and Burns immediately left the class. Going into the small inner room where the books were kept, she returned in half a minute carrying in her hand a bundle of twigs tied together at one end. This ominous tool she presented to Miss Scatcherd with a respectful curtsey. Then she quietly, and without being told, unloosed her pinafore. The teacher instantly and sharply inflicted on her neck a dozen strokes with the bunch of twigs.

I flinched with each blow.

Not a tear rose to Burns's eye and not a feature of her pensive face altered its ordinary expression.

"Hardened girl!" exclaimed Miss Scatcherd, "nothing can correct you of your slatternly habits. Carry the rod away."

Burns obeyed. I looked at her narrowly as she emerged from the book-closet, but her cheeks were dry of tears.

That evening, I wandered as usual among the forms and tables and laughing groups without a companion, yet not feeling lonely. When I passed the windows, I now and then lifted a blind, and looked out, seeing falling snow. It was already forming against the lower panes and, putting my ear close to the window, I could distinguish from the gleeful tumult within the disconsolate moan of the wind outside.

Jumping over forms, and creeping under tables, I made my way to one of the fire-places where, kneeling by the high wire fender, I found Burns, absorbed, silent, and abstracted from all around her.

"What is your name besides Burns?" I asked.

She looked at me in surprise. "Helen," she said.

"You must wish to leave Lowood?" I took up a seat beside her.

"No! Why should I? I was sent to Lowood to get an education."

"But Miss Scatcherd is so cruel to you!"

"Cruel? Not at all! She is severe because she dislikes my faults."

I gazed at her, truly shocked. "If I were in your place I should dislike her," I said. "If she struck me with that rod, I should break it under her nose."

I thought I saw her cheeks flush but it may have been the firelight. "I do not mind," she said.

"You do not mind the flogging?" I repeated, aghast.

Involuntarily I saw her hand reach up to her neck and lightly touch the wound. She winced, but I thought I saw the corner of her mouth tug upwards, almost in a wry smile.

"It is not so bad," she said.

I thought about the long, hard twigs, bundled together at one end and the sharp whistle as they sliced the air and bit into flesh.

"It must hurt."

"Not if you think of other things," Helen whispered.

Suddenly I was reminded of my fight with John Reed, when he had attacked me and I had imagined it was the fervent embraces of my dark-eyed lover. It was my turn to hide my flushed cheeks in the amber glow from the firelight. I wondered how it would feel to have my dark-eyed lover treat me so. I shivered. Once John had tugged my hair sharply in our love making and I had yelped, but the stabbing pain had been followed by an undertone of delicious heat. I wondered whether this was what Helen meant. Though I hated John still with a vengeance, in this desolate, lonely place, I missed a tender touch.

"You say you have faults, Helen, what are they?" I asked to change the subject. "To me you seem very good."

"Then learn from me not to judge by appearances. I am, as Miss Scatcherd said, slatternly. This is very provoking to Miss Scatcherd, who is naturally neat, punctual, and particular."

"And cross and cruel," I added, but Helen Burns would not admit my addition.

"Love your enemies. Bless them that curse you," she said. "Do good to them that hate you and despitefully use you."

I sighed. "Then I should love Mrs. Reed, which I cannot do and I should bless her son John, which is impossible!"

In her turn, Helen asked me to explain, and I proceeded forthwith to pour out the tale of my sufferings and resentments (of course refraining from speaking of my relationship with John).

Helen heard me patiently to the end. I expected she would then make a remark, but she said nothing.

"Well," I asked impatiently, "is not Mrs. Reed a hard-hearted, bad woman?"

"She has been unkind to you because she dislikes your cast of character, as Miss Scatcherd does mine, but how minutely you remember all she has done and said to you! What a singularly deep impression her injustice seems to have made on your heart! You would be happier if you tried to forget her severity, together with the passionate emotions it excited."

A monitor presently came over at that moment and exclaimed in a strong Cumberland accent, "Helen Burns, if you don't go and put your drawer in order and fold up your work this minute, I'll tell Miss Scatcherd to come and look at it!"

Helen sighed and getting up, obeyed the monitor without reply as without delay.

CHAPTER VII

During January, February, and part of March, the deep snows prevented our stirring beyond the garden walls except to go to church. Our clothing was insufficient to protect us from the severe cold and since we had no boots, the snow got into our shoes and melted there. Our ungloved hands became numbed and covered with chilblains, as were our feet and I remember well the distracting irritation I endured from this cause every evening, when my feet inflamed; and the torture of thrusting the swelled, raw, and stiff toes into my shoes in the morning.

The scanty supply of food was also distressing. With the keen appetites of growing children, we had scarcely sufficient to keep alive a delicate invalid. From this deficiency of nourishment resulted an abuse, which pressed hardly on the younger pupils. Whenever the famished great girls had an opportunity, they would coax or menace the little ones out of their portion. Many a time I have shared between two claimants the precious morsel of brown bread distributed at tea-time; and after relinquishing to a third half the contents of my mug of coffee, I have swallowed the remainder with an accompaniment of secret tears, forced from me by the exigency of hunger.

Sundays were dreary days in that wintry season. We had to walk two miles to Brocklebridge Church, where our patron officiated. We set out cold and we arrived at church colder. During the morning service we became almost paralysed.

It was too far to return to dinner so we were forced to stay there. At the close of the afternoon service we returned by an exposed and hilly road, where the bitter winter wind blowing over a range of snowy summits to the north almost flayed the skin from our faces.

How we longed for the light and heat of a blazing fire when we got back! But, to the little ones at least, this was denied. Each hearth in the schoolroom was immediately surrounded by a double row of great girls, and behind them the younger children crouched in groups, wrapping their starved arms in their pinafores.

A little solace came at tea-time, in the shape of a double ration of bread—a whole instead of a half slice—with the delicious addition of a thin scrape of butter. It was the hebdomadal treat to which we all looked forward from Sabbath to Sabbath.

I have not yet alluded to the visits of Mr. Brocklehurst; and indeed that gentleman was from home during the greater part of the first month after my arrival. Perhaps he was prolonging his stay with his friend the archdeacon, but his absence was a relief to me. I need not say that I had my own reasons for dreading his coming, but come he did at last.

One afternoon (I had then been three weeks at Lowood), as I was sitting with a slate in my hand, puzzling over a sum in long division, my eyes, raised in abstraction to the window, caught sight of a figure just passing. I recognised almost instinctively that gaunt outline; and when all the school teachers rose en masse, it was not necessary for me to look up in order to ascertain whose entrance they thus greeted. A long stride measured the schoolroom, and presently beside Miss Temple stood the same man who had frowned on me so ominously from the hearthrug of Gateshead.

I had my own reasons for being dismayed at this

apparition. Too well I remembered the perfidious hints given by Mrs. Reed about my disposition and the promise pledged by Mr. Brocklehurst to apprise Miss Temple and the teachers of my vicious nature. All along I had been dreading the fulfilment of this promise, I had been looking out daily for him whose information respecting my past life and conversation was to brand me as a bad child for ever. Now there he was.

He stood at Miss Temple's side and he was speaking low in her ear. I did not doubt he was making disclosures of my villainy, and I watched her eye with painful anxiety, expecting every moment to see its dark orb turn on me a glance of repugnance and contempt. I listened too; and as I happened to be seated quite at the top of the room, I caught most of what he said. Its import relieved me from immediate apprehension.

"The laundress tells me some of the girls have two clean tuckers in the week. It is too much; the rules limit them to one."

"I think I can explain that circumstance, sir," said Miss Temple. "Agnes and Catherine Johnstone were invited to take tea with some friends at Lowton last Thursday, and I gave them leave to put on clean tuckers for the occasion."

"Well, for once it may pass, I suppose. And there is another thing which surprised me; I find, in settling accounts with the housekeeper, that a lunch consisting of bread and cheese has twice been served out to the girls during the past fortnight. How is this? I looked over the regulations and I find no such meal as lunch mentioned. Who introduced this innovation? and by what authority?"

"I must be responsible for the circumstance, sir," replied Miss Temple. "The breakfast was so ill prepared that the pupils could not possibly eat it and I dared not allow them to remain fasting till dinner-time."

"Madam, allow me an instant. You are aware that my plan in bringing up these girls is not to accustom them to habits of luxury and indulgence, but to render them hardy, patient, self-denying. Should any little accidental disappointment of the appetite occur, such as the spoiling of a meal, they should eat it nonetheless."

Mr. Brocklehurst again paused, perhaps overcome by his feelings. Miss Temple had looked down when he first began to speak to her; but she now gazed straight before her, her face set.

Meantime, Mr. Brocklehurst, standing on the hearth with his hands behind his back, surveyed the whole school. Suddenly his eye gave a blink, as if it had met something that either dazzled or shocked its pupil. Turning, he said in more rapid accents than he had hitherto used, "Miss Temple, Miss Temple, what—*what* is that girl with curled hair? Red hair, ma'am, curled—curled all over?" And extending his cane he pointed to the awful object, his hand shaking as he did so.

"It is Julia Severn," replied Miss Temple, very quietly.

"Julia Severn, ma'am! And why has she, or any other, curled hair? Why, in defiance of every precept and principle of this house, does she conform to the world so openly—here in an evangelical, charitable establishment—as to wear her hair one mass of curls?"

"Julia's hair curls naturally," returned Miss Temple, still more quietly.

"Naturally! Yes, but we are not to conform to nature. I wish these girls to be the children of Grace, and why that abundance? I have again and again intimated that I desire the hair to be arranged closely, modestly, plainly. Miss Temple, that girl's hair must be cut off entirely. I will send a barber to-morrow, and I see others who have far too much of the excrescence—that tall girl, tell her to turn round. Tell all the first form to rise up and direct their faces to the wall."

Miss Temple passed her handkerchief over her lips, as if to smooth away the involuntary smile that curled them and she gave the order.

Leaning a little back on my bench, I could see the looks and grimaces with which the class commented on this manoeuvre. It was a pity Mr. Brocklehurst could not see them too for he would perhaps have felt that, whatever he might do with the outside of the cup and platter, the inside was further beyond his interference than he imagined.

He scrutinised the reverse of these living medals some five minutes, then pronounced sentence. These words fell like the knell of doom, "All those top-knots must be cut off."

Miss Temple seemed to remonstrate.

"Madam," he pursued, "I have a Master to serve whose kingdom is not of this world. My mission is to mortify in these girls the lusts of the flesh and to teach them to clothe themselves with shame-facedness and sobriety, not with braided hair and costly apparel."

I smarted slightly at the mention of "lusts of the flesh" wondering what unearthly punishment Mr. Brocklehurst should condemn me to, should he know of my previous doings. Thankfully he was none the wiser and continued thus, "Each of the young persons before us has a string of hair twisted in plaits which vanity itself might have woven. These, I repeat, *must* be cut off. Think of the time wasted, of—"

Mr. Brocklehurst was here interrupted when three ladies now entered the room. They ought to have come a little sooner to have heard his lecture on dress, for they were splendidly attired in velvet, silk, and furs. The two younger of the trio (fine girls of sixteen and seventeen) had grey beaver hats shaded with ostrich plumes, and from under the brim of this graceful head-dress fell a profusion of light tresses, elaborately curled. The elder lady was enveloped in a costly

velvet shawl trimmed with ermine and she wore a false front
of French curls.

These ladies were deferentially received by Miss Temple
as Mrs. and the Misses Brocklehurst, and conducted to seats
of honour at the top of the room. It seems they had come in
the carriage with their reverend relative, and had been con-
ducting a rummaging scrutiny of the room upstairs, while
he transacted business with the housekeeper, questioned
the laundress, and lectured the superintendent. They now
proceeded to address divers remarks and reproofs to Miss
Smith, who was charged with the care of the linen and the
inspection of the dormitories, but I had no time to listen to
what they said; other matters called off and enchanted my
attention.

Hitherto, while gathering up the discourse of Mr. Brocklehurst and Miss Temple, I had at the same time made pre-
cautions to secure my personal safety by ensuring I eluded
observation. I had sat well back on the form, and while seeming to be busy with my sum, had held my slate in such
a manner as to conceal my face. I might have escaped notice, had not my treacherous slate somehow happened to slip
from my hand, and falling with an obtrusive crash, directly
drawn every eye upon me. I knew it was all over now, and, as
I stooped to pick up the two fragments of slate, I rallied my
forces for the worst. It came.

"A careless girl!" said Mr. Brocklehurst, and immediately
after, "It is the new pupil, I perceive." And before I could
draw breath, "I must not forget I have a word to say respecting her." Then aloud, "Let the child who broke her slate
come forward!"

Of my own accord I could not have stirred. I was paralysed. But the two great girls who sat on each side of me, set
me on my legs and pushed me towards the dread judge. Then
Miss Temple gently assisted me to his very feet, and I caught

her whispered counsel, "Don't be afraid, Jane, I saw it was an accident and you shall not be punished."

The kind whisper went to my heart like a dagger.

"Another minute, and she will despise me for a hypocrite," thought I. An impulse of fury against Reed, Brocklehurst, and Co. bounded in my pulses at the conviction. I was no Helen Burns. I could not withstand any beating.

"Fetch that stool," said Mr. Brocklehurst, pointing to a very high one from which a monitor had just risen. It was brought.

"Place the girl upon it."

And I was placed there, by whom I don't know. I was in no condition to note particulars; I was only aware that they had hoisted me up to the height of Mr. Brocklehurst's nose and that he was within a yard of me.

"Ladies," said he, turning to his family, "Miss Temple, teachers, and children, you all see this girl?"

Of course they did; for I felt their eyes directed like burning-glasses against my scorched skin.

"This is a sad and a melancholy occasion. It becomes my duty to warn you that this girl is not a member of the true flock, but evidently an interloper and an alien. You must be on your guard against her. You must shun her example and if necessary, avoid her company. Exclude her from your sports and shut her out from your converse. Teachers, you must watch her and keep your eyes on her movements, weigh well her words, scrutinise her actions, punish her body to save her soul. This girl is a liar!"

Now came a pause of ten minutes, during which I, by this time in perfect possession of my wits, observed all the female Brocklehursts produce their pocket-handkerchiefs and apply them to their optics, while the elderly lady swayed herself to and fro, and the two younger ones whispered, "How shocking!"

Mr. Brocklehurst resumed. "This I learned from her benefactress. From the pious and charitable lady who adopted her in her orphan state, reared her as her own daughter, and whose kindness and generosity the unhappy girl repaid by an ingratitude so bad, so dreadful, that at last her excellent patroness was obliged to separate her from her own young ones."

With this sublime conclusion, Mr. Brocklehurst adjusted the top button of his surtout, muttered something to his family, bowed to Miss Temple and then all the great people sailed in state from the room. Turning at the door, my judge said, "Let her stand half-an-hour longer on that stool, and let no one speak to her during the remainder of the day."

There was I, then, mounted aloft. I, who had said I could not bear the shame of standing on my natural feet in the middle of the room, was now exposed to general view on a pedestal of infamy. What my sensations were no language can describe; but just as they all rose, stifling my breath and constricting my throat, a girl came up and passed me. In passing, she lifted her eyes.

What a strange light inspired them! What an extraordinary sensation that ray sent through me! How the new feeling bore me up!

Helen Burns asked some slight question about her work of Miss Smith, was chidden for the triviality of the inquiry, returned to her place and smiled at me as she again went by. What a smile! It lit up her marked lineaments, her thin face and her sunken grey eyes like a reflection from the aspect of an angel.

CHAPTER VIII

Five o'clock struck, school was dismissed, and all were gone into the refectory to tea. I now ventured to descend from my pedestal. It was deep dusk and I retired into a corner and sat down on the floor. The spell by which I had been so far supported began to dissolve and soon, so overwhelming was the grief that seized me, I sank prostrate with my face to the ground. Now I wept.

Helen Burns was not here and nothing sustained me. I abandoned myself, and my tears watered the boards. I had meant to be so good and to do so much at Lowood, to make so many friends, to earn respect and win affection. Already I had made visible progress since that very morning I had reached the head of my class and Miss Miller had praised me warmly. Miss Temple had smiled approbation, she had promised to teach me drawing and to let me learn French if I continued to make similar improvement two months longer. Yet now, here I lay again crushed and trodden on. Could I ever rise again?

"Never," I thought, and ardently I wished to die. While sobbing out this wish in broken accents, some one approached. I started up and again Helen Burns was near me. The fading fires just showed her coming up the long, vacant room and she brought my coffee and bread.

"Come, eat something," she said, but I put both away from me, feeling as if a drop or a crumb would have choked me in my present condition. Helen regarded me, probably with surprise and I could not now abate my agitation, though I tried hard. I continued to weep aloud.

She sat down on the ground near me, embraced her knees with her arms, and rested her head upon them; in that attitude she remained silent. I was the first who spoke.

"Helen, why do you stay with a girl whom everybody believes to be a liar?"

"Mr. Brocklehurst is not a great and admired man. He is little liked here and he never took steps to make himself liked. Had he treated you as an especial favourite, you would have found enemies, as it is, the greater number would offer you sympathy if they dared. Teachers and pupils may look coldly on you for a day or two, but friendly feelings are concealed in their hearts."

I did not care; Helen's words merely slid off me, sorrowful as I was. I could only think of the cold, loveless life I had left and how I did not want it to ever return.

"If others don't love me I would rather die than live," I sobbed. "To gain some real affection I would willingly submit to have the bone of my arm broken, or to let a bull toss me, or to stand behind a kicking horse, and let it dash its hoof at my chest—"

"Hush, Jane! You think too much of the love of human beings."

Perhaps I did. My waking hours were consumed with my deep ache for my dark-eyed lover. I craved the affection he symbolised in my mind and relished the hot rush of wanting that forever swept through me as he haunted my thoughts and dreams. I suppose I had been vaguely aware for some time that I thought about him a little too much, but such lonely hearts as that belonging to my childhood cannot be condemned for wanting such a human need as love. Besides, was it not Helen Burns who had told me that when she was whipped she thought of other things? I blushed at the memory. Perhaps those things that occupied her mind were good and homely, perhaps she thought of the family she had once had and not the rough hand of a lover.

Resting my head on Helen's shoulder, I put my arms round her waist. She drew me to her, and we reposed in silence. We had not sat long thus, when Miss Temple entered.

"I came on purpose to find you, Jane Eyre," said she, "I want you in my room and, as Helen Burns is with you, she may come too."

We followed the superintendent through some intricate passages and up a staircase before we reached her apartment, which contained a good fire and looked cheerful. Miss Temple told Helen Burns to be seated in a low arm-chair on one side of the hearth and herself taking another, she called me to her side.

"Is it all over?" she asked, looking down at my face. "Have you cried your grief away?"

"I am afraid I never shall do that."

"Why?"

"Because I have been wrongly accused; and you, ma'am, and everybody else, will now think me wicked."

"We shall think you what you prove yourself to be. Continue to act as a good girl, and you will satisfy us. Now tell me who is the lady whom Mr. Brocklehurst called your benefactress?"

"Mrs. Reed, my uncle's wife. My uncle is dead, and he left me to her care."

"Did she not, then, adopt you of her own accord?"

"No, ma'am; she was sorry to have to do it, but my uncle got her to promise before he died that she would always keep me."

"Well now, Jane, you know, or at least I will tell you, that when a criminal is accused, he is always allowed to speak in his own defence. You have been charged with falsehood; defend yourself to me as well as you can. Say whatever your memory suggests is true, but add nothing and exaggerate nothing."

I resolved, in the depth of my heart, that I would be most moderate—most correct—and, having reflected a few minutes in order to arrange coherently what I had to say, I told her all the story of my sad childhood. Exhausted by emotion, my language was more subdued than it generally was when it developed that sad theme; and mindful of Helen's warnings against the indulgence of resentment, I infused into the narrative far less of gall and wormwood than ordinary. Thus restrained and simplified, it sounded more credible. I felt as I went on that Miss Temple fully believed me.

When I had finished, Miss Temple regarded me a few minutes in silence. She then said, "I know something of the apothecary Mr. Lloyd and I shall write to him. If his reply agrees with the statement you have just given me—of your fit in the red-room—you shall be publicly cleared from every imputation. However to me, Jane, you are clear now."

She kissed me, and still keeping me at her side, she proceeded to address Helen Burns.

"How are you to-night, Helen? Have you coughed much to-day?"

"Not quite so much, I think, ma'am."

"And the pain in your chest?"

"It is a little better."

Miss Temple got up, took her hand and examined her pulse, then she returned to her own seat. As she resumed it, I heard her sigh low. She was pensive a few minutes, then rousing herself, she said cheerfully, "You two are my visitors to-night and I must treat you as such." She rang her bell.

"Barbara," she said to the servant who answered it, "I have not yet had tea, bring the tray and place cups for these two young ladies."

And a tray was soon brought. How pretty, to my eyes, did the china cups and bright teapot look placed on the little round table near the fire! How fragrant was the steam of the beverage, and the scent of the toast!

"Barbara," said Miss Temple, "can you not bring a little more bread and butter? There is not enough for three."

Barbara went out and she returned soon, "Madam, Mrs. Harden says she has sent up the usual quantity."

Mrs. Harden, be it observed, was the housekeeper and a woman after Mr. Brocklehurst's own heart, made up of equal parts of whalebone and iron.

"Oh, very well!" returned Miss Temple, "we must make it do, Barbara, I suppose." And as the girl withdrew she added, smiling, "Fortunately, I have it in my power to supply deficiencies for this once."

Having invited Helen and me to approach the table, and placed before each of us a cup of tea with one delicious but thin morsel of toast, she got up, unlocked a drawer, and taking from it a parcel wrapped in paper, disclosed presently to our eyes a good-sized seed-cake.

"I meant to give each of you some of this to take with you," said she, "but as there is so little toast, you must have it now," and she proceeded to cut slices with a generous hand.

We feasted that evening as on nectar and ambrosia; and not the least delight of the entertainment was the smile of gratification with which our hostess regarded us, as we satisfied our famished appetites on the delicate fare she liberally supplied.

Tea over and the tray removed, she again summoned us to the fire and we sat one on each side of her. Now a conversation followed between her and Helen, which it was indeed a privilege to be admitted to hear. They conversed of things I had never heard of; of nations and times past; of countries far away; of secrets of nature discovered or guessed at; and they spoke of books, oh how many they had read! What stores of knowledge they possessed! They seemed so familiar with French names and French authors, but my amazement reached its climax when Miss Temple asked Helen if she sometimes snatched a moment to recall the Latin her father had taught her, and taking a book from a shelf, bade her read and construe a page of Virgil. She had scarcely finished ere the bell announced bedtime and no delay could be admitted. Miss Temple embraced us both, saying, as she drew us to her heart, "God bless you, my children!"

Helen she held a little longer than me and she let her go more reluctantly. It was Helen her eye followed to the door and it was for her she a second time breathed a sad sigh and for her she wiped a tear from her cheek.

On reaching the bedroom, we heard the voice of Miss Scatcherd examining drawers and she had just pulled out Helen Burns's when we entered. Helen was greeted with a sharp reprimand, and told that to-morrow she should have half-a-dozen of untidily folded articles pinned to her shoulder.

"My things were indeed in shameful disorder," murmured Helen to me, in a low voice, "I intended to have arranged them, but I forgot."

Next morning, Miss Scatcherd wrote in conspicuous characters on a piece of pasteboard the word "Slattern," and bound it like a phylactery round Helen's large, mild, and intelligent forehead. She wore it till evening, patient and unresentful, regarding it as a deserved punishment. The moment Miss Scatcherd withdrew after afternoon school, I ran to Helen, tore it off, and thrust it into the fire. The fury of which she was incapable had been burning in my soul all day, and tears, hot and large, had continually been scalding my cheek; for the spectacle of her sad resignation gave me an intolerable pain at the heart.

About a week subsequently to the incidents above narrated, Miss Temple, who had written to Mr. Lloyd, received his

answer and it appeared that what he said went to corrobo-
rate my account. Miss Temple, having assembled the whole
school, announced that inquiry had been made into the char-
ges alleged against Jane Eyre, and that she was most happy
to be able to pronounce her completely cleared from every
imputation. The teachers then shook hands with me and kissed me, and a murmur of pleasure ran through the ranks of
my companions.

Thus relieved of a grievous load, I from that hour set to
work afresh and resolved to pioneer my way through every
difficulty. In a few weeks I was promoted to a higher class and
in less than two months I was allowed to commence French
and drawing. I learned the first two tenses of the verb *être*, and
sketched my first cottage (whose walls, by-the-bye, outrivalled
in slope those of the leaning tower of Pisa), on the same day.
That night on going to bed, I forgot to picture my dark-eyed
lover, with which I was wont to amuse my inward cravings.
I feasted instead on the spectacle of ideal drawings, which I
saw in the dark. I examined, too, in thought, the possibility of
my ever being able to translate currently a certain little French
story which Madame Pierrot had that day shown me. Thus
my young desire was extinguished with the lure of knowledge
and in this satisfied state, I fell sweetly asleep.

CHAPTER IX

The privations, or rather the hardships, of Lowood lessened. The frosts of winter ceased, the snow melted, the cutting winds ameliorated and spring came. My wretched feet, flayed and swollen to lameness by the sharp air of January, began to heal and subside under the gentler breathings of April. The nights and mornings no longer froze the very blood in our veins. Flowers peeped out amongst the leaves; snow-drops, crocuses, purple auriculas, and golden-eyed pansies. On Thursday afternoons (half-holidays) we now took walks, and found still sweeter flowers opening by the wayside, under the hedges.

April advanced to May and a bright serene May it was. Days of blue sky, placid sunshine, and soft western or southern gales filled up its duration. Vegetation matured with vigour; Lowood shook loose its tresses and it became all green, all flowery. Its great elm, ash, and oak skeletons were restored to majestic life. Woodland plants sprang up profusely in its recesses and unnumbered varieties of moss filled its hollows. All this I enjoyed often and fully, free, unwatched, and almost alone. Have I not described a pleasant site for a dwelling when I speak of it as bosomed in hill and wood, rising from the verge of a stream? Assuredly pleasant enough, but whether healthy or not is another question.

That forest-dell where Lowood lay was the cradle of fog and fog-bred pestilence; which, quickening with the quickening spring, crept into the Orphan Asylum and breathed typhus through its crowded interior. Semi-starvation and neglected colds had predisposed most of the pupils to receive infection. Forty-five out of the eighty girls lay ill at one time. Classes were broken up, rules relaxed. Miss Temple's whole attention was absorbed by the patients and she lived in the sick-room, never quitting it except to snatch a few hours' rest at night. The teachers were fully occupied with packing up and making other necessary preparations for the departure of those girls who were fortunate enough to have friends and relations able and willing to remove them from the seat of contagion. Many, already smitten, went home only to die. Some died at the school, and were buried quietly and quickly, the nature of the malady forbidding delay.

I, and the rest who continued well, enjoyed fully the beauties of the scene and season. They let us ramble in the wood like gipsies from morning till night and we did what we liked and went where we liked. Mr. Brocklehurst and his family never came near Lowood now and household matters were not scrutinised into. The cross housekeeper was gone, driven away by the fear of infection and her successor, who had been matron at the Lowton Dispensary, provided with comparative liberality. When there was no time to prepare a regular dinner, which often happened, she would give us a large piece of cold pie, or a thick slice of bread and cheese, and this we carried away with us to the wood, where we each chose the spot we liked best, and dined sumptuously.

And where in the meantime was Helen Burns? Why did I not spend these sweet days of liberty with her? Had I forgotten her? Or was I so worthless as to have grown tired of her pure society? Never. Helen was one of the many ill. For some weeks she had been removed from my sight to I knew not what room upstairs. She was not, I was told, in the hospital portion of the house with the fever patients for her complaint was consumption, not typhus. By consumption I, in my ignorance, understood something mild, which time and care would be sure to alleviate.

Without Helen I grew lonely, for in her I had found the love of a friend, a love I had never before possessed or imagined. My loneliness struck me bitterly and I would traipse the grounds of Lowood mournfully, wondering at my lost playmate. It was at this time that I came across an altogether different playmate.

Jack was the stable lad who tended to the ponies at Lowood, which were kept by the teachers for bringing goods and deliveries from Lowton. I would not have met him if it were not for the typhus, since we girls were chaperoned at all times and kept separate from the servants lest we got in the way. But as it was, I was in the midst of one of my mournful rambles when I happened upon Jack, sitting on a low stone wall. There was no one else about so when he said, "Good evening," I had no choice but to reply.

A conversation transpired in which Jack teased out of me the reason for my sadden mood and he lamented greatly the terrible illness that had taken over Lowood, claiming that he would escape here could he find work elsewhere, but that being unlikely, he was forced to stay.

I liked the easy way in which he talked and his gentle manner derived from a lifetime dealing with shying colts and skittish mares. He had large, soft hands and widely-set green eyes. He was not handsome with his dirty, fair hair and stocky, rough frame, but then I was not pretty and we saw in each other a mutual loneliness.

After that first meeting, I would often find Jack on that wall on my daily wanderings around Lowood and always I would stop to speak to him. I gathered that he often watched the young ladies of the school going about their lives but never had he a chance to talk to one and thus I became elevated in his eyes; a delicate delight that made up for the fact that I was no beauty.

I cannot remember the exact moment that he first touched me, or pressed his chapped lips against mine, but I can remember that I wanted him to desperately. It had been a year since I had been with a man and Jack was older and altogether nicer than John Reed. I did not love him, but I liked him and we began meeting twice a week and comforting each other with fervent kisses and hot embraces.

I usually met Jack on the low stone wall and together we would walk across Lowood's scrubland and eventually tumble under the shelter of an overhanging tree, stripping off our clothes and hungrily grasping for each other.

One evening at the beginning of June, however, Jack said, "There's a stable free."

I was just turning to take our usual route and his words took me by surprise.

"It'll be warmer than lying out this evening," he added.

It was, indeed, a little chilly. I nodded and followed him along the low stone wall, towards the stables. We had never laid together so near the main house before and the thrill of being discovered sent shivers down my spine.

"Jane, you're smiling," he said, tugging on my hand as we entered a dark, wooden outbuilding. "I believe that is a first."

"There is not much to smile about," I replied, trying to work the corners of my mouth down with the guilty thought that while I lay with a lover, my dear friend lay sick in her bed.

"You cannot control everything." And with those words he shut the stable door and pulled me down onto a stack of fresh, soft hay.

We had not met anyone in the yard nor was there a sound in the stable save the gentle chewing of a pony in the next stall and the distant buzz of a fly, but the thought of being discovered still sent pulses of excitement tingling from my heart to my groin. With trembling fingers, I tore off Jack's loose, dirty shirt. His manual labour had made him thick and defined and my hands ran up and down his vast, muscled chest, catching the tufts of his fair chest hair in my nails. I bit them into his shoulders gently and he groaned, pushing his lips to mine.

They were rough but tender, and they worked against mine in hunger. Desire sparked inside me, pushing my breasts hard against my stays so that they swelled beneath my dress. Jack stroked them over my uniform, each of his large hands softly caressing and groping them until my breath came out in hurried gasps. Meanwhile his tongue coaxed mine, touching the inside of my mouth and encouraging my own.

Thick, hot desire pooled in my stomach and the muscles in the deepest part of me clenched in anticipation. He put his great, thick arms around me and hauled me against his body over the hay. One hand remained stroking my breasts, while the other slid upwards to tug at my hair.

The rustle of hay as we moved was the only sound that punctuated the stillness of the stable. The light filtering through the rickety wood of the roof spilt dabbled yellow over our bodies and the air smelt sweetly of summertime.

Gripping Jack's large forearm with one hand, I used the other to caress his face and glide it slowly into his hair. Pinning me against the hay, he gently broke free so that he was leaning over me, staring into my eyes. I held his green gaze as he placed both hands on my legs and slowly slid them up, underneath my dress.

My skin burnt with his touch and my hips ached for him. His fingers an inch from between my legs, he paused and smiled at me, knowing how much I wanted him. I gasped, still holding his gaze and quickly he dipped one of his fingers inside of me whilst pushing his lips against mine and pressing me harder over the hay. I groaned as he moved his finger slowly in and out of me and I clawed at the hay around us.

Suddenly he stopped and began planting kisses across my jaw. I gently bent forward and bit his neck, pinching the skin with my teeth. He responded by pulling my hand over his firm, bulging erection. I tugged his breeches down and took it in my grasp, running my fingers up and down him teasingly.

He moaned and hitched my dress up further, maneuvering himself so that he was between my legs, about to enter. I arched my hips, slamming him inside me and hooked my arms around his neck. He grunted and moved in and out of me exquisitely slowly, sending shoots of pleasure shivering up my body.

He sped up and I moaned, meeting his thrusts. He grasped my head between his hands and kissed me hard, pressing his teeth into my lips. He shifted slightly and I could feel something building deep in the knot of desire at the pit of my stomach. My mind drew a blank, all of my wits scattered, and all I could feel was the sensation of him thrusting deeply in and out of me, rocking my body against the hay.

Suddenly he pulled out of me and came with a groan. Abruptly my desire vanished and I was left panting and unsatisfied.

"Oh Jane," he breathed, reclining on the hay next to me.

I looked down on his stocky, rough body and said nothing.

A little while later when I left the stables, it was dark outside, which surprised me. The moon had risen and in its light I saw a pony, which I knew to be the surgeon's, standing at the garden door as I approached the main building of Lowood. I supposed some one must be very ill, as Mr. Bates had been sent for at that time of the evening.

I heard the front door open and Mr. Bates came out, and with him was a nurse. After she had seen him mount his horse and depart, she was about to close the door, but I ran up to her.

"How is Helen Burns?" I asked.

"Very poorly," was the answer.

"Is it her Mr. Bates has been to see?"

"Yes."

A pang of guilt tore through my chest. While I had been indulging in pleasure, my friend was writhing in pain. I slowly lifted a hand to my hair and gingerly extracted a strand of hay, breaking it in two in my hands and throwing it to the ground.

"What does Mr. Bates say about her?" I asked, my heart thudding.

"He says she'll not be here long."

I experienced a shock of horror, then a strong thrill of grief and then necessity to see her. I asked in what room she lay.

"She is in Miss Temple's room," said the nurse.

"May I go up and speak to her?"

"Oh no, child! It is time for you to come in. You'll catch the fever if you stop out when the dew is falling."

The nurse closed the front door and I went in by the side entrance which led to the schoolroom. All was quiet and creeping along, I set off in quest of Miss Temple's room. It was at the other end of the house, but I knew my way and the light of the unclouded summer moon enabled me to find it without difficulty. I dreaded being discovered and sent back, for I *must* see Helen. I must embrace her before she died. I must exchange with her one last word.

Having descended a staircase, traversed a portion of the house below and succeeded in opening and shutting two doors without noise, I reached Miss Temple's room. A light

shone through the keyhole and from under the door, a profound stillness pervaded the vicinity. Coming near, I found
the door slightly ajar; probably to admit some fresh air into
the close abode of sickness. Indisposed to hesitate and full
of impatient impulses I put it back and looked in. My eye
sought Helen and feared to find death.

Close by Miss Temple's bed and half covered with its
white curtains, there stood a little crib. I saw the outline of a
form under the clothes, but the face was hid by the hangings.
The nurse I had spoken to in the garden sat in an easy-chair
asleep; an unsnuffed candle burnt dimly on the table. Miss
Temple was not to be seen and I found afterwards that she
had been called to a delirious patient in the fever-room. I advanced, then paused by the crib side, my hand on the curtain,
but I preferred speaking before I withdrew it. I still recoiled
at the dread of seeing a corpse.

"Helen!" I whispered softly, "are you awake?"

She stirred herself, put back the curtain, and I saw her
face—pale, wasted, but quite composed. She looked so little
changed that my fear was instantly dissipated.

"Can it be you, Jane?" she asked, in her own gentle voice.

I got on to her crib and kissed her. Her forehead was cold,
and her cheek both cold and thin, and so were her hands and
wrists; but she smiled as of old.

"Why are you come here, Jane? It is past eleven o'clock.
I heard it strike some minutes since."

"I came to see you, Helen. I heard you were very ill and
I could not sleep till I had spoken to you."

"You came to bid me good-bye and you are just in time
probably."

"Are you going somewhere, Helen? Are you going home?"

"Yes, to my long home—my last home."

"No, no, Helen!" I stopped, distressed. While I tried to
devour my tears, a fit of coughing seized Helen. It did not,

however, wake the nurse and when it was over, she lay some minutes exhausted. Then she whispered, "Jane, your little feet are bare; lie down and cover yourself with my quilt."

I did so. She put her arm over me, and I nestled close to her. After a long silence, she resumed still whispering, "I am very happy, Jane; and when you hear that I am dead, you must be sure and not grieve because there is nothing to grieve about. I have only a father; and he is lately married, and will not miss me. By dying young, I shall escape great sufferings."

"And shall I see you again, Helen, when I die?"

"You will come to the same region of happiness and be received by the same mighty, universal Parent, no doubt, dear Jane."

I clasped my arms closer round Helen and she seemed dearer to me than ever. She had afforded me a little of the love that I had always craved and I did not know what I should do without her. Who would love me now? I felt as if I could not let her go and I lay with my face hidden on her neck. Presently she said, in the sweetest tone , "How comfortable I am! That last fit of coughing has tired me a little; I feel as if I could sleep. But don't leave me, Jane. I like to have you near me."

"I'll stay with you, dear Helen, and no one shall take me away."

"Are you warm?"

"Yes."

"Good-night, Jane."

"Good-night, Helen."

She kissed me, and we both soon slumbered.

When I awoke it was day and an unusual movement roused me. I looked up and I was in somebody's arms; the nurse held me; she was carrying me through the passage back to the dormitory. I was not reprimanded for leaving my bed; people had something else to think about. A day or two afterwards I learned that Miss Temple, on returning to her own room at dawn, had found me laid in the little crib; my face against Helen Burns's shoulder, my arms round her neck. I was asleep and Helen was dead.

Her grave is in Brocklebridge churchyard and for fifteen years after her death it was only covered by a grassy mound, but now a grey marble tablet marks the spot, inscribed with her name and the word "Resurgam."

CHAPTER X

When the typhus fever had fulfilled its mission of devastation at Lowood, it gradually disappeared from thence; but not till the number of its victims had drawn public attention on the school. Inquiry was made into the origin of the scourge, and by degrees various facts came out which excited public indignation in a high degree. The unhealthy nature of the site, the quantity and quality of the children's food, the brackish, fetid water used in its preparation and the pupils' wretched clothing and accommodations—all these things were discovered and the discovery produced a result mortifying to Mr. Brocklehurst, but beneficial to the institution.

Several wealthy and benevolent individuals in the county subscribed largely for the erection of a more convenient building in a better situation. New regulations were made, improvements in diet and clothing introduced and the funds of the school were intrusted to the management of a committee. Mr. Brocklehurst, who, from his wealth and family connections, could not be overlooked, still retained the post of treasurer; but he was aided in the discharge of his duties by gentlemen of rather more enlarged and sympathising minds: his office of inspector. The school, thus improved, became in time a truly useful and noble institution. I remained an inmate of its walls after its regeneration for three years: two as pupil, and one as teacher. In both capacities I bear my testimony to its value and importance.

During these three years, my life was uniform but not unhappy. I had the means of an excellent education placed within my reach, a fondness for some of my studies and a desire to excel in all, together with a great delight in pleasing my teachers. Some months after Helen Burns's death, Jack sought me and told me that he was leaving. We had not seen much of each other since the lax rules were once again tightened after the typhus epidemic died down and though I was disappointed that I could no longer seek solace in his arms, I was happy for him to leave under the prospects of finding a better position elsewhere than a lowly stable lad. He did sheepishly suggest that perhaps I should wish to run away with him, but I would not have left Lowood with its prospects of an education for anything. In time I almost forgot about Jack completely, throwing myself into my studies instead and rising to be the first girl of the first class. I was then invested with the office of teacher, which I discharged with zeal for a year, but at the end of that time, I altered.

Miss Temple, through all changes, had thus far continued superintendent of the seminary. However, at this period she married, removed with her husband (a clergyman, an excellent man, almost worthy of such a wife) to a distant county, and consequently was lost to me. From the day she left I was no longer the same and with her was gone every settled feeling, every association that had made Lowood in some degree a home to me. I now remembered that the real world was wide and that a varied field of hopes and fears, of sensations and excitements, awaited those who had courage to go forth and seek it.

I wanted to explore the hilly horizon I could see from my bedroom window. I longed to surmount those blue peaks; all within their boundary of rock and heath seemed prison-ground, exile limits. My vacations had all been spent at school since Mrs. Reed had never sent for me to Gateshead

and neither she nor any of her family had ever been to visit
me. I had had no communication by letter or message with
the outer world: school-rules, school-duties, school-habits,
notions, voices, faces, phrases, costumes, and preferences was
all I knew of existence. And now I felt that it was not enough.
I tired of the routine of three years and I desired liberty.

That night I sat up in bed and then I proceeded to think
with all my might.

"What do I want?" I asked myself. "A new place, in a new
house amongst new faces, under new circumstances. What
do people do to get a new place?"

I could not tell and nothing answered me. I then ordered
my brain to find a response and quickly. It worked and worked
faster. I felt the pulses throb in my head and temples, but for nearly an hour it worked in chaos and no result came of its efforts.
Feverish with vain labour, I got up and took a turn in the room,
undrew the curtain, noted a star or two, shivered with cold and
again crept to bed.

A kind fairy in my absence had surely dropped the required suggestion on my pillow; for as I lay down, it came quietly and naturally to my mind: "Those who want situations
advertise; you must advertise in the -shire Herald."

The next day I was up early. I had my advertisement written, enclosed, and directed before the bell rang to rouse the
school and it ran thus: "A young lady accustomed to tuition
is desirous of meeting with a situation in a private family
where the children are under fourteen" (I thought that as
I was barely nineteen, it would not do to undertake the gui-
dance of pupils nearer my own age). "She is qualified to teach
the usual branches of a good English education, together with
French, Drawing, and Music" (in those days, Reader, this
now narrow catalogue of accomplishments, would have been
held tolerably comprehensive). "Address, J.E., Post-office,
Lowton, -shire."

This document I took to the post-office that afternoon.

The succeeding week seemed long, but it came to an end at last, and towards the close of a pleasant autumn day, I found myself afoot on the road to Lowton. A picturesque track it was, lying along the side of the beck and through the sweetest curves of the dale, but that day I thought more of the letters that might or might not be awaiting me at the little burgh whither I was bound, than of the charms of lea and water.

"Are there any letters for J.E.?" I asked at the post-office.

The lady peered at me over her spectacles, and then she opened a drawer and fumbled among its contents for a long time, so long that my hopes began to falter. At last, having held a document before her glasses for nearly five minutes, she presented it across the counter—it was for J.E.

"Is there only one?" I demanded.

"There are no more," said she.

I put it in my pocket and turned my face homeward. I could not open it then; rules obliged me to be back by eight and it was already half-past seven.

Various duties awaited me on my arrival. I had to sit with the girls during their hour of study, then it was my turn to read prayers, then to see them to bed and afterwards I supped with the other teachers. Finally alone in my room, I took out my letter with the seal initial F and broke it. The contents were brief:

"If J.E., who advertised in the -shire Herald of last Thursday, possesses the acquirements mentioned, and if she is in a position to give satisfactory references as to character and competency, a situation can be offered her where there is but one pupil, a little girl under ten years of age. The salary is thirty pounds per annum. J.E. is requested to send references, name, address, and all particulars to the direction: Mrs. Fairfax, Thornfield, near Millcote, -shire."

I went to the superintendent immediately.

A fortnight later, my place at Thornfield with Mrs. Fair-fax having been secured, I sat in my room with the little pos-sessions I owned packed in a box before me. I was anxious for my new life and could not settle to wait for the carriage that would come to fetch me tomorrow.

"Miss," said a servant, entering, "a person below wishes to see you."

"The carrier, no doubt," I thought, and ran downstairs without inquiry. I was passing the back-parlour which was half open to go to the kitchen, when some one ran out.

"It's her, I am sure! I could have told her anywhere!" cried the individual who stopped my progress and took my hand.

I looked and I saw a woman attired like a well-dressed servant, matronly, yet still young; very good-looking with black hair and eyes, and lively complexion.

"Well, who is it?" she asked, in a voice and with a smile I half recognised; "you've not quite forgotten me, I think, Miss Jane?"

In another second I was embracing and kissing her rapturously. "Bessie! Bessie! Bessie!" that was all I said. Whereat she half laughed, half cried, and we both went into the parlour. By the fire stood a little fellow of two years old, in plaid frock and trousers.

"That is my little boy," said Bessie directly.

"Then you are married, Bessie?"

"Yes, nearly five years since to Robert Leaven, the coach-man."

"And you don't live at Gateshead?"

"I live at the lodge since the old porter has left."

"Well, and how do the Reeds all get on? Tell me everyth-ing about them. But sit down first and Bobby, come and sit on my knee, will you?" but Bobby preferred sidling over to his mother.

"You're not grown so very tall, Miss Jane, nor so very stout," continued Mrs. Leaven. "I dare say they've not kept you too well at school. Miss Reed is the head and shoulders taller than you are, and Miss Georgiana would make two of you in breadth."

"Georgiana is handsome, I suppose, Bessie?"

"Very. She went up to London last winter with her mama, and there everybody admired her and a young lord fell in love with her. But his relations were against the match so he and Miss Georgiana made it up to run away, but they were found out and stopped."

"And what of John Reed?"

I thought very little about my childhood lover, for I did not remember him in a fond light, but I was intrigued as to his circumstances now.

"Oh, he is not doing so well as his mama could wish. He went to college and his uncles wanted him to be a barrister and study the law, but he is such a dissipated young man, they will never make much of him, I think."

"What does he look like?"

"He is very tall and some people call him a fine-looking young man, but he has such thick lips."

"And Mrs. Reed?"

"Missis looks stout and well enough in the face, but I think she's not quite easy in her mind. Mr. John's conduct does not please her—he spends a deal of money."

"Did she send you here, Bessie?"

"No, indeed, but I have long wanted to see you! When I heard that there had been a letter from you, and that you were going to another part of the country, I thought I'd just set off, and get a look at you before you were quite out of my reach."

"I am afraid you are disappointed in me, Bessie," I said this laughing. I perceived that Bessie's glance, though it expressed regard, did in no shape denote admiration.

"No, Miss Jane, not exactly. You are genteel enough, you look like a lady, and it is as much as ever I expected of you. You were no beauty as a child."

I smiled at Bessie's frank answer. I felt that it was correct, but I confess I was not quite indifferent to its import. At nineteen most people wish to please, and the conviction that they have not an exterior likely to second that desire brings anything but gratification.

"I dare say you are clever, though," continued Bessie, by way of solace. "What can you do? Can you play on the piano?"

"A little."

There was one in the room and Bessie went and opened it. She asked me to sit down and give her a tune so I played a waltz or two, and she was charmed.

"The Miss Reeds could not play as well!" said she exultingly. "I always said you would surpass them in learning. Can you draw?"

"That is one of my paintings over the chimney-piece." It was a landscape in water colours, of which I had made a present to the superintendent and which she had framed and glazed.

"Well, that is beautiful, Miss Jane! It is as fine a picture as any Miss Reed's drawing-master could paint, let alone the young ladies themselves, who could not come near it. Have you learnt French?"

"Yes, Bessie, I can both read it and speak it."

"And you can work on muslin and canvas?"

"I can."

"Oh, you are quite a lady, Miss Jane! I knew you would be. You will get on whether your relations notice you or not. There was something I wanted to ask you, have you ever heard anything from your father's kinsfolk, the Eyres?"

"Never in my life."

"Well, you know Missis always said they were poor and quite despicable? They may be poor, but I believe they are as much gentry as the Reeds are for one day, nearly seven years ago, a Mr. Eyre came to Gateshead and wanted to see you. Missis said you were to school fifty miles off and he seemed so much disappointed, for he could not stay. He was going on a voyage to a foreign country, and the ship was to sail from London in a day or two. He looked quite a gentleman, and I believe he was your father's brother."

"What foreign country was he going to, Bessie?"

"An island thousands of miles off, where they make wine—the butler did tell me—"

"Madeira?" I suggested.

"Yes, that is it—that is the very word."

"So he went?"

"Yes, he did not stay many minutes in the house. Missis was very high with him and she called him afterwards a 'sneaking tradesman.' My Robert believes he was a wine-merchant."

"Very likely," I returned, "or perhaps clerk or agent to a wine-merchant."

Bessie and I conversed about old times an hour longer, and then she was obliged to leave me. I saw her again for a few minutes the next morning at Lowton, while I was waiting for the coach. We parted finally at the door of the Brocklehurst Arms there and each went her separate way. She set off for the brow of Lowood Fell to meet the conveyance which was to take her back to Gateshead and I mounted the vehicle which was to bear me to new duties and a new life in the unknown environs of Millcote.

CHAPTER XI

Having travelled from Lowton to Millcote and being dropped at an inn there, I had expected a separate carriage to be waiting for me, that would bear me to my new home. Anxiously, I looked about me, wondering what I should do and at last I entered the inn and enquired.

"Is there a place in this neighbourhood called Thornfield?" I asked of a waiter.

"Thornfield? I don't know, ma'am. I'll inquire at the bar." He vanished, but reappeared instantly.

"Is your name Eyre, Miss?"

"Yes."

"There is a person here waiting for you."

I jumped up, took my muff and umbrella, and hastened into the inn-passage. A man was standing by the open door, and in the lamp-lit street I dimly saw a one-horse conveyance.

"This will be your luggage, I suppose?" said the man rather abruptly when he saw me, pointing to my trunk in the passage.

"Yes."

He hoisted it on to the vehicle, which was a sort of car, and then I got in. Before he shut me up, I asked him how far it was to Thornfield.

"A matter of six miles."

"How long shall we be before we get there?"

"An hour and a half."

He fastened the car door, climbed to his own seat outside, and we set off. Our progress was leisurely and gave me ample time to reflect. I was content to be at length so near the end of my journey and as I leaned back in the comfortable though not elegant conveyance, I meditated much at my ease.

"I suppose," thought I, "judging from the plainness of the servant and carriage, Mrs. Fairfax is not a very dashing person and so much the better. I never lived amongst fine people but once, and I was very miserable with them. I pray God Mrs. Fairfax may not turn out a second Mrs. Reed."

I let down the window and looked out; Millcote was behind us, judging by the number of its lights. We were now, as far as I could see, on a sort of common, but there were houses scattered all over the district and I felt we were in a different region to Lowood, more populous and less picturesque. More stirring and less romantic.

The roads were heavy, the night misty and my conductor let his horse walk all the way. I verily believe it took two hours till at last, he turned in his seat and said, "You're noan so far fro' Thornfield now."

About ten minutes after, the driver got down and opened a pair of gates, which we passed through, and they clashed to behind us. We now slowly ascended a drive and came upon the long front of a house. Candlelight gleamed from one curtained bow-window, but all the rest were dark. The car stopped at the front door and it was opened by a maid-servant. I alighted and went in.

"Will you walk this way, ma'am?" said the girl, and I followed her across a square hall with high doors all round. She ushered me into a room whose double illumination of fire and candle at first dazzled me. When I could finally see, a cosy and agreeable picture presented itself to my view.

A snug small room with an arm-chair high-backed and old-fashioned, wherein sat the neatest imaginable little elderly lady, in widow's cap, black silk gown and snowy muslin apron. It was exactly as I had fancied Mrs. Fairfax, only less stately and milder looking. She was occupied in knitting and a large cat sat demurely at her feet. Nothing in short was wanting to complete the beau-ideal of domestic comfort. As I entered, the old lady got up and promptly and kindly came forward to meet me.

"How do you do, my dear? You must be cold, come to the fire."

"Mrs. Fairfax, I suppose?" said I.

"Yes, you are right, do sit down."

She conducted me to her own chair, and then said, "You've brought your luggage with you, haven't you, my dear?"

"Yes, ma'am."

"I'll see it carried into your room," she said, and bustled out.

"She treats me like a visitor," thought I. "I little expected such a reception. I anticipated only coldness and stiffness. This is not like what I have heard of the treatment of governesses; but I must not exult too soon."

She returned and cleared her knitting apparatus and a book or two from the table, to make room for the tray of food which the servant, Leah, now brought for me. Then she herself handed me the refreshments. I felt rather confused at being the object of more attention than I had ever before received, and shown by my employer and superior as well, but I did not fuss.

"Shall I have the pleasure of seeing Miss Fairfax to-night?" I asked, when I had partaken of what she offered me.

"What did you say, my dear? I am a little deaf," returned the good lady, approaching her ear to my mouth.

I repeated the question more distinctly.

"Miss Fairfax? Oh, you mean Miss Varens! Varens is the name of your future pupil."

"Indeed! Then she is not your daughter?"

"No, I have no family."

I should have followed up my first inquiry by asking in what way Miss Varens was connected with her, but I recollected it was not polite to ask too many questions. Besides, I was sure to hear in time.

"I am so glad," she continued, as she sat down opposite to me and took the cat on her knee, "I am so glad you are come. It will be quite pleasant living here now with a companion. Leah is a nice girl to be sure, and the man who brought you, John and his wife are very decent people, but then you see they are only servants, and one can't converse with them on terms of equality. I'm sure last winter (it was a very severe one, if you recollect, and when it did not snow, it rained and blew), not a creature but the butcher and postman came to the house, from November till February, and I really got quite melancholy. In spring and summer one get on better. Sunshine and long days make such a difference. Now you are here, I shall be quite gay."

My heart really warmed to the worthy lady as I heard her talk and I drew my chair a little nearer to her, and expressed my sincere wish that she might find my company as agreeable as she anticipated.

"But I'll not keep you sitting up late to-night," said she, "it is on the stroke of twelve now, and you have been travelling all day, you must feel tired. If you have got your feet well warmed, I'll show you your bedroom. I've had the room next to mine prepared for you; it is only a small apartment, but I thought you would like it better than one of the large front chambers, they are dreary and solitary."

I thanked her for her considerate choice, and as I really felt fatigued with my long journey, expressed my readiness to retire. She took her candle, and I followed her from the room.

When I awoke, it was broad day. The chamber looked such a bright little place to me as the sun shone in between the gay blue chintz window curtains, showing papered walls and a carpeted floor, so unlike the bare planks and stained plaster of Lowood, that my spirits lifted at the view.

I rose and dressed myself with care, obliged to be plain— for I had no article of attire that was not made with extreme simplicity. It was not my habit to be disregardful of appearance or careless of the impression I made. On the contrary, I ever wished to look as well as I could, and to please as much as my want of beauty would permit. I sometimes regretted that I was not handsomer. I sometimes wished to have rosy cheeks, a straight nose and small cherry mouth; I desired to be tall, stately, and finely developed in figure. I felt it a misfortune that I was so little, so pale, and had features so irregular and so marked. However, when I had brushed my hair very smooth, and put on my black frock—which Quakerlike as it was at least had the merit of fitting to a nicety—and adjusted my clean white tucker, I thought I should do respectably enough to appear before Mrs. Fairfax, and that my new pupil would not at least recoil from me. Having opened my chamber window, and seen that I left all things straight and neat on the toilet table, I ventured forth.

Traversing the long and matted gallery, I descended the slippery steps of oak. Everything appeared very stately and imposing to me, but then I was so little accustomed to grandeur. The hall-door, which was half of glass, stood open and I stepped over the threshold. It was a fine autumn morning and the early sun shone serenely through the windows. I looked out and surveyed the front of the mansion. It was three storeys high, of proportions not vast, though considerable: a gentleman's manor-house, not a nobleman's seat. Battlements round the top gave it a picturesque look. Its grey front stood out well from the background of a rookery, who-

se cawing tenants were now on the wing and they flew over
the lawn and grounds. Farther off were hills, not so lofty as
those round Lowood nor so craggy, but seeming to embrace
Thornfield with a seclusion I had not expected to find exis-
tent so near the stirring locality of Millcote.

I was yet enjoying the calm prospect and pleasant fresh
air and thinking what a great place it was for one lonely
little dame like Mrs. Fairfax to inhabit, when that lady appeared at the door.

"What! Out already?" said she. "I see you are an early
riser."

I went up to her, and was received with an affable kiss
and shake of the hand.

"How do you like Thornfield?" she asked.

I told her I liked it very much.

"Yes," she said, "it is a pretty place, but I fear it will be
getting out of order, unless Mr. Rochester should take it into
his head to come and reside here permanently. Great houses
and fine grounds require the presence of the proprietor."

"Mr. Rochester!" I exclaimed. "Who is he?"

"The owner of Thornfield," she responded quietly. "Did
you not know he was called Rochester?"

Of course I did not—I had never heard of him before,
but the old lady seemed to regard his existence as a univer-
sally understood fact, with which everybody must be acquainted by instinct.

"I thought," I continued, "Thornfield belonged to you."

"To me? Bless you, child, what an idea! To me! I am only
the housekeeper—the manager."

"And the little girl—my pupil!"

"She is Mr. Rochester's ward and he commissioned me to
find a governess for her. He intended to have her brought up
in -shire, I believe. Here she comes, with her 'bonne', as she
calls her nurse."

The enigma then was explained: this affable and kind little widow was no great dame, but a dependant like myself. I did not like her the worse for that, on the contrary, I felt better pleased than ever. The equality between her and me was real and not the mere result of condescension on her part. So much the better—my position was all the freer.

As I was meditating on this discovery, a little girl, followed by her attendant came running up the lawn. I looked at my pupil, who did not at first appear to notice me. She was quite a child, perhaps seven or eight years old, slightly built, with a pale, small-featured face, and a redundancy of hair falling in curls to her waist.

"Good morning, Miss Adele," said Mrs. Fairfax. "Come and speak to the lady who is to teach you, and to make you a clever woman some day."

She approached.

"C'est le ma gouverante!" said she, pointing to me, and addressing her nurse, who answered, "Mais oui, certainement."

"Are they foreigners?" I inquired, amazed at hearing the French language.

"The nurse is a foreigner, and Adele was born on the Continent. I believe she never left it till within six months ago. When she first came here she could speak no English; now she can make shift to talk it a little, but I don't understand her since she mixes it so with French, but you will make out her meaning very well, I dare say."

Fortunately I had had the advantage of being taught French by a French lady; and as I had always made a point of conversing with Madame Pierrot as often as I could, I had acquired a certain degree of readiness and correctness in the language, and was not likely to be much at a loss with Mademoiselle Adele. She came and shook hand with me when she heard that I was her governess; and as I led her in to breakfast, I addressed some phrases to her in her own tongue. She replied briefly at first, but after we were seated at the table and she had examined me some ten minutes with her large hazel eyes, she suddenly commenced chattering fluently.

"Ah!" cried she, in French, "you speak my language as well as Mr. Rochester does. I can talk to you as I can to him, and so can Sophie. She will be glad, nobody here understands her and Madame Fairfax is all English. Sophie is my nurse; she came with me over the sea in a great ship with a chimney that smoked—how it did smoke!—and I was sick, and so was Sophie, and so was Mr. Rochester. Mr. Rochester lay down on a sofa in a pretty room called the salon, and Sophie and I had little beds in another place. I nearly fell out of mine; it was like a shelf."

"Can you understand her when she runs on so fast?" asked Mrs. Fairfax.

I understood her very well and nodded.

"I wish," continued the good lady, "you would ask her a question or two about her parents. I wonder if she remembers them?"

"Adele," I inquired, "with whom did you live when you were in that pretty clean town you spoke of?"

"I lived long ago with mama; but she is gone to the Holy Virgin. Mama used to teach me to dance and sing, and to say verses. A great many gentlemen and ladies came to see mama, and I used to dance before them, or sit on their knees and sing to them. I liked it. Shall I let you hear me sing now?"

She had finished her breakfast, so I permitted her to give a specimen of her accomplishments. Descending from her chair, she came and placed herself on my knee and then, folding her little hands demurely before her, shaking back her curls and lifting her eyes to the ceiling, she commenced singing a song from some opera. It was the strain of a forsaken lady, who, after bewailing the perfidy of her lover, calls pride to her aid and desires her attendant to deck her in her brightest jewels and richest robes, and resolves to meet the false one that night at a ball, and prove to him, by the gaiety of her demeanour, how little his desertion has affected her. The subject seemed strangely chosen for an infant singer; but I suppose the point of the exhibition lay in hearing the notes of love and jealousy warbled with the lisp of childhood; and in very bad taste that point was. At least I thought so.

Adele sang the canzonette tunefully enough, and with the naïvete of her age. This achieved, she jumped from my knee and said, "Now, Mademoiselle, I will repeat you some poetry."

Assuming an attitude, she began, "La Ligue des Rats: fable de La Fontaine." She then declaimed the little piece with an attention to punctuation and emphasis, a flexibility of voice and an appropriateness of gesture, very unusual indeed at her age, and which proved she had been carefully trained.

"Was it your mama who taught you that piece?" I asked.

"Yes, and she just used to say it in this way: 'Qu' avez vous donc? lui dit un de ces rats; parlez!' She made me lift my hand to remind me to raise my voice at the question. Now shall I dance for you?"

"No, that will do: but after your mama went to the Holy Virgin, as you say, with whom did you live then?"

"With Madame Frederic and her husband. I was not long there. Mr. Rochester asked me if I would like to go and live with him in England, and I said yes; for I knew Mr. Rochester was always kind to me and gave me pretty dresses and toys. But you see he has not kept his word, for he has brought me to England, and now he is gone back again himself, and I never see him."

After breakfast, Adele and I withdrew to the library, which room, it appears, Mr. Rochester had directed should be used as the schoolroom. Most of the books were locked up behind glass doors; but there was one bookcase left open containing everything that could be needed in the way of elementary works. In this room, too, there was a cabinet piano, quite new and of superior tone; also an easel for painting and a pair of globes.

I found my pupil sufficiently docile, though disinclined to apply. She had not been used to regular occupation of any kind. I felt it would be injudicious to confine her too much at first; so when the morning had advanced to noon, I allowed her to return to her nurse. I then proposed to occupy myself till dinner-time in drawing some little sketches for her use.

As I was going upstairs to fetch my portfolio and pencils, Mrs. Fairfax called to me: "Your morning school-hours are over now, I suppose." She was in a room, the folding-doors of which stood open. I went in when she addressed me. It was a large, stately apartment with purple chairs and curtains. Mrs. Fairfax was dusting some vases of fine purple spar, which stood on a sideboard.

"What a beautiful room!" I exclaimed, as I looked round.

"Yes, this is the dining-room. I have just opened the window, to let in a little air and sunshine. Though Mr. Rochester's visits here are rare, they are always sudden and unexpected so I thought it best to keep the rooms in readiness."

"Do you like Mr. Rochester? Is he generally liked?"

"Oh, yes; the family have always been respected here. Almost all the land in this neighbourhood, as far as you can see, has belonged to the Rochesters time out of mind."

"But, leaving his land out of the question, do you like him? Is he liked for himself?"

"I have no cause to do otherwise than like him."

"But has he no peculiarities? What, in short, is his character?"

"Oh! His character is unimpeachable, I suppose. He is

rather peculiar, perhaps. He has travelled a great deal, and seen a great deal of the world, I should think. I dare say he is clever, but I never had much conversation with him."

"In what way is he peculiar?"

"I don't know—it is not easy to describe—nothing striking, but you feel it when he speaks to you. You cannot be always sure whether he is in jest or earnest, whether he is pleased or the contrary. You don't thoroughly understand him, but he is a good master."

This was all the account I got from Mrs. Fairfax of her employer and mine. Mr. Rochester was Mr. Rochester in her eyes; a gentleman and a landed proprietor—nothing more.

When we left the dining-room, she proposed to show me over the rest of the house; and I followed her upstairs and downstairs, admiring as I went; for all was well arranged and handsome. I liked the hush, the gloom and the quaintness of the large front rooms upstairs in the day, but I by no means coveted a night's repose on one of those wide and heavy beds. Some of them were shut in with doors of oak, others with wrought old English hangings crusted with thick work, portraying effigies of strange flowers, stranger birds, and strangest human beings—all which would have looked strange, indeed, by the pallid gleam of moonlight.

"Do the servants sleep in these rooms?" I asked.

"No, they occupy a range of smaller apartments to the back. No one ever sleeps here and one would almost say that, if there were a ghost at Thornfield Hall, this would be its haunt."

"So you have no ghost, then?"

"None that I ever heard of," returned Mrs. Fairfax, smiling.

"Nor any traditions of one? No legends or ghost stories?"

"I believe not."

I followed her up a very narrow staircase to the attics, and thence by a ladder and through a trap-door to the roof of the hall. I was now on a level with the crow colony, and could see into their nests. Leaning over the battlements and looking far down, I surveyed the grounds laid out like a map: the bright and velvet lawn closely girdling the grey base of the mansion, the field, wide as a park, dotted with its ancient timber and the wood, dun and sere. The horizon was bounded by a propitious sky, azure, marbled with pearly white. No feature in the scene was extraordinary, but all was pleasing. When I turned from it and repassed the trap-door, I could scarcely see my way down the ladder and the attic seemed black as a vault compared with that arch of blue air to which I had been looking up.

Mrs. Fairfax stayed behind a moment to fasten the trap-door and I lingered in the long passage to which this led. It was narrow, low and dim, with only one little window at the far end, and looking, with its two rows of small black doors all shut, like a corridor in some Bluebeard's castle.

While I paced softly on, the last sound I expected to hear in so still a region—a laugh—struck my ear. It was a curious laugh; distinct, formal, mirthless. I stopped and the sound ceased, only for an instant before it began again, louder. It passed off in a clamorous peal that seemed to wake an echo in every lonely chamber; though it originated but in one, and I could have pointed out the door whence the accents issued.

"Mrs. Fairfax!" I called out, for I now heard her descending the great stairs. "Did you hear that loud laugh? Who is it?"

"Some of the servants, very likely," she answered. "Perhaps Grace Poole."

"Did you hear it?" I again inquired.

"Yes, plainly. I often hear her since she sews in one of these rooms. Sometimes Leah is with her and they are frequently noisy together."

The laugh was repeated in its low, syllabic tone, and terminated in an odd murmur.

"Grace!" exclaimed Mrs. Fairfax.

I really did not expect any Grace to answer; for the laugh was as tragic, as preternatural a laugh as any I ever heard.

The door nearest me opened and a servant came out—a woman of between thirty and forty; a set, square-made figure, red-haired, and with a hard, plain face. Any apparition less romantic or less ghostly could scarcely be conceived.

"Too much noise, Grace," said Mrs. Fairfax. "Remember directions!" Grace curtseyed silently and went in.

"She is a person we have to sew and assist Leah in her housemaid's work. By-the-bye, how have you got on with your new pupil this morning?"

The conversation thus turned on Adele, continued till we reached the light and cheerful region below. Adele came running to meet us in the hall, exclaiming

"Mesdames, vous etes servies!" adding, "J'ai bien faim, moi!"

We found dinner ready, and waiting for us in Mrs. Fairfax's room.

CHAPTER XII

Mrs. Fairfax turned out to be what she appeared; a placid-tempered, kind-natured woman of competent education and average intelligence. My pupil was a lively child, who had been spoilt and indulged and therefore was sometimes wayward, but as she was committed entirely to my care she soon forgot her little ways and her manner changed. I became quite attached to them both, but despite Adele and Mrs. Fairfax, I felt lonely. For three years I had been without male company at Lowood and since Jack left, I had not missed it. I was too busy learning and drinking in all the knowledge that was offered to me to wish for the tender touch of another or writhing bodies of ecstasy. But now, circumstance had changed and I looked earnestly for another that could quench the hungry desire that burnt deeply in my chest. I wanted to be loved in a way that was not for-filled by the admiration of my student or the companionship of the old widow. I went about my life as usual, but my yearning was strong and hot inside me.

When alone in these months, I often heard Grace Poole's laugh. The same peal, the same low, slow *ha! ha!* which when first heard had thrilled me. I heard too her eccentric murmurs; stranger than her laugh. There were days when she was quite silent, but there were others when I could not account for the sounds she made. Sometimes I saw her and she would come out of her room with a basin or a plate or a tray in her hand, go down to the kitchen and shortly return. I made some attempts to draw her into conversation, but she seemed a person of few words. A monosyllabic reply usually cut short every effort of that sort.

October, November, and December passed away. One afternoon in January, Mrs. Fairfax begged a holiday for Adele because she had a cold and, as Adele seconded the request with an ardour that reminded me how precious occasional holidays had been to me in my own childhood, I accorded it. It was a fine, calm day though very cold and I was tired of sitting still in the library through a whole long morning. Mrs. Fairfax had just written a letter which was waiting to be posted so I put on my bonnet and cloak and volunteered to carry it to Hay. The distance of two miles would be a pleasant winter afternoon walk. Having seen Adele comfortably seated in her little chair by Mrs. Fairfax's parlour fireside, and given her her best wax doll to play with, I set out.

The ground was hard, the air was still and my road was lonely. I walked fast till I got warm, and then I walked slowly to enjoy and analyse the species of pleasure brooding for me in the hour and situation. It was three o'clock; the church bell tolled as I passed under the belfry and the charm of the hour lay in its approaching dimness, in the low-gliding and pale-beaming sun. I was a mile from Thornfield, in a lane noted for wild roses in summer and if a breath of air stirred, it made no sound here.

This lane inclined up-hill all the way to Hay and having reached the middle, I sat down on a stile which led thence into a field. Gathering my mantle about me, and sheltering my hands in my muff, I did not feel the cold, though it froze keenly. From my seat I could look down on Thornfield and I lingered till the sun went down amongst the trees, and sank crimson and clear behind them. I then turned eastward.

On the hill-top above me sat the rising moon; pale as a cloud, but brightening momentarily. Hay was yet a mile distant, but in the absolute hush I could hear plainly its thin murmurs of life.

A rude noise broke on these fine ripplings and whisperings, at once so far away and so clear. A positive *tramp, tramp*. A metallic clatter, which effaced the soft wave-wanderings. This din on the causeway meant a horse was coming. The windings of the lane yet hid it and I sat still on the stile to let it go by, but as this horse approached, I was suddenly hit with a bout of fear that clutched at my insides. I suddenly remembered the nursery tales of Betty and the red-room and the manic laugh at Thornfield. It echoed through my mind, but I could not tell you, Reader, why.

The *tramp, tramp*, grew nearer and I heard a rush under the hedge. Close down by the hazel stems glided a great dog whose black and white colour made him a distinct object against the trees. I gasped for it was a lion-like creature with long hair and a huge head. It passed me, however, quietly enough and the horse followed; a tall steed, and on its back, a man.

He passed in a thunder of hooves and grunts. My fear subsiding slightly, I went on a few steps but then I heard a sliding sound and an exclamation of "What the deuce is to do now?"

A clatter, a tumble, and then quiet.

I turned back and saw that the man and horse were down; they had slipped on the sheet of ice which glazed the causeway. The dog came bounding back, and seeing his master in a predicament, and hearing the horse groan, barked till the evening hills echoed the sound. He snuffed round the prostrate group and then he ran up to me. I obeyed him and walked down to the traveller who was struggling himself free of his steed. His efforts were so vigorous, I thought he could not be much hurt, but I asked him the question, "Are you injured, sir?"

I think he was swearing, but I am not certain. Howe-ver, he was pronouncing some formula which prevented him from replying to me directly.

"Can I do anything?" I asked again.

"You must just stand on one side," he answered as he rose to his feet.

It was then that I had some view of his features since when he had passed me thence, his face was in shadow and just now, he had been stuck under the horse. I gasped shar-ply at the likeness and glanced all around me, wondering if this was some dreadful apparition, perhaps a trick of my mind. I suddenly wished that I had not watched the sun set or thought about Grace Poole's eerie laugh.

"Down, Pilot!" The traveller now, stooping, felt his foot and leg, as if trying whether they were sound. Apparently something ailed them, for he halted to the stile whence I had just risen, and sat down.

His shout brought me to my senses and I gathered that he was indeed real flesh and blood. It had been many years since I had seen a portrait of a dark-eyed man in the drawing room of my aunt's house and I had almost forgotten my ob-session with the image, but his breathing likeness was before me now.

He groaned and clutched his leg.

"If you are hurt, and want help, sir, I can fetch some one either from Thornfield Hall or from Hay," I said in a strang-led, hushed voice.

"Thank you, I shall do. I have no broken bones, only a sprain." He stood up and tried his foot, but the result extor-ted an involuntary "Ugh!"

His figure was enveloped in a riding cloak, fur collared and steel clasped; its details were not apparent, but I traced the general points of middle height and considerable breadth of chest. He had a dark face with stern features and a heavy brow. He was perhaps thirty-five and did not possess the soft, fresh handsomeness of youth, rather the rugged, swarthy look of travelled experience. His unruly dark hair to his chin and his sweep of stubble were exactly that of the portrait, but it was his eyes, the darkness of them; so dark that they were almost black, and smoldering, that rung so clearly with the image in my mind. I could not help but stare at him, mesmerised and he noticed my fascination.

His gaze locked with mine and I found myself drawn into the blackness of his eyes, unable to tear myself away. There was something thrilling and torturous about them; something I did not understand.

"Could you hand me my whip," he said, his deep voice husky. "It is just under that hedge."

Obediently, I walked slowly to the hedge and pulled out his riding crop, my eyes never leaving his as I did so. I stopped a few paces from him and extended my arm, offering the tail end. He snatched at it and pulled hard so that I stumbled forward, knocking against his chest. He grabbed me to stop me from falling and held me still, pressed up against him.

My breath tore from my throat in hurried gasps and created ragged, silver clouds in the cool, evening air. I was so close to him that I could smell his faint scent of sweat and leather and I could see the dampness about his brow. His eyes burnt into mine in a way I had never known. My thoughts scattered, I could no longer contemplate whether this was a true stranger I had encountered on the road or a figment of my imagination and as a rush of excitement spiked my stomach, I did not care.

"You do not need to say anything," he whispered, bringing his face a little closer to mine and throwing the whip aside. "I can read everything I need to know." And he briefly glanced left and right to check that we were alone save his great dog, Pilot, and the panting, sweaty stallion.

Before I could transpire the meaning of this, he grabbed my hand roughly and pulled me down into the frozen ditch at the side of the causeway. There he stood over me, under the shelter of a tall oak tree, hidden by the dusk of the evening.

"I am going to kiss you," he said.

He brushed his thumb across my bottom lip and I began to tremble with anticipation. I had never laid with a stranger before, but this man did not seem unknown to me. He was my young desire come alive.

His dark eyes gleaming with excitement, he brought his soft, full lips firmly down onto mine, forcing my teeth apart with his tongue and tasting the sweetness of my mouth. I was breathless and my chest heaved in the confines of my stays, my breasts almost bursting over my corset. With one hand he cupped my chin, whilst the other tore off my bonnet and began to rake through my hair.

I whimpered and moaned into his mouth, feeling his grip on my chin tighten.

He abruptly pulled back from me and his eyes bore into mine, their intensity thrilling. Slowly and gently, he pushed me down so that I was lying against the cold, hard ground and he moved over me. Silently, he tilted my head back to gain access to my throat and let his lips glide down to my chest, kissing and nipping my tender skin.

A hotness gathered in my groin and filled me with hungry desire. As his lips moved across my chest and back to my neck—to the soft, small dip at the base of my throat, I closed my eyes. He was nothing like the inexperienced clutching of John Reed or the clumsy, coarse touching of Jack. His lips and hands moved expertly over me, feather-light, yet firm at the same time, teasing my senses.

He paused and I opened my eyes, losing myself in the mysterious depths of his. Emboldened, I reached up a hand

and knotted it in his hair, bringing his lips firmly back to mine. I thrust my hips against his, feeling the hardness of his erection through my dress and petticoat, which sent shivers up my body. My hips began writhing and swaying of their own accord in the same rhythm of his mouth against mine.

"Keep still," he growled.

I obediently stopped, my nerve endings tingling.

Slowly, he pulled my legs apart and slid his hands underneath my dress. He gently rolled my stockings down and I winced at the coolness of the evening air on my bare skin. Above me, all I could see was the duskiness of the sky and a scattering of stars.

He reached between my legs and rubbed his thumb up and down me, watching my reaction. I fidgeted uncontrollably, a tight feeling of wanting coiling inside. He bent over me, hitching my dress up further so that from my navel down I was completely bare, and ran his tongue across the tops of my thighs. Suddenly he dipped between my legs and I could not help but cry out in surprise and pleasure as he moved his tongue in slow, tantalising circles. Teasing me until I thought I might burst.

My hands clenched into fists and I panted. When I thought that I could not go on any further, he stopped and undid his breeches. I let out an involuntary gasp of shock at the size of his erection and he grinned. I ran my hands up and down it gently at first and then harder, angling it towards me.

Suddenly, he grasped both of my legs and pulled them onto his shoulders, lifting my hips off the ground. I glanced at him in confusion, but before I could speak, he thrust himself inside of me and I could but moan with rapture. I convulsed as he pulled out of me and then sunk slowly in again, pushing deeper than anything I had experienced before.

It was too much and I began losing myself and my

senses, only conscious of the delicious thrusting between my legs. I felt heat and desire building in my stomach and flooding my groin, pulling me into a hazy, fractured place where I had no control. I was clutching his cloak desperately, wishing that I could run my hands over his body and feel his broad chest.

He started to move hard and fast. My insides felt like they were being wrung raw and I squirmed with built-up pleasure, waiting to burst as he pounded into me deeper and harder. He leant forward and kissed me so softly, his mouth caressing mine, before taking my bottom lip in his teeth and biting down hard.

Suddenly I exploded into tiny pieces as he heaved into me once more and collapsed back onto the cold ground, barely knowing who or what I was. It was an ecstasy of pleasure I had never felt before and I whimpered and sighed as I slowly recovered.

He pulled out of me and grunted, coming.

We were both still for a moment as he lay over me.

Finally, he lifted his eyes to mine, those deep, dark eyes and I asked, "Is your ankle better, sir?"

He let out a bark of laughter and pulled down my dress. "I'll live," he said.

I frowned as he hurriedly stood up and pulled his breeches back on. I did not want him to leave. I could not bear to return to the silent nunnery that was Thornfield Hall.

"I should think you ought to be at home," said he suddenly, "if you have a home in this neighbourhood. Where do you come from?"

"From just below."

"You live just below—do you mean at that house with the battlements?" pointing to Thornfield Hall, on which the moon cast a hoary gleam.

"Yes, sir."

He became very still. "Whose house is it?" he asked.

"Mr. Rochester's."

"Do you know Mr. Rochester?"

"No, I have never seen him."

"Are you a servant?"

"I am a governess."

"Ah, the governess!" he repeated thoughtfully. There was something newly rushed and detached about his manor. He righted his cloak, which had slipped aside and dipped his head at me. "Good evening," he said, turning and climbing out of the ditch.

I watched him go, my heart sinking.

As I pulled my stockings back on I heard the jangle of a horse bit and the soft pad of Pilot who had apparently been waiting patiently on the causeway for his master.

"Onwards!" came the gruff command and I heard the stallion neigh, and then the thunder of hooves as it galloped on.

I did not like re-entering Thornfield later that evening. I lingered at the gates, I lingered on the lawn, and I paced backwards and forwards on the pavement. I could not forget my meeting with the man on the lane.

At last, I pulled my wits together and entered the hall. I hastened to Mrs. Fairfax's room where there was a fire I could warm myself, but I found no Mrs. Fairfax and no candles. Instead, all alone, sitting upright on the rug and gazing with gravity at the blaze, I beheld a great black and white long-haired dog.

I gasped.

"Pilot?" I said in a high, anxious voice.

The thing got up, came to me and snuffed me. Before I could think anything more, Leah entered.

"What dog is this?" I asked in a shaking, affected voice.

"He came with master."

"With whom?"

"With master—Mr. Rochester—he is just arrived."

"Indeed! And is Mrs. Fairfax with him?"

"Yes, and Miss Adele. They are in the dining-room, and John is gone for a surgeon for master has had an accident. His horse fell and his ankle is sprained."

I fled to my room.

CHAPTER XIII

That night and the next morning, I trembled continuously. I dreamt fitfully of clutching fingers and hot caresses and ghostly lovers. I was now sure that the man I had laid with yesterday evening in the ditch near Hay was Mr. Rochester, but part of me still considered him to be a dream; a manifestation of my intense desire. I wondered fervently what was to become of me, whether he would dismiss me in disgrace or lay with me again and I am ashamed to admit that I keenly wished for the latter.

By the surgeon's orders, the returned master of Thornfield Hall went to bed early so he was not present when I finally left my room that evening and he did not rise early the next morning either. I was in limbo, walking about the house with permanent flushed cheeks, wondering what my fate would be. Though I had been intimate with this man, I knew nothing about him or his temper and thus I did not know how he would react. He must have realised that I was a resident of his house when I said that I had come from Thornfield; perhaps he was currently pondering what to do with me. I pleaded that he would keep me here, for my foolish, young fancy of my dark-eyed lover had returned and having finally found his human likeness, I could not bear to be sent away.

Adele was not easy to teach that day; she could not apply and I was a sullen, distracted teacher. She kept running to the door and looking to see if she could get a glimpse of Mr. Rochester, which constantly threw me into a fit of anxiety. When I got a little angry and made her sit still, she continued to talk incessantly of her "ami, Monsieur Edouard Fairfax de Rochester," as she dubbed him and to conjecture what presents he had brought her.

However, he did not appear or call for her all day and when evening came upon us, I and my pupil dined as usual in Mrs. Fairfax's parlour. At dark I allowed Adele to put away books and work, and to run downstairs. Left alone, I walked to the window, but nothing was to be seen thence, only twilight and snowflakes together thickening the air. I let down the curtain and went back to the fireside.

I was staring into the flames when Mrs. Fairfax suddenly entered.

"Mr. Rochester would be glad if you and your pupil would take tea with him in the drawing-room this evening," said she. "He has been so much engaged all day that he could not ask to see you before."

A rush of dread swept through me, but the thought of seeing those dark, brooding eyes once more kept me from fleeing as I had last night.

"When is his tea-time?" I inquired in a steady tone.

"Oh, at six o'clock, he keeps early hours in the country. You had better change your frock now and I will go with you and fasten it. Here is a candle."

"Is it necessary to change my frock?" I asked, thinking that it was good enough for him yesterday, but such thoughts only increased my anxiousness.

"Yes, you had better. I always dress for the evening when Mr. Rochester is here."

I repaired to my room and with Mrs. Fairfax's aid, replaced my black stuff dress by one of black silk. Luckily, she did not appear to notice my shaking, fumbling fingers.

"You want a brooch," she said when I was dressed. I had a single little pearl ornament which Miss Temple gave me as a parting keepsake and I put it on. Then we went downstairs and I let Mrs. Fairfax precede me into the dining-room, keeping in her shade as we crossed that apartment, my legs trembling.

Two wax candles stood lighted on the table and two on the mantelpiece. Basking in the light and heat of a superb fire, lay Pilot with Adele knelt near him. Half reclined on a couch appeared Mr. Rochester, his foot supported by a cushion. He must have been aware of the entrance of Mrs. Fairfax and myself, but it appeared he was not in the mood to notice us, for he never lifted his head as we approached. This threw me at once for it was the last reaction I had expected and I almost doubted what had happened yesterday.

"Here is Miss Eyre, sir," said Mrs. Fairfax.

He bowed, still not taking his eyes from the group of the dog and child.

"Let Miss Eyre be seated," said he, and there was something in the forced stiff bow, in the impatient yet formal tone, which seemed further to express, "What the deuce is it to me whether Miss Eyre be there or not? At this moment I am not disposed to accost her."

I sat down quite embarrassed.

He neither spoke nor moved. Mrs. Fairfax seemed to think it necessary that some one should be amiable and she began to talk. Kindly, as usual and, as usual, rather trite. She condoled with him on the pressure of business he had had all day, on the annoyance it must have been to him with that painful sprain and then she commended his patience and perseverance in going through with it.

"Madam, I should like some tea," was the sole rejoinder she got. She hastened to ring the bell and when the tray

came, she proceeded to arrange the cups and spoons with as-
siduous celerity. I and Adele went to the table, but the master
did not leave his couch.

"Will you hand Mr. Rochester's cup?" said Mrs. Fairfax
to me, "Adele might perhaps spill it."

I took the tea from her, my hands shaking and jingling
the china. I used my other hand to steady it so as not to be
noticed and slowly walked over to Mr. Rochester. I stopped
before him and for the first time that evening, his dark eyes
met mine. I almost gasped aloud for a great throb of desire
tore through my stomach. His eyes were even blacker by firelight and there seemed to be a hint of amusement within
them, as if he knew my discomfort and it pleased him.

Carefully he took the cup from me, making sure to press
his fingers against mine. It sent a thrilling ripple of tingling
heat up my arm and the skin where we had touched was
scorched. Involuntarily I licked my lips. His likeness to my
dark-eyed lover was so accurate, that I wondered briefly if he
were a Rochester ancestor.

"N'est-ce pas, monsieur," Adele suddenly cried out, making me jump and breaking my musings. "Qu'il y a un cadeau pour Mademoiselle Eyre dans votre petit coffre?"

"Who talks of cadeaux?" said he gruffly. "Did you expect
a present, Miss Eyre? Are you fond of presents?" He searched
my face with eyes and I became breathless and hot.

"I hardly know, sir," I whispered. "I have little experience
of them, but they are generally thought pleasant things."

"Oh, don't fall back on over-modesty! I have examined
Adele and find you have taken great pains with her. She is not
bright, she has no talents and yet in a short time she has made
much improvement."

"Sir, you have now given me my 'cadeau'—praise of my
pupils' progress. There is no better present to a teacher."

"Humph!" said Mr. Rochester, and he took his tea in silence.

He did not speak again until the tray was taken away, and Mrs. Fairfax had settled into a corner with her knitting, while Adele played with Pilot.

"Come here," he said to me, gesturing to a chair.

I obeyed, and we sat opposite each other, bathed in firelight. The heat from his gaze and the fire was almost too much and I felt my skin redden under their glare.

"You have been resident in my house three months?" he asked.

I wondered if he would confront me about yesterday now, perhaps he had not at first recognised me, but there was something still in his expression that was playful.

"Yes, sir."

"And you came from . . . ?"

"From Lowood school."

"Ah! A charitable concern. How long were you there?"

"Three years."

"Three years! No wonder you have rather the look of another world. I marvelled where you had got that sort of face. When you came on me in Hay Lane last night, I thought unaccountably of fairy tales, and had half a mind to demand whether you had bewitched my horse. I am not sure yet."

I jumped slightly, startled by his mentioning our meeting in front of Adele and Mrs. Fairfax. I glanced at both who seemed not to have noticed and were quietly and individually absorbed in what they were doing. I let out a shaky breath and wrung my hands, my nerves almost at their ends.

"Who recommended you to come here?" he continued.

I swallowed hard before I again allowed myself to look on him. "I advertised, and Mrs. Fairfax answered my advertisement."

"Miss Eyre, if you indeed went to Lowood then you have lived the life of a nun. No doubt you are well drilled in religious forms. Brocklehurst, who I understand directs Lowood, is a parson, is he not?"

"Yes, sir."

I felt he was making a point and asking how it could be possible that the girl who had attended Lowood for three years was the very same that had lain in a ditch with him in ecstasy. I did not have the answer, but I knew that I had never experienced such pleasure as he had induced by any one else before. Even the thought made the muscles in my thighs clench.

"Adele showed me some sketches this morning, which she said were yours," he carried on, forever switching from subject to subject as if to confuse me and lead me to reveal something. "I don't know whether they were entirely of your doing, probably a master aided you?"

"No, indeed!" I interjected.

"Ah! That pricks pride. Well, fetch me your portfolio, if you can vouch for its contents being original, but don't pass your word unless you are certain. I can recognise patchwork."

"Then I will say nothing, and you shall judge for yourself, sir."

I brought the portfolio from the library.

"Approach the table," said he, and I wheeled it to his couch.

He deliberately scrutinised each sketch and painting. Three he laid aside; the others, when he had examined them, he swept from him.

"Where did you get your copies?"

"Out of my head."

"That head I see now on your shoulders?"

"Yes, sir."

He spread the pictures before him and again surveyed them alternately.

They were in water-colours and of a wild and peculiar nature, being supernatural in subject rather than depicting a pretty view or a pretty subject. In these pieces, I had allowed my imagination to run wild and create desolate hills, raging seas, eerie moonlight, and floating corpses.

"Were you happy when you painted these pictures?" asked Mr. Rochester presently.

"I was absorbed, sir. To paint them, in short, was to enjoy one of the keenest pleasures I have ever known."

"That is not saying much. Your pleasures, by your own account have been few, but I daresay you did exist in a kind of artist's dreamland while you blent and arranged these strange tints. Did you feel self-satisfied with the result of your ardent labours?"

"Far from it. I was tormented by the contrast between my idea and my handiwork."

He regarded me for a moment before barking, "It is nine o'clock. What are you about, Miss Eyre, to let Adele sit up so long? Take her to bed."

He suddenly seemed indifferent to me and wishing that I was out of his sight.

Adele went to kiss him before quitting the room and he endured the caress, but scarcely seemed to relish it more than Pilot would have done.

"I wish you all good-night, now," said he, making a movement of the hand towards the door, in token that he was tired of our company and wished to dismiss us. Mrs. Fairfax folded up her knitting, I took my portfolio, and we curtseyed to him, received a frigid bow in return, and so withdrew.

"How do you find Mr. Rochester?" asked Mrs. Fairfax, when I rejoined her in her room, after putting Adele to bed.

I looked the other way and tried to hide my flushed cheeks in the firelight. "He is very changeful and abrupt," I finally answered.

"True, no doubt he may appear so to a stranger, but I am so accustomed to his manner that I never think of it. And then, if he has peculiarities of temper, allowance should be made."

"Why?"

"Family troubles, for one thing."

"But he has no family."

"Not now, but he has had. He lost his elder brother a few years since."

"His elder brother?"

"Yes. The present Mr. Rochester has not been very long in possession of the property, only about nine years."

"Nine years is a tolerable time. Was he so very fond of his brother as to be still inconsolable for his loss?"

"Why no, perhaps not. I believe there were some misunderstandings between them. Mr. Rowland Rochester and Old Mr. Rochester combined to bring Mr. Edward into what he considered a painful position for the sake of making his fortune. What the precise nature of that position was I never clearly knew, but his spirit could not brook what he had to suffer in it. He is not very forgiving and he broke with his family, and now for many years he has led an unsettled kind of life. I don't think he has ever been resident at Thornfield for a fortnight together, since the death of his brother."

"Why should he shun it?"

"Perhaps he thinks it gloomy."

The answer was evasive. I should have liked something clearer, but Mrs. Fairfax either could not, or would not give me more explicit information. It was evident, indeed, that she wished me to drop the subject, which I did accordingly.

It seemed clear to me now, however, that Mr. Rochester did not wish to dismiss me for the events of yesterday. What he would do with me though, I was not sure.

CHAPTER XIV

For several subsequent days I saw little of Mr. Rochester. In the mornings he seemed much engaged with business, and in the afternoon, gentlemen from Millcote or the neighbourhood called and sometimes stayed to dine with him. When his sprain was well enough to admit of horse exercise, he rode out a good deal, probably to return these visits and he generally did not come back till late at night.

During this interval even Adele was seldom sent for to his presence, and all my acquaintance with him was confined to an occasional rencontre in the hall, on the stairs, or in the gallery, when he would pass me haughtily and coldly, just acknowledging my presence by a distant nod or a cool glance. This startled and upset me and I thought earnestly of our night in the ditch on the causeway, almost as if it were a dream.

One day, however, he rang the bell and a message came that I and Adele were to go downstairs. I was at once nervous again, least this should be the moment of my dismissal. I told myself that I should be relieved that Mr. Rochester kept me at such a distance, but I would rather be sent away then to forever be treated coldly by him.

As we descended the stairs, Adele cajoled me at length with wanderings whether the petit coffre was finally come, for, owing to some mistake, its arrival had hitherto been delayed. She was gratified when we entered the dining room since there it stood; a little carton, on the table. She appeared to know it by instinct.

"Ma boite! Ma boite!" exclaimed she, running towards it.

"Yes, there is your 'boite' at last. Take it into a corner, you genuine daughter of Paris, and amuse yourself with disembowelling it," said the deep and rather sarcastic voice of Mr. Rochester, proceeding from the depths of an immense easy-chair at the fireside. "And mind," he continued, "don't bother me with any details of the anatomical process, or any notice of the condition of the entrails. Let your operation be conducted in silence: tiens-toi tranquille, enfant; comprends-tu?"

Adele seemed scarcely to need the warning, she had already retired to a sofa with her treasure and was busy untying the cord which secured the lid. Having removed this impediment, and lifted certain silvery envelopes of tissue paper, she merely exclaimed, "Oh ciel! Que c'est beau!" and then remained absorbed in ecstatic contemplation.

"Is Miss Eyre there?" now demanded the master, half rising from his seat to look round to the door near which I still stood.

"Ah! Well, come forward and be seated here." He drew a chair near his own. "I am not fond of the prattle of children," he continued, "it would be intolerable to me to pass a whole evening tête-à-tête with a brat. Don't draw that chair farther off, Miss Eyre, sit down exactly where I placed it."

As he rang and despatched an invitation to Mrs. Fairfax, I stared at him uncertainly. I could not see where this warmth of character had suddenly sprung from or why he was now directing so much attention on me.

Mrs. Fairfax soon arrived, knitting-basket in hand.

"Good evening, madam, I sent to you for a charitable purpose. I have forbidden Adele to talk to me about her presents and she is bursting with repletion. Have the goodness to serve her as auditress and interlocutrice and it will be one of the most benevolent acts you ever performed."

Adele no sooner saw Mrs. Fairfax than she summoned her to her sofa and there, quickly filled her lap with the porcelain, the ivory and the waxen contents of her "boite," pouring out explanations and raptures in such broken English as she was mistress of.

"Now I have performed the part of a good host," pursued Mr. Rochester, "I ought to be at liberty to attend to my own pleasure. Miss Eyre, draw your chair still a little farther forward, you are yet too far back and I cannot see you."

I did as I was bid, wondering what he might do. He was wearing that playful, mocking expression once more but his cold looks of the days past weighed on my mind, making me guarded. I could not understand what he wanted from me. I knew what I hoped for, but his recent behavior did not warrant such thoughts.

He had been looking two minutes at the fire, and I had been looking the same length of time at him, when turning suddenly, he caught my gaze fastened on his physiognomy.

"You examine me, Miss Eyre," said he, "do you think me handsome?"

I should, if I had deliberated, have replied to this question by something conventionally vague and polite, but the answer somehow slipped from my tongue before I was aware, fueled by the bitter resentment I had harbored over the last few days of being ignored.

"No, sir."

"Ah! By my word! There is something singular about you," said he. "You have the air of a little nonnette; quaint, quiet, grave and simple, as you sit with your hands before you and your eyes generally bent on the carpet. When one asks you a question, or makes a remark to which you are obliged to reply, you rap out a round rejoinder, which if not blunt, is at least brusque. What do you mean by it?"

"Sir, I was too plain and I beg your pardon. I ought to have replied that beauty is of little consequence, or something of that sort."

"You ought to have replied no such thing. Beauty of little consequence, indeed! Go on, what fault do you find with me, pray? I suppose I have all my limbs and all my features like any other man?"

"Mr. Rochester, allow me to disown my first answer, it was only a blunder."

"No, no, you shall be answerable for it. Criticise me, does my forehead not please you?"

He lifted up the dark sable waves of hair which lay horizontally over his brow, and showed a smooth, alabaster stretch of skin. I wished to tug his hair back myself and kiss it. A shiver went through my body and I said nothing.

"You look very much puzzled, Miss Eyre, and though you are not pretty any more than I am handsome, yet a puzzled air becomes you. Besides, it is convenient, for it keeps those searching eyes of yours away from my physiognomy so puzzle on. Young lady, I am disposed to be gregarious and communicative to-night."

With this announcement he rose from his chair and stood, leaning his arm on the marble mantelpiece. I am sure that others would not have found him handsome and that is what I had meant, I suppose, when I answered him before. He had none of the freshness of youth and his features were rough and rugged, but I found in their form an exciting, dashing quality. His air and manor was confident and magnetic and I was taken away by him completely.

"I am disposed to be gregarious and communicative to-night," he repeated, sitting back down "and that is why I sent for you. Pilot cannot talk, Adele is a degree better, but still far below the mark, Mrs. Fairfax ditto, but you, I am persuaded, can suit me if you will. It would please me now to learn more of you, therefore speak."

Instead of speaking, I smiled, and not a very complacent or submissive smile either.

"Speak," he urged.

"What about, sir?"

"Whatever you like. I leave both the choice of subject and the manner of treating it entirely to yourself."

Accordingly I sat and said nothing.

"Stubborn?" he said.

I stood up.

"Where are you going?"

"To put Adele to bed, it is past her bedtime."

"You are afraid of me, because I talk like a Sphynx."

"Your language is enigmatical, sir, but I am certainly not afraid."

"Do you never laugh, Miss Eyre? Don't trouble yourself to answer—I see you laugh rarely, but you can laugh very merrily. Believe me, you are not naturally austere any more than I am naturally vicious. The Lowood constraint still clings to you somewhat, controlling your features, muffling your voice and restricting your limbs. You fear in the presence of a man to smile too gaily, speak too freely, or move too quickly, but in time, I think you will learn to be natural with me. I see at intervals the glance of a curious sort of bird through the close-set bars of a cage; a vivid, restless, resolute captive is there. Were it but free, it would soar cloud-high. You are still bent on going?"

"It has struck nine, sir."

"Wait a minute, Adele is not ready to go to bed yet. While talking to you, I have also occasionally watched her and she pulled out of her box about ten minutes ago, a little pink silk frock. 'Il faut que je l'essaie!' cried she, 'et e l'instant meme!' and she rushed out of the room. She is now with Sophie, undergoing a robing process and in a few minutes she will re-enter. I know what I shall see—a miniature of Celine Varens as she used to appear . . . but never mind that. My tenderest feelings are about to receive a shock."

Ere long, Adele's little foot was heard tripping across the hall. She entered, transformed as her guardian had predicted. A dress of rose-coloured satin, very short, and as full in the skirt as it could be gathered, replaced the brown frock she had previously worn, a wreath of rosebuds circled her forehead and her feet were dressed in small white satin sandals.

"Est-ce que ma robe va bien?" cried she, bounding forwards; "et mes souliers? et mes bas? Tenez, je crois que je vais danser!"

And spreading out her dress, she chasseed across the room till, having reached Mr. Rochester, she wheeled lightly round before him on tip-toe, then dropped on one knee at his feet, exclaiming, "Monsieur, je vous remercie mille fois de votre bonte," then rising, she added, "C'est comme cela que maman faisait, n'est-ce pas, monsieur?"

"Pre-cise-ly!" was the answer, "and, 'comme cela,' she charmed my English gold out of my British breeches' pocket. I have been green, Miss Eyre. My Spring is gone, however, but it has left me that French floweret on my hands, which in some moods, I would fain be rid of. I keep it and rear it rather on the Roman Catholic principle of expiating numerous sins, great or small, by one good work. I'll explain all this some day. Good-night."

CHAPTER XV

M^r. Rochester did, on a future occasion, explain it. It was one afternoon when he chanced to meet me and Adele in the grounds, and while she played with Pilot and her shuttlecock, he asked me to walk up and down a long beech avenue within sight of her. Again, our intercourse since the last conversation and this had been cold and silent. I did not know if Mr. Rochester purposely treated me thus as a punishment for my previous wanton behavior or if he was naturally inconsistent. My hopes of ever laying with him again as we once had in a ditch under the filmy moon were rapidly decreasing and the prospect made me dull and gloomy. I simply could not figure him out.

As we walked that afternoon he told me that Adele was the daughter of a French opera-dancer, Celine Varens, towards whom he had once cherished what he called a "grande passion." This passion Celine had professed to return with even superior ardour.

"And, Miss Eyre, so much in love was I that I installed her in an hotel, gave her a complete establishment of servants, a carriage and diamonds &c. In short, I began the process of ruining myself in the received style, like any other spoony. However, happening to call one evening when Celine did not expect me, I found her out, but as it was a warm night and I was tired with strolling through Paris, I sat down in her boudoir and waited."

I did not know why he was telling me this, but I listened quietly. Perhaps he wished me to be aware of my pupil's background, but I felt that such detail did not warrant this reason. There was something more. I found myself wondering if maybe Mr. Rochester was at the same time giving me an account of his own character.

"While in a boudoir, I heard a carriage outside the open window and I recognised the sound of the 'voiture' I had given Celine," he carried on. "She was returning and of course, my heart thumped with impatience to see her. I went to the window and leant out, watching the carriage stop at the hotel door. I knew her instantly by her little foot, seen peeping from the skirt of her dress, as she skipped from the carriage-step. Bending out of the window further, I was about to murmur "Mon ange" in a tone which should be audible to the ear of love alone, when a figure jumped from the carriage after her. It was cloaked, but a spurred heel was heard which rung on the pavement and a hatted head now passed under the arched porte cochere of the hotel. It was a man . . . You never felt jealousy, did you, Miss Eyre? Of course not, I need not ask you, because you never felt love."

This was not true. Upon his mentioning the beautiful Celine, I had indeed felt a crude stab of jealousy that made my knees weak, but I had not wished to show it. It was clear that I was nothing to Mr. Rochester, merely an encounter on the causeway that he had hoped never to run into again. I would then have been lost in a torrent of my own dark lament had I not noticed the sinister change in the man before me.

He ground his teeth and was silent, then he arrested his step and struck his boot against the hard ground. Some hated thought seemed to have him in its grip and to hold him so tightly that he could not advance. Lifting his eye to the battlements of Thornfield, he cast over them a glare such as I never saw before or since. Pain, shame, ire, impatience, disgust, and detestation seemed momentarily to hold a quivering conflict in the large pupil dilating under his ebon eyebrow. Wild was the wrestle which should be paramount, but another feeling rose and triumphed, something hard and cynical.

Adele here ran before him with her shuttlecock. "Away!" he cried harshly, "keep at a distance or go in to Sophie!"

Adele and I both jumped, but she soon scuttled away whereas I remained.

Continuing then to pursue his walk in silence, I ventured to recall him to the point whence he had abruptly diverged. I was curious as to the change in his mood and the rest of the story.

"Did you leave the boudoir, sir?" I asked, returning to his tale.

I almost expected a rebuff for this hardly well-timed question, but on the contrary, waking out of his scowling abstraction, he turned his eyes towards me and the shade seemed to clear off his brow. "Oh, I had forgotten Celine! Well, to resume. When I saw my charmer thus come in accompanied by a cavalier, I seemed to hear a hiss and the green snake of jealousy rose within me. I remained in the boudoir waiting for them and hid behind a curtain, leaving only an opening through which I could take observations. The couple entered and there was 'the Varens,' shining in satin and jewels—my gifts of course—and there was her companion in an officer's uniform. I knew him for a young roue of a vicomte, a brainless and vicious youth whom I had sometimes met in society and had never thought of hating because I despised him so absolutely. On recognising him, the fang of the snake Jealousy was instantly broken because at the same moment, my love for Celine sank under an extinguisher. A woman who could betray me for such a rival was not worth contending for and she deserved only scorn."

Adele here came running up again.

"Monsieur, John has just been to say that your agent has called and wishes to see you."

"Ah," said Mr. Rochester, turning to me. "In that case, I must quickly abridge and be off—throwing back the curtain, I revealed myself and liberated Celine from my protection. I gave her notice to vacate her hotel, offered her a purse for immediate exigencies, disregarded screams, hysterics, prayers, protestations, convulsions and made an appointment with the vicomte for a meeting at the Bois de Boulogne. Next morning I had the pleasure of encountering him, left a bullet in one of his poor arms and then thought I had done with the whole crew. But unluckily the Varens, six months before, had given me this filette Adele, who she affirmed was my daughter and perhaps she may be, though I see no proofs of such grim paternity written in her countenance. Pilot is more like me than she. Some years after I had broken with the mother, she abandoned her child and ran away to Italy with a musician or singer. I acknowledged no natural claim on Adele's part to be supported by me, but hearing that she was quite destitute, I e'en took the poor thing out of the slime and mud of Paris and transplanted it here. Mrs. Fairfax found you to train it, but now you know that it is the illegitimate offspring of a French opera-girl, you will perhaps think differently of your post and protégée?"

"No, Adele is not answerable for either her mother's faults or yours. I shall cling closer to her than before."

He looked long and hard at me for a moment, staring deep into my eyes so that something stirred in the pit of my stomach.

"Oh," he simply said. "I must go in now and you too, it darkens."

I did not understand Mr. Rochester or his behavior towards me and that night, I tossed and turned in a fitful sleep. Half of me felt that I should leave and be free of this control he had over me; the need to make him happy and the constant hope that he would take me in his arms once more. I did not like the thought of being a slave to him, nor being a slave to anyone, but I knew that I could not go. I had found something here that I had been searching for a long time and I could not leave yet.

"Mrs. Fairfax said he seldom stayed here longer than a fortnight at a time, and he has now been resident eight weeks," I said to myself in the darkness. "Could I dare hope that he stays for interest in me?" The thought seemed unlikely given the spontaneous attention he delivered. Rather I seemed an interesting pet like Pilot, but I could not help but hope I at least had something to do with his extended stay.

I hardly know whether I slept or not after this musing, at any rate, I started wide awake on hearing a vague murmur, which sounded just above me. I wished I had kept my candle burning since the night was drearily dark and my spirits were depressed. I rose and sat up in bed, listening. The sound was hushed.

I tried again to sleep, but my heart beat anxiously and my inward tranquillity was broken. The clock far down in the hall struck two. Just then, it seemed my chamber-door was touched as if fingers had swept the panels in groping a way along the dark gallery outside.

I said, "Who is there?"

Nothing answered and I was chilled with fear.

I lay down. Silence composes the nerves and as an unbroken hush now reigned again through the whole house, I began to feel the return of slumber. But it was not fated that I should sleep that night. A dream had scarcely approached my ear when it fled affrighted, scared by a marrow-freezing incident enough.

This was a demoniac laugh—low, suppressed and deep— uttered, as it seemed, at the very keyhole of my chamber door. The head of my bed was near the door, and I thought at first the goblin-laugher stood at my bedside, or rather, crouched by my pillow. I rose, looked round, and could see nothing but as I still gazed, the unnatural sound was reiterated and I knew it came from behind the panels. My first impulse was to rise and fasten the bolt, my next, again to cry out, "Who is there?"

Something gurgled and moaned. Ere long, steps retreated up the gallery towards the third-storey staircase and a door opened and closed.

"Was that Grace Poole? Is she possessed with a devil?" thought I.

Impossible now to remain longer by myself, I knew that I must go to Mrs. Fairfax. I hurried on my frock and a shawl and withdrew the bolt, opening the door with a trembling hand. There was a candle burning just outside, and I was surprised at this circumstance, but still more was I amazed to perceive the air quite dim as if filled with smoke. I suddenly became further aware of a strong smell of burning.

Something creaked—it was a door ajar and that door was Mr. Rochester's and more still, the smoke rushed in a cloud from thence. I thought no more of Mrs. Fairfax, I thought no more of Grace Poole, or the laugh, I thought only of him and in an instant, I was within the chamber. As I entered I saw tongues of flame darted round the bed, the curtains immersed in fire. In the midst of blaze and vapour, Mr. Rochester lay stretched motionless, in deep sleep.

"Wake! wake!" I cried. I shook him, but he only murmured and turned since the smoke had stupefied him. Not a moment could be lost and I rushed to his basin and ewer which were both filled with water. I heaved them up, deluged the bed and its occupant, flew back to my own room, brought my own water-jug, baptized the couch afresh, and succeeded in extinguishing the flames which were devouring it.

The hiss of the quenched element and the splash of the shower-bath I had liberally bestowed, finally roused Mr. Rochester. Though it was now dark, I knew he was awake because I heard him fulminating strange anathemas at finding himself lying in a pool of water.

"Is there a flood?" he cried.

"No, sir," I answered, "but there has been a fire. Get up and I will fetch you a candle."

"Is that Jane Eyre?" he demanded. "What have you done with me, witch, sorceress? Who is in the room besides you? Have you plotted to drown me?"

"I will fetch you a candle, sir and, in Heaven's name, get up. Somebody has plotted something and you cannot too soon find out who and what it is."

I brought the candle which still remained in the gallery and he took it from my hand. Holding it up, he surveyed the bed, all blackened and scorched, the sheets drenched and the carpet round swimming in water.

The sight was shocking, but there was a closer sight which still shocked and thrilled me more. I could now see Mr. Rochester plainly, bathed in the golden light from the candle and he looked like a brooding angel; his features softened by the buttery glow and his dark eyes glinting. The water had drenched his nightshirt and it stuck to the deep contours in his chest, sculpting his broad shoulders and lean torso. A tremor of heat shuddered through me and I longed to touch the muscled bumps of his stomach and rake my fingernails down his strong, curved spine.

He turned to look at me and I started slightly, my cheeks flushing pink.

"What is it? And who did it?" he asked.

I briefly related to him what had transpired: the strange laugh I had heard in the gallery, the step ascending to the third storey, the smoke, the smell of fire which had conducted me to his room and in what state I had found matters there.

He listened very gravely, his face, as I went on, expressed more concern than astonishment and he did not immediately speak when I had concluded.

"Shall I call Mrs. Fairfax?" I asked.

"Mrs. Fairfax? Not at all. Just be still. If you are not warm enough, you may take my cloak yonder, wrap it about you and sit down in the arm-chair."

He passed the cloak to me and I flushed, remembering the last time I had seen him wearing it, when we were lying together in the ditch on the causeway. Despite the seriousness of this situation, I thought I noticed a flash of a smile across his face, but it was fleeting and he was once again sombre.

"I am going to leave you a few minutes and I shall take the candle," he said. "Remain where you are till I return and be as still as a mouse. I must pay a visit to the second storey. Don't move or call any one."

He went and I watched the light withdraw. He passed up the gallery very softly, unclosed the staircase door with as little noise as possible, shut it after him and the last ray vanished. I was left in total darkness. I listened for some noise, but heard nothing.

A very long time elapsed and I grew weary. I wrapped his thick cloak around me and breathed deeply his rich scent of leather and sweat. I closed my eyes and imagined we were back together on the causeway as I had often done since. I felt a tingling stirring within me, but I tried to ignore it. I was on the point of risking Mr. Rochester's displeasure by disobeying his orders, when the light once more gleamed dimly on the gallery wall, and I heard his unshod feet tread the matting.

He re-entered, pale and very gloomy. "I have found it all out," said he, setting his candle down on the washstand. "It is as I thought."

"How, sir?"

He made no reply, but stood with his arms folded, looking on the ground. At the end of a few minutes he inquired in rather a peculiar tone, "I forget whether you said you saw anything when you opened your chamber door?"

"No, sir, only the candlestick on the ground."

"But you heard an odd laugh? You have heard that laugh before, I should think, or something like it?"

"Yes, sir. There is a woman who sews here called Grace Poole and she laughs in that way. She is a singular person."

"Just so. Grace Poole—you have guessed it. I am glad that you are the only person, besides myself, acquainted with the precise details of to-night's incident. You are no talking fool so say nothing about it. Now return to your own room. I shall do very well on the sofa in the library for the rest of the night. It is near four and in two hours the servants will be up."

I at once felt dejected and full of sorrow. I could not bear for us to be so close like this but still master and servant and nothing more.

"Good-night, then, sir," said I quietly, making to go.

He seemed surprised. "What!" he exclaimed. "Are you quitting me already, and in that way?"

"You said I might go, sir."

"You have saved my life, Jane. I have a pleasure in owing you so immense a debt. I cannot say more."

My heart quickened in my chest and my breath fluttered from my mouth in gasps. Fixing his dark eyes upon me, he took a step closer and the hairs on the back of my neck tingled.

"Sir . . ." I whispered, but found that I could not go on.

He reached out a hand gently, taking hold of my waist and never breaking his gaze, he pulled me in to him so that I was crushed deliciously against his damp chest. The wet material soaked through my nightgown and felt cold against my bare breasts. My nipples hardened and I pressed myself against him feeling his heart beat and the warmth of his body against mine. I deliberately skimmed my tongue across my bottom lip, wishing he would kiss it and I was rewarded when his eyes widened and glinted wickedly.

Suddenly, his grip tightened on my waist and he wrenched me towards him, clamping his lips to mine. Then delicately he pushed his tongue into my mouth and moved it in soft circles, leaving a scalding heat of desire wherever he touched. I sucked hard on his tongue and heard him grunt in a pleasurable laugh, he returned the gesture by pinning me firmly against his hip so that I could feel his long, hard erection across my belly.

I ran my hands down his nightshirt, noticing the enticing undulations of muscles across his stomach and crept my fingers further, past the soft humps of his hip bones to his bulging erection. His eyes closed briefly and I felt his whole body stiffen with anticipation. Gently I ran my fingers up and down it, feeling its smooth, hard texture.

Abruptly he took his hands away from my waist and closed them over mine. "Like this," he whispered huskily, closing my hands into a firm grip and moving them up and down.

He moaned quietly as I carried on and moved his hands back to my waist and then up into my hair. I had never done anything like this before and the thought that I was giving him such pleasure sent scorching waves of desire rippling through my body. He began kissing me in rhythm to my hands tugging him, and pulling gently on my hair. This was unlike anything I had ever done with John Reed or Jack and I felt completely in control.

I suddenly pulled back from his kisses and he glanced at me in shock. Tilting my head slightly, I kissed his neck passionately and began working my way down his body. I left a hot trail of kisses across his torso and down between his legs where I paused, and slowly knelt on the wooden floor of his room at his feet.

He looked down at me, breathing heavily, his great chest heaving and his dark eyes full of yearning. With slow deliberation, I leant forward and placed my lips around him tentatively, running my tongue over the tip of him. His mouth dropped open slightly and his breathing increased.

Gently I sucked and he was soft and hard all at once. His hips flexed into my mouth and I pulled him in deeper. He let out a low groan as I pulled out, twirled my tongue against the tip and then sucked him quickly back into my mouth. My hands grasped his thighs as I pulled him into me deeper and deeper, loving the sensation of his fingers grasping my hair in ecstasy. I sucked harder and harder, feeling him writhing and glanced up at him; his eyes were blisteringly hot into mine, filled with hungry need.

I pulled the tip of his erection to the back of my throat and felt him convulse with pleasure. He grunted and slammed his hips against my mouth as warm, salty liquid oozed down my throat. After a second, I swallowed and he sighed.

I moved away from him and stood up, pleased that his brow was damp with sweat and his eyes were glazed with pleasure.

"Jane . . ." he whispered, "lie down on the bed."

I shook my head. "Another time," I heard myself say and I felt myself grin. "Soon," I added, before bobbing him a curtsey and leaving the room.

CHAPTER XVI

I both wished and feared to see Mr. Rochester on the day which followed this sleepless night. I had lost some of the confidence I had adopted last night, full of control. I wanted to hear his voice again, yet feared what either of us would say or do. As I took my lessons with Adele, often distracted, I almost expected him to enter the schoolroom.

But the morning passed just as usual and nothing happened to interrupt the quiet course of Adele's studies. Only soon after breakfast, I heard some bustle in the neighbourhood of Mr. Rochester's chamber with exclamations from Mrs. Fairfax's voice and Leah's and the cook's—John's wife—and even John's own gruff tones. They gasped, "What a mercy master was not burnt in his bed!"—"It is always dangerous to keep a candle lit at night."—"I wonder he waked nobody!" &c.

To much confabulation succeeded a sound of scrubbing and setting to rights, and when I passed the room in going downstairs to dinner, I saw through the open door that all was again restored to complete order. Leah stood up in the window-seat, rubbing the panes of glass dimmed with smoke and I was about to address her when I saw a second person in the chamber—a woman sitting on a chair by the bedside, sewing. That woman was no other than Grace Poole.

She was intent on her work and in her commonplace features, there was nothing either of the paleness or desperation one would have expected to see marking the countenance of a woman who had attempted murder. I was amazed and confounded. She looked up, while I still gazed at her and I perceived no start, no increase or failure of colour betrayed emotion. She said, "Good morning, Miss," in her usual brief manner, and went on with her sewing.

"Good morning, Grace," I replied. "Has anything happened here? I thought I heard the servants all talking together a while ago."

"Only master had been reading in his bed last night and he fell asleep with his candle lit. The curtains got on fire, but fortunately, he awoke before the bed-clothes or the wood-work caught, and contrived to quench the flames with the water in the ewer."

"A strange affair!" I said, in a low voice and then looked at her fixedly. "Did Mr. Rochester wake nobody? Did no one hear him move?"

She again raised her eyes to me and this time there was something of consciousness in their expression. She seemed to examine me warily, then she answered, "Mrs. Fairfax's room and yours are the nearest to master's, but Mrs. Fairfax said she heard nothing." She paused and then added with a sort of assumed indifference, but still in a marked and significant tone, "But you are young, Miss, and I should say a light sleeper; perhaps you may have heard a noise?"

"I did," said I, dropping my voice, so that Leah, who was still polishing the panes, could not hear me, "and at first I thought it was Pilot, but Pilot cannot laugh. I am certain I heard a laugh, and a strange one."

She took a new needleful of thread, waxed it carefully, threaded her needle with a steady hand, and then observed, with perfect composure, "You must have been dreaming."

"I was not dreaming," I said, with some warmth, for her brazen coolness provoked me.

Again she looked at me with the same scrutinising and conscious eye.

"You did not think of opening your door and looking out into the gallery?"

Her question threw me and I was on my guard.

"On the contrary," said I, "I bolted my door."

"Then you are not in the habit of bolting your door every night before you get into bed?"

I replied sharply, "I did not think it necessary. I was not aware any danger or annoyance was to be dreaded at Thornfield Hall, but in future I shall take good care to make all secure before I venture to lie down."

"It will be wise so to do," was her answer.

I was about to say something more when the cook entered.

"Mrs. Poole," said she, addressing Grace, "the servants' dinner will soon be ready. Will you come down?"

The cook here turned to me, saying that Mrs. Fairfax was waiting for me and so I departed.

I hardly heard Mrs. Fairfax's account of the curtain conflagration during dinner, so much was I occupied in puzzling my brains over the enigmatical character of Grace Poole, and still more in pondering the problem of her position at Thornfield and questioning why she had not been given into custody that morning, or at the very least dismissed from her master's service. He had almost as much as declared his conviction of her criminality last night: what mysterious cause withheld him from accusing her? A cold thought went through me that perhaps she too satisfied the master's needs—perhaps she too was a servant he had first met on the causeway and she had set his curtains alight in a bout of jealous rage. I immediately dismissed it, partly through hurt and partly because deep down, I did not think it possible. Grace Poole was no beauty and though neither was I handsome, I at least had youth. I could not imagine the wild, reckless ways of my master finding solace in the doughy plainness that was Grace. Though I admit, I could not think of another reason why he should protect her.

I waited all day to be called for by Mr. Rochester. I wanted desperately to speak to him and ask him about Grace Poole and . . . continue our love making. When dusk actually closed, and Adele left me to go and play in the nursery with Sophie, I listened keenly for the bell to ring below. I listened for Leah coming up with a message and I fancied sometimes I heard Mr. Rochester's own tread. I turned to the door, expecting it to open and admit him, but the door remained shut.

A tread creaked on the stairs at last and Leah made her appearance, but it was only to intimate that tea was ready in Mrs. Fairfax's room. Thither I repaired, glad at least to go downstairs for that brought me at least a little nearer to Mr. Rochester's presence.

"You must want your tea," said the good lady, as I joined her, "you are not well to-day, you look flushed and feverish."

"Oh, I am quite well! I never felt better."

She did not look convinced but she changed the subject, commenting, "It is fair to-night though not starlight; Mr. Rochester has, on the whole, had a favourable day for his journey."

I felt a rush of dread run through me.

"Journey! Is Mr. Rochester gone anywhere? I did not know he was out."

"Oh, he set off the moment he had breakfasted. He is gone to the Leas, Mr. Eshton's place, ten miles on the other side of Millcote. I believe there is quite a party assembled there with Lord Ingram, Sir George Lynn, Colonel Dent, and others."

"Do you expect him back to-night?"

"No, nor to-morrow either and I should think he is very likely to stay a week or more. When these fine, fashionable people get together, they are so surrounded by elegance and gaiety that they are in no hurry to separate. Gentlemen especially are often in request on such occasions and Mr. Rochester is so talented and so lively in society that I believe he is a general favourite, particularly with the ladies."

I thought I might drop my cup, since a stab of pain shot through my chest, but I managed to keep myself composed. "Are there ladies at the Leas?" I asked quietly.

"There is Mrs. Eshton and her three daughters—very elegant young ladies indeed and there is the Honourable Blanche and Mary Ingram—most beautiful women. Blanche came here to a Christmas ball and party Mr. Rochester gave some years ago and she was considered the belle of the evening."

"You saw her, you say, Mrs. Fairfax?" I could not help but ask. "What was she like?"

"Yes, I saw her. She was tall and fine with sloping shoulders, a long, graceful neck, olive complexion and eyes rather like Mr. Rochester's: large and black. She had such a fine head of hair; raven-black and so becomingly arranged."

"She was greatly admired, of course?" I almost choked on my words.

"Yes, indeed, and not only for her beauty, but for her accomplishments. She was one of the ladies who sang and a gentleman accompanied her on the piano. She and Mr. Rochester sang a duet."

"And this beautiful and accomplished lady, she is not yet married?"

"It appears not. I fancy neither she nor her sister have very large fortunes."

I was about to elude to the dreaded union between Mr. Rochester and the beautiful Blanche but Adele came in, and the conversation was turned into another channel.

When once more alone, I grieved for what I had heard keenly. That night I wept into my pillow for I had been weak and stupid and wrong. I should not have followed my passions and nor should I ever have. Such men as Mr. Rochester did not fall in love with such plain, ugly beasts as Jane Eyre. It is madness in all women to let a secret love kindle within them, which, if unreturned and unknown, must devour the life that feeds it, and if discovered and responded to, must lead, ignis-fatus-like, into miry wilds whence there is no extrication.

I now felt extremely foolish for my behavior of the night before and I endeavored to forget it, for I fully expected Mr. Rochester had.

CHAPTER XVII

A week passed and no news arrived of Mr. Rochester: ten days, and still he did not come. I balmed my wounded heart in his absence and convinced myself to adhere to my old solitary life. Mrs. Fairfax said she should not be surprised if he were to go straight from the Leas to London, and thence to the Continent and not show his face again at Thornfield for a year to come. When I heard this, I was beginning to feel a strange chill and failing at the heart. I was actually permitting myself to experience a sickening sense of disappointment, but rallying my wits and recollecting my principles, I at once called my sensations to order and it was wonderful how I got over the temporary blunder.

Mr. Rochester had been absent upwards of a fortnight when the post brought Mrs. Fairfax a letter.

"It is from the master," said she, as she looked at the direction. "Now I suppose we shall know whether we are to expect his return or not."

And while she broke the seal and perused the document, I went on taking my coffee as if I did not care. Why my hand shook and why I involuntarily spilt half the contents of my cup into my saucer, I did not choose to consider.

"Mr. Rochester will be back in three days' time next Thursday, he says, and not alone either. I don't know how many of the fine people at the Leas are coming with him, but he sends directions for all the best bedrooms to be prepared and the library and drawing-rooms are to be cleaned out. We shall have a full house of it!" after exclaiming this, Mrs. Fairfax swallowed her breakfast and hastened away to commence operations.

The next three days were, as she had foretold, busy enough. I had thought all the rooms at Thornfield beautifully clean and well arranged, but it appears I was mistaken. Three women were got to help and such scrubbing, such brushing, such washing and such polishing I never beheld either before or since. I was expected to help and I found solace in the monotonous housework that did not allow me to think too much of Mr. Rochester or Blanche Ingram. At night I wept into my pillow but in the daylight at least, I was kept busy.

On the second day I chanced to see the third-storey staircase door (which of late had always been kept locked) open slowly and give passage to the form of Grace Poole. I watched her glide along the gallery, mutter something to a charwoman and then pass on. She would thus descend to the kitchen once a day, eat her dinner, smoke a moderate pipe on the hearth and go back carrying her pot of porter with her to her own gloomy, upper haunt. Only one hour in the twenty-four did she pass with her fellow-servants below and all the rest of her time was spent in some low-ceiled, oaken chamber of the second storey.

The strangest thing of all was that not a soul in the house except me noticed her habits or seemed to marvel at them. No one discussed her position or employment and no one pitied her solitude or isolation. I once overheard part of a dialogue between Leah and one of the charwomen of which Grace formed the subject. Leah had been saying something I had not caught, and the charwoman remarked, "She gets good wages, I guess?"

"Yes," said Leah. "I wish I had as good, but it is not every one could fill her shoes even for all the money she gets."

"That it is not!" was the reply. "I wonder whether the master—"

The charwoman was going on, but here Leah turned, perceived me and she instantly gave her companion a nudge.

"Doesn't she know?" I heard the woman whisper.

Leah shook her head and the conversation was, of course, dropped. All I had gathered from it amounted to this: there was a mystery at Thornfield Hall, but I had yet to discover what it was.

Thursday came and we all wandered about the house that day, waiting for our master's return in the evening. At last, wheels were heard and I leant out of a window on the second-storey to see four equestrians galloping up the drive with two open carriages following. Mr. Rochester was astride his black horse, Mesrour, Pilot bounding before him and at his side rode a beautiful lady. Her purple riding-habit almost swept the ground, her veil streamed long on the breeze and gleaming through it shone rich raven ringlets.

"Miss Ingram!" exclaimed Mrs. Fairfax beside me, and away she hurried.

Adele, who stood by me also, petitioned to go down, but I took her on my knee and gave her to understand that she must not on any account think of venturing in sight of the ladies, either now or at any other time unless expressly sent for by Mr. Rochester. She was most upset about this, but I remained firm.

A joyous stir was now audible in the hall and gentlemen's deep tones and ladies' silvery accents blent harmoniously together. Distinguishable above all, though not loud, was the sonorous voice of the master of Thornfield Hall, welcoming his fair and gallant guests under its roof. At the sound of his familiar tones, I felt my knees go weak and I became light-headed, but I told myself to be strong.

"What beautiful ladies!" cried Adele in English. "Oh, I wish I might go to them! Do you think Mr. Rochester will send for us by-and-bye, after dinner?"

"No, indeed, I do not. Mr. Rochester has other things to think about. Never mind the ladies to-night, perhaps you will see them to-morrow."

That evening, Adele and I sat upstairs listening to the joy and commotion unfolding beneath us. I told her stories to pass the time, but she often seemed distracted. I too found it difficult to concentrate; memories of my childhood with the Reeds drifted into my mind and threw me into a melancholy mood. When the evening was far advanced, the sound of music issued from the drawing-room and Adele and I fell quiet to listen. Presently a voice blent with the rich tones of the piano and a lady sang sweetly. The solo over, a duet followed and I listened long, suddenly discovering that my ear was wholly intent on analysing the mingled sounds, trying to discriminate amidst the confusion of accents those of Mr. Rochester, but I could not.

The clock struck eleven and finally, Adele and I went to bed.

The next day was as fine as its predecessor and it was devoted by the party to an excursion to some site in the neighbourhood. Miss Ingram was the only lady riding and as before, Mr. Rochester galloped at her side. I watched the two ride a little apart from the rest away from Thornfield and pointed out this circumstance to Mrs. Fairfax, who was standing at the window with me, "Mr. Rochester evidently prefers her to any of the other ladies."

"No doubt he admires her."

"And she him," I added, trying to keep all forms of jealousy and sadness at bay. "Look how she leans her head towards him as if she were conversing confidentially. I wish I could see her face, I have not had a glimpse of it yet."

"You will see her this evening," answered Mrs. Fairfax. "I happened to remark to Mr. Rochester how much Adele wished to be introduced to the ladies, and he said: 'Oh! Let her come into the drawing-room after dinner and request Miss Eyre to accompany her.'"

"I need not go, I am sure," I answered quickly, my panic rising.

"Well, I observed to him that you were unused to company, and he replied, 'Nonsense! If she resists, say I shall come and fetch her.'"

I was confused as to the meaning of this. Did he wish purely to gloat in front of me and give me pain? It was cruelty at the highest, but I could not refuse my master.

"I will go, if no better may be, but I don't like it. Shall you be there, Mrs. Fairfax?"

"No, I pleaded off and he admitted my plea. If you do not wish to be seen, slip into the drawing-room while it is empty, choose your seat in a quiet nook and just let Mr. Rochester see you are there, then come away. Nobody will notice you."

I sighed wearily, not at all pleased with these circumstances. I did not wish to see Mr. Rochester for the first time since our night together in a room full of strangers, but perhaps it would be for the best. Surrounded by others, the embarrassment of such a thing would most certainly be of little importance and neither of us would have the opportunity to talk about it.

"Will these people remain long, do you think?" I asked.

"Perhaps two or three weeks, certainly not more."

Thus it was with some trepidation that I perceived the hour approach when I was to repair with my charge to the drawing-room. Adele had been in a state of ecstasy all day after hearing she was to be presented to the ladies in the evening and it was not till Sophie commenced the operation of dressing her that she sobered down. I too tried to look my best for the occasion wearing a silver-grey dress purchased for Miss Temple's wedding, smoothing my hair and wearing my sole ornament: the pearl brooch. When we were both ready, we descended.

Fortunately we found the drawing-room vacant and while Adele sat down, without a word on a footstool, I retired to a window-seat. Taking a book from a table near, I endeavoured to read and not be noticed.

A soft sound of rising now became audible and a band of ladies entered the drawing room. There were but eight, yet somehow, as they flocked in, they gave the impression of a much larger number. Some of them were very tall, many were dressed in white and all had a sweeping amplitude of array that seemed to magnify their persons as a mist magnifies the moon. I rose and curtseyed to them and one or two bent their heads in return. The others only stared at me.

They dispersed about the room, reminding me of a flock of white plumy birds. Some of them threw themselves in half-reclining positions on the sofas and ottomans, some bent over the tables and examined the flowers and books, and the rest gathered in a group round the fire. I knew their names afterwards, and may as well mention them now.

First, there was Mrs. Eshton and two of her daughters. She had evidently been a handsome woman in her youth and was well preserved still. Of her daughters, the eldest, Amy, was rather little, naive and child-like in face and manner. The second, Louisa, was taller and more elegant in figure with a very pretty face. Both sisters were fair as lilies.

Lady Lynn was a large and stout personage of about forty, very erect, very haughty-looking, and richly dressed in a satin robe of changeful sheen. Her dark hair shone glossily under the shade of an azure plume and within the circlet of a band of gems.

Mrs. Colonel Dent was less showy but, I thought, more lady-like. She had a slight figure, a pale, gentle face, and fair hair. Her black satin dress, her scarf of rich foreign lace and her pearl ornaments, pleased me better than the rainbow radiance of the titled dame.

But the three most distinguished—partly perhaps because they were the tallest figures of the band—were the Dowager Lady Ingram and her daughters, Blanche and Mary. The Dowager might be between forty and fifty, her shape was still fine, her hair still black and her teeth too were still apparently perfect. Most people would have termed her a splendid woman of her age physically speaking, but then there was an expression of almost insupportable haughtiness in her bearing and countenance. Blanche and Mary too were straight and tall as poplars. Mary was too slim for her height, but Blanche was moulded like a Dian. I regarded her, of course, with special interest. She was undeniably beautiful. The noble bust, the sloping shoulders, the graceful neck, the dark eyes and black ringlets were all there, but her face? Her face was like her mother's with the same sneering pride. However, I thought that most men would admire her and I knew too well that Mr. Rochester did for there was much to admire. I could not find fault with her physically and nor could I match up to such beauty; I felt that only too keenly.

You are not to suppose, Reader, that Adele had all this time been sitting motionless on a stool. No, when the ladies entered, she rose and advanced to meet them, saying with gravity, "Bon jour, mesdames."

Miss Ingram looked down at her with a mocking air, and exclaimed, "Oh, what a little puppet!"

Lady Lynn remarked, "It is Mr. Rochester's ward, I suppose."

Mrs. Dent kindly took her hand, and given her a kiss.

Amy and Louisa Eshton cried out simultaneously, "What a love of a child!"

And then they had called her to a sofa where she sat ensconced between them, chattering alternately in French and broken English, getting spoilt to her heart's content.

At last coffee was brought in, and the gentlemen were summoned. The collective appearance of them, like that of the ladies, was very imposing. They were all costumed in black; most of them tall and some young. Henry and Frederick Lynn were very dashing sparks indeed and Colonel Dent was a fine soldierly man. Mr. Eshton, the magistrate of the district, was gentleman-like with white hair and dark whiskers, while Lord Ingram, like his sisters, was very tall and handsome.

And where was Mr. Rochester?

He came in at last and I jumped slightly in my seat at the sight of him. I had forgotten the magnetic nature of his presence, which seeped across the room and seemed to grasp my heart in a breath-taking clutch. Images of our last night together flashed through my mind, mingling with my memories of our evening on the causeway and I saw his drenched shirt in candlelight as I knelt before him, desire burning in his eyes, and then his dark features gleaming in the moonlight as I lay beneath him and he thrust into me. My fingers began to shake.

He did not turn to look at me once, indeed, it was as if I was not there. I suppose he could not with the beauty of Miss Ingram before him. I bent my head and tried desperately not to weep. I had been telling myself since he left that he did not care for me and I should delude my fantasies not longer but somehow having it confirmed in such a way was deeply painful.

"Mr. Rochester, I thought you were not fond of children?" said Miss Blanche Ingram, walking across the room to stand beside him as the other guests chattered between themselves.

"Nor am I."

"Then, what induced you to take charge of such a little doll as that?" (pointing to Adele). "Where did you pick her up?"

"I did not pick her up, she was left on my hands."

"You should have sent her to school."

"I could not afford it. Schools are so dear."

"Why, I suppose you have a governess for her. I saw a person with her just now, is she gone? Oh, no! There she is still, behind the window-curtain. You pay her, of course and I should think it quite as expensive."

I feared the allusion to me would make Mr. Rochester glance my way and I involuntarily shrank farther into the shade, but he never turned his eyes. With such beauty before him as Miss Ingram, I did not wish him to see me.

"I have not considered the subject," said he indifferently, staring straight ahead.

"You should hear mama speak of governesses! Mary and I have had, I should think, a dozen at least in our day and half of them detestable and the rest ridiculous. All were incubi were they not, mama?"

"My dearest, don't mention governesses," returned the Dowager Lady Ingram. "The very word makes me nervous. I thank Heaven I have now done with them!"

Mrs. Dent here bent over to the pious lady and whispered something in her ear. I suppose from the answer elicited, it was a reminder that one of the anathematised race was present.

"I hope it may do her good!" said her ladyship. "I noticed her; I am a judge of physiognomy and in hers, I see all the faults of her class."

"What are they, madam?" inquired Mr. Rochester.

"I will tell you in your private ear," replied she.

"My curiosity will not last."

"Ask Blanche, she is nearer you than I."

"Oh, don't refer him to me, mama! I have just one word to say of the whole tribe—they are a nuisance. Am I right, Baroness Ingram, of Ingram Park?"

"My lily-flower, you are right now, as always."

"Then no more need be said—change the subject."

Why don't you give us some music, sweet?" suggested her mother.

She smiled gallantly and both she and Mr. Rochester walked to the piano. While Miss Ingram played, they both began to sing.

"Now is my time to slip away," thought I, but the tones that then severed the air arrested me. Mrs. Fairfax had said Mr. Rochester possessed a fine voice and he did; a mellow, powerful bass into which he threw his own feeling, his own force. I waited till the last deep and full vibration had expired and the tide of talk resumed its flow before I could leave. I then quitted my sheltered corner and made my exit by the side-door, which was fortunately near. Thence a narrow passage led into the hall and in crossing it, I perceived my sandal was loose. I stopped to tie it and heard the dining-room door unclose. A gentleman came out and rising hastily, I stood face to face with him. It was Mr. Rochester.

"How do you do?" he asked.

"I am very well, sir."

"Why did you not come and speak to me in the room?"

I might have asked him the same question but, looking down, I merely answered, "I did not wish to disturb you as you seemed engaged, sir."

"What have you been doing during my absence?"

"Nothing particular. Teaching Adele as usual."

"And getting a good deal paler than you were as I saw at first sight. What is the matter?"

Oh how could he ask me that question? I wished to scream out, but I stayed calm.

"Nothing at all, sir."

"Return to the drawing-room, you are deserting too early."

"I am tired, sir."

He looked at me for a minute.

"And a little depressed," he said. "What about? Tell me."

"Nothing. Nothing, sir. I am not depressed."

"But I affirm that you are so much depressed that a few more words would bring tears to your eyes. Well, to-night I excuse you, but understand that so long as my visitors stay, I expect you to appear in the drawing-room every evening. It is my wish and don't neglect it. Now go and send Sophie for Adele. Good-night my—" He stopped, bit his lip, and abruptly left me.

CHAPTER XVIII

I wondered what they were going to do the next evening for a change of entertainment was proposed and they spoke of playing charades. All that day they had been engaged in riding about the countryside around Thornfield and they returned that evening, wishing for amusement. The servants were called down, the dining-room tables wheeled away and chairs placed in a semicircle in the drawing-room. While Mr. Rochester and the other gentlemen directed these alterations, the ladies were running up and down stairs ringing for their maids. Mrs. Fairfax was summoned to give information respecting the resources of the house in shawls, dresses, and draperies of any kind, and wardrobes of the third storey were ransacked for their contents.

Meantime, Mr. Rochester had again summoned the ladies round him, and was selecting certain of their number to be of his party. "Miss Ingram is mine, of course," said he and afterwards he looked at me and said, "Will you play?"

I shook my head and he did not insist, which I rather feared he might.

He and his party now disappeared to ready themselves for the first game. One of the gentlemen left in the room, Mr. Eshton, observing me, seemed to propose that I should be asked to join them, but Lady Ingram instantly negatived the notion.

"No," I heard her say, "she looks too stupid for any game of the sort."

Ere long a bell tinkled, and Mr. Rochester and his party entered once more. Adele (who had insisted on being one of her guardian's party), bounded forward, scattering round her the contents of a basket of flowers she carried on her arm. Then appeared the magnificent figure of Miss Ingram, clad in white, a long veil on her head and a wreath of roses round her brow. By her side walked Mr. Rochester and together they drew near the table. They knelt while Mrs. Dent and Louisa Eshton, dressed also in white, took up their stations behind them. A ceremony followed in dumb show, which was easily recognised as the pantomime of a marriage. At its termination, Colonel Dent and his party consulted in whispers for two minutes, then the Colonel called out: "Bride!"

Mr. Rochester bowed, and I completely lost interest in the whole thing. I shrank back into the corner in which I was sitting and took to my book. I could not bear to see the two of them together or watch Miss Ingram throw herself at Mr. Rochester so completely. The game went on but I took no more notice and nor did I make a sound for the rest of the evening.

The next day it was verging on dusk and the clock had already given warning of the hour to dress for dinner, when little Adele, who knelt by me in the drawing-room window-seat, suddenly exclaimed

"Voile, Monsieur Rochester, qui revient!"

Mr. Rochester had been away on business all day and left his guests to themselves at Thornfield. While the others had seemed to relish a period of relaxation, Miss Ingram had been restless.

I turned at Adele's words and Miss Ingram darted forwards from her sofa. The others, too, looked up from their several occupations and the crunching of wheels and splashing tramp of horse-hoofs became audible on the wet gravel. A post-chaise was approaching.

"What can possess him to come home in that style?" said Miss Ingram. "He rode Mesrour when he went out and Pilot was with him—what has he done with the animals?"

As she said this, she approached her tall person and ample garments so near the window where I was sitting that I was obliged to bend back almost to the breaking of my spine. In her eagerness she did not observe me at first, but when she did, she curled her lip and moved to another casement. We watched the post-chaise stop and a gentleman alighted attired in travelling garb, but it was not Mr. Rochester.

"How provoking!" exclaimed Miss Ingram. "You tiresome monkey!" (apostrophising Adele), "Who perched you up in the window to give false intelligence?" and she cast on me an angry glance, as if I were in fault.

Some parleying was audible in the hall, and soon the newcomer entered.

"It appears I come at an inopportune time, madam," said he. "My friend, Mr. Rochester, is from home, but I arrive from a very long journey and I think I may presume so far on old and intimate acquaintance as to install myself here till he returns."

His manner was polite, but his accent in speaking struck me as being somewhat unusual, not precisely foreign, but still not altogether English. His age might be about Mr. Rochester's and his complexion was singularly sallow, otherwise he was a fine-looking man.

The sound of the dressing-bell then dispersed the party and it was not till after dinner that I saw him again when he then seemed quite at his ease. However, there was something about him on second-inspection that repelled me exceedingly. As I sat in my usual nook, I looked at him in the arm-chair opposite from me, drawn close to the fire as if he were cold, and compared him with Mr. Rochester. I think the contrast could not be much greater between a sleek gander and a fierce falcon, between a meek sheep and the rough-coated keen-eyed dog, its guardian. He had spoken of Mr. Rochester as an old friend. A curious friendship theirs must have been.

Two or three of the gentlemen sat near him, and I caught at times scraps of their conversation across the room. At first I could not make much sense of what I heard, but I presently gathered that the new-comer was called Mr. Mason. I learned that he was but just arrived in England from some hot country which was the reason, doubtless, his face was so sallow and he sat so near the hearth. Presently the words Jamaica, Kingston, and Spanish Town indicated the West Indies as his residence and it was with no little surprise I gathered, ere long, that he had there first seen and become acquainted with Mr. Rochester.

I was pondering this when an incident, and a somewhat unexpected one, broke the thread of my musings. Mr. Mason, shivering as some one chanced to open the door, asked for more coal to be put on the fire which had burnt out its flame. The footman who brought the coal, in going out, stopped near Mr. Eshton's chair and said something to him in a low voice, of which I heard only the words, "old woman . . . quite troublesome."

"Tell her she shall be put in the stocks if she does not take herself off," replied the magistrate.

"No, stop!" interrupted Colonel Dent. "Don't send her away, Eshton. Better consult the ladies." And speaking aloud, he continued, "ladies, you talked of going to Hay Common to visit the gipsy camp; Sam here says that one of the old Mother Bunches is in the servants' hall at this moment and insists upon being brought in to tell fortunes. Would you like to see her?"

"Surely, colonel," cried Lady Ingram, "you would not encourage such a low impostor? Dismiss her, by all means, at once!"

"But I cannot persuade her to go away, my lady," said the footman. "Nor can any of the servants. Mrs. Fairfax is with her just now, entreating her to be gone, but she has taken a chair in the chimney-corner, and says nothing shall stir her from it till she gets leave to come in here."

"What does she want?" asked Mrs. Eshton.

"To tell the gentry their fortunes, she says, ma'am."

"What is she like?"

"A shockingly ugly old creature, almost as black as a crock."

"Why, she's a real sorceress!" cried Frederick Lynn. "Let us have her in, of course."

"I cannot possibly countenance any such inconsistent proceeding," chimed in the Dowager Ingram.

"Indeed, mama, but you can and will," pronounced the haughty voice of Blanche. "I have a curiosity to hear my fortune told. Sam, order the beldame forward."

"Yes, yes, yes!" cried all the juveniles, both ladies and gentlemen. "Let her come! It will be excellent sport!"

The footman still lingered. "She looks such a rough one," said he.

"Go!" shouted Miss Ingram, and the man went.

Excitement instantly seized the whole party and a running fire of raillery and jests was proceeding when Sam returned.

"She won't come now," said he. "She says it's not her mission to appear before the 'vulgar herd' (them's her words). I must show her into a room by herself, and then those who wish to consult her must go to her one by one."

"You see now, my queenly Blanche," began Lady Ingram, "she encroaches. Be advised, my angel girl and—"

"Show her into the library, of course," cut in the angel girl. "It is not my mission to listen to her before the vulgar herd either. I mean to have her all to myself. Is there a fire in the library?"

"Yes, ma'am."

"Do my bidding."

Again Sam vanished and mystery, animation, expectation rose to full flow once more.

"She's ready now," said the footman, as he reappeared. "She wishes to know who will be her first visitor."

"I think I had better just look in upon her before any of the ladies go," said Colonel Dent. "Tell her, Sam, a gentleman is coming."

Sam went and returned.

"She says, sir, that she'll have no gentlemen. And no ladies either, except the young and single."

"By Jove, she has taste!" exclaimed Henry Lynn.

Miss Ingram rose solemnly. "I go first," she said.

"Oh, my best! Oh, my dearest! Pause and reflect!" was her mama's cry, but she swept past her in stately silence, passed through the door which Colonel Dent held open and we heard her enter the library.

A comparative silence ensued and the minutes passed very slowly. Fifteen were counted before the library-door again opened and Miss Ingram returned to us through the arch. All eyes met her with a glance of eager curiosity and she met all eyes with one of rebuff and coldness. She looked neither flurried nor merry and she walked stiffly to her seat, taking it in silence.

"Well, Blanche?" said Lord Ingram.

"What did she say, sister?" asked Mary.

"What did you think? How do you feel?" demanded the Misses Eshton.

"Now, now, good people," returned Miss Ingram, "don't press upon me. Really you seem to believe we have a genuine witch in the house who is in close alliance with the old gentleman. I have seen a gipsy vagabond; she has practised in hackneyed fashion the science of palmistry and told me what such people usually tell. My whim is gratified and now I think Mr. Eshton will do well to put the hag in the stocks to-morrow morning, as he threatened."

Miss Ingram took a book, leant back in her chair and declined further conversation. I watched her for nearly half-an-hour and during all that time she never turned a page. Her face grew darker, more dissatisfied and more sourly expressive of disappointment. She had obviously not heard anything to her advantage.

Meantime, Mary Ingram, Amy and Louisa Eshton, declared they dared not go alone and so they went all together. Their visit was not so still as Miss Ingram's had been and we heard hysterical giggling and little shrieks proceeding from the library. In half an hour they burst back into the room, breathless.

"I am sure she is something not right!" they cried, one and all. "She told us such things! She knows all about us!" and they sank into the various seats the gentlemen hastened to bring them.

In the midst of the tumult, and while my eyes and ears were fully engaged in the scene before me, I heard a hem close at my elbow. I turned and saw Sam.

"If you please, miss, the gipsy declares that there is another young single lady in the room who has not been to her yet and she swears she will not go till she has seen all. I thought it must be you as there is no one else for it. What shall I tell her?"

"Oh, I will go by all means," I answered, and I was glad of the unexpected opportunity to gratify my much-excited curiosity. I slipped out of the room, unobserved by any eye and closed the door quietly behind me.

"If you like, miss," said Sam, "I'll wait in the hall for you, and if she frightens you, just call and I'll come in."

"Do not worry Sam, return to the kitchen. I am not in the least afraid."

Nor was I, but I was a good deal interested and excited.

CHAPTER XIX

The library looked tranquil as I entered it and the gipsy was seated snugly enough in an easy-chair at the chimney-corner. She had on a red cloak and a broad-brimmed gipsy hat tied down with a striped handkerchief under her chin. I stood on the rug before her and warmed my hands at the fire. I felt now as composed as ever I did in my life as there was nothing indeed in the gipsy's appearance to trouble one's calm. She shut her book and slowly looked up. Her hat-brim partially shaded her face, yet I could see as she raised it that it was a strange one. It looked all brown and black and elf-locks bristled out from beneath a white band which passed under her chin.

"Well, and you want your fortune told?" she said, in a voice as decided as her glance and as harsh as her features.

"I don't care about it, you may please yourself."

"It's like your impudence to say so, I expected it of you. Why don't you tremble?"

"I'm not cold."

"Why don't you turn pale?"

"I am not sick."

"Why don't you consult my art?"

"I'm not silly."

The old crone laughed and then drew out a short black pipe and lighting it, began to smoke. Having indulged a while in this sedative, she raised her bent body, took the pipe from her lips, and said very deliberately, "You are very near happiness, yes, within reach of it. The materials are all prepared, there only wants a movement to combine them."

"I don't understand enigmas. I never could guess a riddle in my life."

"If you wish me to speak more plainly, show me your palm."

"And I must cross it with silver, I suppose?"

"To be sure."

I gave her a shilling and she put it into an old stocking-foot which she took out of her pocket. She then arched her face to my palm and poured over it without touching it.

"It is too fine," said she. "I can make nothing of such a hand as that. Besides, what is in a palm? Destiny is not written there."

"I believe you."

"I wonder what thoughts are busy in your heart during all the hours you sit in that window-seat. You see I know your habits," said she, changing track.

"You have learned them from the servants," I replied, unconvinced.

"Ah! You think yourself sharp. Well, perhaps I have. I have an acquaintance with one of them, Mrs. Poole—"

I started when I heard the name.

"Don't be alarmed," continued the strange being, "she's a safe hand, is Mrs. Poole. But, as I was saying, sitting in that window-seat, do you have no present interest in any of the company who occupy the sofas and chairs before you? Is there not one face you study? One figure whose movements you follow with at least curiosity?"

"I like to observe all the faces and all the figures."

"But do you never single one from the rest? Or two?"

"I do frequently when the gestures or looks of a pair seem telling a tale. It amuses me to watch them."

"What tale do you like best to hear?"

"Oh, I have not much choice! They generally run on the same theme: courtship and promise to end in the same catastrophe—marriage."

"And do you like that monotonous theme?"

"It is nothing to me."

"Nothing to you? When a lady, young and full of life and health, charming with beauty and endowed with the gifts of rank and fortune, sits and smiles in the eyes of a gentleman you—"

"I what?"

"—you know and perhaps think well of."

"I don't know the gentlemen here. I have scarcely interchanged a syllable with one of them."

"Will you say that of the master of the house?"

I felt my cheeks flush, but I tried desperately not to give myself away and I answered calmly, "He is not at home."

"A profound remark! A most ingenious quibble! He went to Millcote this morning and will be back here to-night or to-morrow. Does that circumstance exclude him from the list of your acquaintance?"

"No, but I can scarcely see what Mr. Rochester has to do with the theme you had introduced."

"I was talking of ladies smiling in the eyes of gentlemen and, of late, so many smiles have been shed into Mr. Rochester's eyes."

"Mr. Rochester has a right to enjoy the society of his guests."

"True. He is so willing to receive them and looks so grateful for the pastime given him, you have noticed this?"

"Grateful! I cannot remember detecting gratitude in his face."

"Detecting! You have analysed, then. And what did you detect, if not gratitude?"

I said nothing.

"You have seen love, have you not? And looking forward you have seen him married and beheld his bride happy?"

"Humph! Not exactly. Your witch's skill is rather at fault sometimes."

"What the devil have you seen, then?"

"Never mind. I came here to inquire, not to confess. Is it known that Mr. Rochester is to be married?" I asked.

"Yes, and to the beautiful Miss Ingram."

"Shortly?"

"Appearances would warrant that conclusion and no doubt they will be a happy pair. He must love such a handsome, noble, witty, accomplished lady, and probably she loves him or if not his person, at least his purse. I know she considers the Rochester estate eligible to the last degree, though I told her something on that point about an hour ago which made her look wondrous grave—the corners of her mouth fell half an inch."

Such thoughts of their marriage made my heart sink and I could not help but look very grave as well.

"I did not come to hear Mr. Rochester's fortune. I came to hear my own and you have told me nothing of it."

"Your fortune is yet doubtful. Chance has meted you a measure of happiness, but it depends on yourself to stretch out your hand and take it up. Whether you will do so, is the problem I study. Kneel on the rug."

I knelt and she did not stoop towards me, but only gazed, leaning back in her chair. I looked into her eyes and they were dark, mysterious, and familiar.

"Rise, Miss Eyre and leave me. The play is played out."

Where was I? Had I been dreaming? Did I dream still? The old woman's voice had changed and her accent and her gesture were all familiar to me now. I got up, but did not go.

"Well, Jane, do you know me?" asked a gruff voice.

"Only take off the red cloak, sir."

Mr. Rochester stepped out of his disguise and I gasped.

"Now, sir, what a strange idea!" I said, flushing and wondering if I had revealed too much in our conversation.

"It was a mere folly. Do you forgive me for it, Jane?"

"I cannot tell till I have thought it all over."

He stood abruptly and moved closer to me, his eyes boring into mine. "I will make it up to you," he breathed. "I believe I owe you a favour."

My blood rushed to my head and my abdominal muscles clenched with excitement. My head told me not to adhere to the wishes of this man that treated me so inconsistently and was practically the bridegroom of Miss Ingram, but I could not help it. I wanted every last moment I could snatch with my master before he was completely lost to me.

"And what favour would that be?" I asked, my voice trembling slightly.

His eyes blackened with desire and burnt into mine with such blistering heat that I had never before known. I was gasping although he was not touching me and yearning pumped through my whole body, filling me with desperate need.

"Come to me, Jane," he whispered, holding out his hand.

I shook my head. "No, you come to me," I said.

He raised his eyebrows in surprise but the corners of his mouth tugged up in a devilish smile and he obediently crossed the distance between us, wrapping his great arms around me swiftly and slamming his lips against mine. My breath hitching in my throat, I surrendered myself to his violent passion and let his hands run the length of my body, caressing my breasts through my dress and tearing at my hair.

I let out a yelp of pleasure as he bit down hard on my lip and sucked and smoothed it better with his tongue. Then suddenly, he bent down and scooped me into his arms, his lips still fiercely pressing against mine, his tongue darting in and out of my mouth. He carried me over to the table and laid me down upon it.

"Stay still," he instructed, leaning over me and delicately brushing my hair back from my face.

Then slowly, he peeled back my dress and petticoat. I lay against the cold, hard table wishing that I were completely bare and he too so that I could finally run my hands across the skin and dark hair on his broad chest. We had never been completely bare with each other before and I suddenly wanted it like nothing else.

I tried to move my hands back to unlace my dress, but he stopped me.

"Not now, Jane," he said with a wicked grin. "Later. Right now, this is you only."

I gently sank back against the table in sweet rapture as he trailed kisses across my neck and chest, tenderly kissing, sucking, and nipping the skin so that my senses quaked and shivered with longing. He ran his hands down the length of my body and slid them beneath my skirts. Then he pulled down my stockings ever so slowly, kissing each bare piece of skin as it exposed itself and licking the length of my thighs.

I moaned softly and convulsed, quivering.

He began kissing my ankle and then gliding his lips up my calf before pausing and doing the same on the other foot, teasing me.

"Please," I begged.

Without responding, he kissed up my calf again and then carried on across my inner thigh, pushing my legs apart. I gasped, desire strong in me and my whole body tingling with coiled anticipation.

He took each of my legs and hooked them over his shoulders, pushing them even farther apart and I writhed. Softly he pressed his lips between them and then very gently, he ran them up and down as I shuddered and groped with delight. He waited calmly for me to pause and then, locking his eyes with mine, he plunged his tongue inside me.

My body sung from the deep touch and bowed uncontrollably with pleasure. He circled his tongue, grating against me and building up a steady, torturous rhythm. I found that I could no longer regulate myself. I gave myself up to him completely. Every part of me was solely concentrated on the scorching heat between my legs and my body was ridged with ecstasy.

He dipped his tongue back inside me and I panted and whimpered. His tongue flexed in wide circles, pulling me luxuriously apart and sending ripples of heat shooting through me. It was too much and my body begged for relief. Letting go, everything slipped away and I was lost in lust and the strength of my intense euphoria. My insides clenched to a climax and I cried out before they released blissfully.

Mr. Rochester stepped away from me and grinned.

I could barely respond except to sigh a satisfied sigh.

"That will do for now," he said.

I gingerly sat up and began rolling my stockings on. Mr. Rochester watched me, deep in thought.

"Tell me," he said suddenly. "What do you believe the people in the drawing-room yonder are doing?"

"Discussing the gipsy, I daresay," I responded still a little breathless, "and speaking to . . . oh, are you aware Mr. Rochester, that a stranger has arrived here since you left this morning?"

"A stranger! I expected no one. Is he gone?"

"No, he said he had known you long and that he could take the liberty of installing himself here till you returned."

"The devil he did! Did he give his name?"

"His name is Mason, sir, and he comes from the West Indies."

The smile on his lips froze and apparently a spasm caught his breath. The mood in the library quickly altered and I wished I had said nothing.

"Mason! The West Indies!" he gasped. ". . . Mason! The West Indies!" he reiterated and he went over the syllables three times, growing whiter than ashes.

"Go back now into the room," he said, his voice cold. "Step quietly up to Mason and whisper in his ear that Mr. Rochester is come and wishes to see him. Show him in here and then leave me."

We were master and servant once more and I lowered my head meekly.

"Yes, sir," I replied.

"Jane," he called, just as I was departing.

I paused.

"We will resume this later—I have not forgotten."

CHAPTER XX

Good God! What a cry!

Awakening in the dead of the night, I opened my eyes. The night's silence was rent in twain by a savage, sharp, shrilly sound that ran from end to end of Thornfield Hall.

My pulse stopped and my heart stood still. The cry died and was not renewed. It came out of the third storey for it passed overhead, and overhead in the room just above my chamber-ceiling, I now heard a struggle, a deadly one it seemed from the noise. A half-smothered voice shouted, "Help! Help! Help!" three times rapidly.

"Will no one come?" it cried, and then, while the staggering and stamping went on wildly, I distinguished through plank and plaster, "Rochester! Rochester! For God's sake, come!"

A chamber-door opened and someone ran along the gallery. Another step stamped on the flooring above and something fell. Then there was silence.

I put on some clothes, though horror shook all my limbs, and issued from my apartment. The sleepers were all aroused and terrified murmurs sounded in every room. Door after door unclosed and one looked out and another looked out and the gallery filled. Gentlemen and ladies alike had quitted their beds saying, "Oh! What is it?"—"Who is hurt?"—"What has happened?" The confusion was inextricable.

"Where the devil is Rochester?" cried Colonel Dent. "I cannot find him in his bed."

"Here!" was shouted in return. "Be composed, all of you. I'm coming."

And the door at the end of the gallery opened, and Mr. Rochester advanced with a candle. One of the ladies ran to him directly, seizing his arm: it was Miss Ingram.

"What awful event has taken place?" said she. "Speak! Let us know the worst at once!"

"All's right!" he cried, as the other ladies began to cry shrilly. "A servant has had a nightmare, that is all. I must see you all back into your rooms for, till the house is settled, she cannot be looked after. Gentlemen, have the goodness to set the ladies the example."

And so, by dint of alternate coaxing and commanding, he contrived to get them all once more enclosed in their separate dormitories. I did not wait to be ordered back to mine, but retreated unnoticed, as unnoticed I had left it. Not to go to bed, on the contrary, I dressed myself carefully. The sounds I had heard after the scream, and the words that had been uttered had probably been heard only by me for they had proceeded from the room above mine, but they assured me that it was not a servant's dream which had thus struck horror through the house.

When dressed, I sat a long time by the window looking out over the silent grounds and silvered fields and waiting for I knew not what. It seemed to me that some event must follow the strange cry, struggle, and call.

No. Stillness returned and each murmur and movement ceased gradually. In about an hour, Thornfield Hall was again as hushed as a desert. It seemed that sleep and night had resumed their empire. Suddenly, a cautious hand tapped low at the door.

"Am I wanted?" I asked.

"Are you up?" asked a familiar voice.

I felt a lusty thrill rush through me.

"Yes, sir."

"And dressed?"

"Yes."

Although I almost wished I was not.

"Come out, then, quietly."

I obeyed and found Mr. Rochester standing in the gallery, holding a light.

"I want you," he said. "Come this way, take your time and make no noise."

We glided up the gallery and up the stairs, then stopped in the dark, low corridor of the fateful third storey. I was a little confused for I had assumed that we would be retiring to his room.

"Have you a sponge in your room?" he asked in a whisper.

My puzzlement mounted for I could not see why our love making might need a sponge. "Yes, sir," I answered.

"Have you any salts—volatile salts?"

"Yes."

"Go back and fetch both."

I did as he asked, now sure that he had not brought me here for love's purposes and though I was intrigued as well, I was overridden with disappointment.

"You don't turn sick at the sight of blood?" he asked, as I returned.

"I think not."

"Just give me your hand," he said, "it will not do to risk a fainting fit."

I put my fingers into his and felt their scorching heat. I dearly wished to lace mine into his and kiss his knuckles but I sensed that his mind was elsewhere.

We entered a room I had been in once before, when Mrs. Fairfax showed me over the house. It was hung with tapestry, but the tapestry was now looped up in one part and there was a door apparent, which had then been concealed.

This door was open and a light shone out of the room within.
I heard thence a snarling, snatching sound, almost like a dog
quarrelling. Mr. Rochester put down his candle and said to
me, "Wait a minute."

He went forward to the inner apartment and a shout of
laughter greeted his entrance; noisy at first, then terminating
in Grace Poole's own goblin *ha! ha!* She then was there. All
quelling of desire left me in an instant and I was afraid.
Mr. Rochester made some sort of arrangement without
speaking, though I heard a low voice address him and he
came out and closed the door behind him.

"Here, Jane!" he said, and I walked round to the other
side of a large bed, which with its drawn curtains concealed
a considerable portion of the chamber. An easy-chair was
near the bed-head and a man sat in it, his head leant back,
his eyes closed. Mr. Rochester held the candle over him
and I recognised in his pale and seemingly lifeless face the
stranger, Mason. I saw too that his linen on one side, and
one arm, was almost soaked in blood.

"Hold the candle," said Mr. Rochester, and taking my
smelling-bottle, he held it under Mason's nose.

He shortly unclosed his eyes and groaned. Then
Mr. Rochester opened the shirt of the wounded man, and
began to sponge away blood, trickling fast down.

"Is there immediate danger?" murmured Mr. Mason.

"No, a mere scratch. Don't be so overcome, man, bear up!
I'll fetch a surgeon for you now, myself. Jane?"

"Sir?"

"I shall have to leave you in this room with this gentleman, for an hour, or perhaps two hours. You will sponge
the blood as I do when it returns and if he feels faint, you
will put the glass of water on that stand to his lips. You will
not speak to him on any pretext and Richard, it will be at
the peril of your life if you speak to her."

Again the poor man groaned and he looked as if he dared not move. Fear, either of death or of something else appeared almost to paralyse him. Mr. Rochester put the now bloody sponge into my hand and I proceeded to use it as he had done. He watched me a second, then saying, "Remember! No conversation," he left the room. I experienced a strange feeling as the key grated in the lock, and the sound of his retreating step ceased to be heard.

Then my own thoughts worried me. What crime was this that lived incarnate in this sequestered mansion, and could neither be expelled nor subdued by the owner? And this man I bent over, how had he become involved in the web of horror? In the darkened room, all sorts of fiendish thoughts troubled me.

"When will Mr. Rochester come? When will he come?" I cried inwardly, as the night lingered and lingered, as my bleeding patient drooped, moaned, sickened, and neither day nor aid arrived. I had again and again held the water to Mason's white lips and again and again offered him the stimulating salts, but my efforts seemed ineffectual. He moaned so and looked so weak, wild, and lost that I feared he was dying. However, still we said not a word to each other.

At last, I heard Pilot bark far below and hope was revived. In five minutes more the grating key and the yielding lock warned me my watch was relieved. It could not have lasted more than two hours, but many a week has seemed shorter.

Mr. Rochester entered, and with him the surgeon he had been to fetch.

"Now, Carter, be on the alert," he said to this last: "I give you but half-an-hour for dressing the wound, fastening the bandages, getting the patient downstairs and all."

"But is he fit to move, sir?"

"No doubt of it. Come, set to work."

Carter undid the bandages saying, "I wish I could have got here sooner, he would not have bled so much. But how is this? The flesh on the shoulder is torn as well as cut. This wound was not done with a knife: there have been teeth here!"

"She bit me," murmured the patient. "She worried me like a tigress, when Rochester got the knife from her."

"I warned you," was his friend's answer. "Carter, hurry! The sun will soon rise and I must have him off."

"Directly, sir. But I must look to this other wound in the arm for she has had her teeth here too, I think."

"She sucked the blood. She said she'd drain my heart," murmured Mason.

I saw Mr. Rochester shudder and a singularly marked expression of disgust, horror, and hatred, warped his countenance almost to distortion, but he only said, "Be silent, Richard and never mind her gibberish. Don't repeat it."

There was silence as Carter worked on his patient. After a few minutes he was finished and all breathed a sigh of relief for Mason looked markedly better, although still weak. Then plans were made for him to be taken to the surgeon's house until complete recovery when he would return to Jamaica.

"Take care of him," said Mr. Rochester, as Carter supported Mason and both walked to the door. "I shall ride over in a day or two to see how he gets on. Richard, how is it with you?"

Mason sighed. "Let her be taken care of, friend, and let her be treated as tenderly as may be. Let her—" he stopped and burst into tears.

"I'll do my best," was the answer.

The two men left the room to travel down to a coach that was waiting for them at the back door of the kitchen.

For the first time since reentering the room, Mr. Rochester looked in my direction. I had been standing in the corner through all of this, watching and listening in fear.

"You have passed a strange night, Jane."

"Yes, sir."

In some inexplicable way, when he looked at me, I did not feel so afraid.

"You look pale—were you afraid when I left you alone with Mason?"

"I was afraid of someone coming out of the inner room."

"But I had fastened the door and I had the key in my pocket. You were safe."

I did not reply, instead I was caught by the change in his dark eyes; the way they seemed to pull me towards them and glitter in the low candlelight. Leisurely, he took a key from his pocket and walked over to the door. He slotted it into the lock and turned it with a flick of his wrist.

"We need not be disturbed," he said.

It was remarkable how quickly all the horrors of the night slid from my mind and I became aware that I was standing before him in just my nightdress and shawl. My breath became shallow and I found I could not move.

He too was wearing his white nightshirt and breeches and I longed to finally pull them off and see him completely unclothed; our bare skin pressing hot and warm against each other.

"Before that commotion set about, I am aware that I promised we would resume our meeting later," he said, walking steadily towards me.

I clenched my fingers in rich anticipation and felt my heart beat rapidly in my chest. For once I was not burdened by my corset and my breasts heaved with excited, hurried breaths.

Still he moved closer to me, taking his time and enjoying my obvious, violent lust. I wanted to step forward and quickly remove the distance between us, but I found I could not. His dark eyes hypnotized me to the spot. Instead I felt my nerve endings quiver and a throb tore through my groin, tingling and deep.

"You look different without your stiff dresses, Jane," he said huskily, reaching out a hand with his last step and tracing the curve of my cheek.

I started with pleasure at his warm touch and a wave of desire burst through me.

Gently, he undid my plait and worked my hair out with his fingers, locking his eyes on mine as he did so, until it was completely free and I was gasping quietly. He brushed it over my shoulder and let it hang down my back.

"I think it would look better against your bare skin," he said darkly.

In quick, fervent movements, he tore off my nightdress and undergarments and threw them to the floor. Then he stood back and his inky black eyes darted to every part of my naked body, drinking me in. Lust flamed in the redness of his cheeks and he slid his hand around the arch of my hip to the warm dip in my lower back.

I took his hand away and he frowned in confusion, but then I tugged on his nightshirt.

"It is your turn, sir," I whispered quietly and seductively in his ear.

He shivered slightly and grinned. "As you wish, Jane," he said.

He undid his breeches and let them fall to the floor, unleashing his large erection and then he whipped his shirt over his head, revealing his great, broad chest. I sucked my breath in upon seeing his carved, firm pack of muscles and could not help but reach out and run my fingers through the tufts of dark hair, down the humped skin of his stomach to the flat, smoothness of his hips.

"Lower, Jane," he breathed.

Obediently, I let my fingers glide lower and taking him in both hands, I slowly tugged. He grunted and convulsed, running his hands up and down my spine in tickling, sweeping motions in return and wrapping my locks of hair around his wrists.

I let my hands move faster, feeling him harden and pulse beneath my fingers and feeling his breathing get heavier against my neck. Abruptly I stopped and my hands went back to caressing his toned chest. I giggled softly at his disgruntled expression.

Suddenly, he pulled my hair sharply, throwing my head back and then pressed his mouth to mine. His tongue gently prised my teeth apart and tasted the walls of my mouth, teasing my wanting from me. As he did so, I felt his hands drift down my sides leaving a trail of scorching heat, to my hips, where he reached around and clasped my buttocks, cupping the soft cheeks and fingering the crease between my thighs. Putting each of his hands on the backs of my legs, he pulled me up against him with a grunt, thrusting his tongue further down my throat and pressing his throbbing erection to me.

I returned his kisses eagerly, taking his bottom lip between my teeth and biting down gently. This produced another groan and his fingers clenched my bare skin. He hoisted me up further and I wrapped my legs around his torso, returning his kisses with an even greater fever. He carried me over to the bed and threw me down, standing over me. I looked up at him gasping against the soft, clean sheets.

Holding my gaze, he removed a curtain tie from one of the bedsteads. I was confused when he uttered huskily, "Put your hands out in front of you."

I obeyed. Quickly he wrapped the golden curtain tie around my wrists and pulled the knot tight, then he pushed my hands up over my head, pinning me in place. He took my nightgown from the floor and folded it into a long strip, then bending over me, he placed it over my eyes and secured it at the back of my head so that I was unable to see anything.

"Relax and enjoy this, Jane," he whispered in my ear as arousal coursed through me.

Beginning at my hips, he ran his hands up my body and paused at my breasts. He fingered the smooth skin of my nipples, letting them harden under his touch, and ran his thumb down the deep well between my breasts. I could not see any of this and each caress was unexpected and erotically heightened.

Suddenly I felt him lick my right nipple while his free hand pinched and flicked the other. I gasped as he let his tongue circle my breast and then blew gently on it, making me shudder with delight. Then I felt him sucking hard and flicking his tongue backwards and forwards and it was all that I could do to stop myself from crying out. He gently and carefully took my nipple between his teeth and bit it.

He paused and allowed me to recover a little before shifting slightly and suddenly, I felt him doing the same to my left breast; licking, sucking and nipping it until I was in a frenzy of passion. I clawed at the bed sheets above my head and tried to bring my hands in front of me so that I could touch and clutch him back, but I could not.

As my lust began building, I flexed my hips against him, aching for him to be inside me.

"Please . . ." I heard myself beg.

I could not see, but I felt that he grinned back at me wickedly.

He left my breasts and his fingers traced languidly across my belly and lower abdominal instead. I began to pant as slowly, he let them creep over my hips and between my legs.

I could not see and so each touch was magnified and a deep, extreme pleasure raged through my body. He gently ran his finger up and down before suddenly dipping two fingers inside me.

I convulsed and my body bowed with pleasure, my wrists straining against the curtain tie. As he moved his fingers in and out of me, I pushed against him, lifting my hips up, begging. His fingers moved faster before stopping completely and leaving me in a hazy, hungry state, gasping and wriggling with desire.

"All right, Jane," I heard him say softly.

I felt him shifting and suddenly, he plunged himself inside me. I cried out from the suddenness of it and came instantly and then again and again as he pounded deliciously into me, hooking my legs over his back and pulling him deeper.

I could barely believe it as I felt something new building with each thrust. A hot spasm pooled in my groin and I clenched my teeth as it coiled into more. It tightened and tightened before I climaxed luxuriously and shattered into tiny fragments, collapsing back onto the sheets, exhausted. My senses were wrung raw and my body tingled with the aftermath of pleasure, my head light and dizzy.

I felt him pull out of me and I heard him grunt as he came.

After a moment, my vision was restored and my wrists freed. I glanced around the room with weak, delirious eyes and felt my chaffed wrists which were imprinted with the pattern of the curtain tie.

"Thank you, Jane," said Mr. Rochester, lying beside me.

"Thank you, sir," I replied and we were quiet for a few minutes.

"Little friend," said he in quite a changed tone. His face changed too, losing all its softness and gravity and becoming harsh and sarcastic. "You have noticed my tender penchant for Miss Ingram, don't you think if I married her she would regenerate me with a vengeance?"

I stared at him, aghast. I felt my cheeks redden and a bitter stab of hurt swept through my body, wiping away all desire.

"Well?" he probed.

"Yes, sir."

"She's a rare one, is she not, Jane?"

"Yes, sir."

"A strapper, a real strapper. Big, brown, and buxom with hair just such as the ladies of Carthage must have had."

I felt sick. I snatched at my nightgown which was nearby and hurried into it, while he remained lying on the bed, silent. I was foolish to believe that Mr. Rochester harbored any tender feelings for me. To him I was a means of satisfaction only. He could not possibly conceive that I could be anything more. I should hand in my resignation and find a position elsewhere, but I could not for I loved him.

"Good night, sir," I said in a small voice before leaving the room.

I am not even sure that he replied.

CHAPTER XXI

I stayed as far away from Mr. Rochester as I could for the next few days and I never once raised my eyes to his. I was deeply hurt and pained by what he had said after such a pleasurable, joyful union and I did not want him to see my sorrow.

On one day when I was in the midst of teaching Adele, I was summoned downstairs by a message that some one wanted me in Mrs. Fairfax's room. On repairing thither, I found a man waiting for me having the appearance of a gentleman's servant. He was dressed in deep mourning and a hat that he held in his hand was surrounded with a crape band.

"I daresay you hardly remember me, Miss," he said, rising as I entered. "My name is Leaven and I was the coachman with Mrs. Reed when you were at Gateshead."

"Oh, Robert! How do you do? I remember you very well, how is Bessie? You are married to Bessie?"

"Yes, my wife is very hearty, thank you, Miss."

"And are the family well at the house, Robert?"

"I am sorry I can't give you better news of them, Miss, they are very badly at present and in great trouble. Mr. John died last week at his chambers in London."

"Mr. John?"

"Yes."

I thought of my old, cruel lover. I was neither greatly sad nor happy to hear this news, merely curious.

"How does his mother bear it?" I asked.

"Not well, although it is not such a surprise, Miss. He ruined his health and his estate amongst the worst men and the worst women. He got into debt and into jail, which his mother helped him out of twice, but as soon as he was free he returned to his old companions and habits. He came down to Gateshead about three weeks ago and wanted Missis to give up all to him. Missis refused, her means have long been much reduced by his extravagance, so he went back again and the next news was that he was dead. How he died, God knows! They say he killed himself."

I was silent, contemplating these awful things.

Robert Leaven resumed, "Missis had been out of health herself for some time. The information about Mr. John's death and the manner of it brought on a stroke. She was three days without speaking, but last Tuesday she seemed rather better. She appeared as if she wanted to say something and kept making signs to my wife and mumbling. It was only yesterday morning, however, that Bessie understood she was pronouncing your name and at last she made out the words, 'Bring Jane, fetch Jane Eyre.' I left Gateshead yesterday and if you can get ready, Miss, I should like to take you back with me early to-morrow morning."

It was the perfect way to escape Mr. Rochester.

"Yes, Robert, I shall be ready. It seems to me that I ought to go."

"I suppose you will have to ask leave before you can get off?"

"Yes and I will do it now."

I directed him to the servants' hall and went in search of Mr. Rochester for the first time since we had last laid together.

He was not in any of the lower rooms and he was not in the yard, the stables, or the grounds. I finally asked Mrs. Fairfax if she had seen him and she replied that she believed he was playing billiards with Miss Ingram. To the billiard-room I hastened, trying to quell the bitter feeling that surged through my breast. I entered to the click of balls and the hum of voices, seeing Mr. Rochester, Miss Ingram, the two Misses Eshton, and their admirers all busied in the game.

As I approached the master where he stood at Miss Ingram's side, she turned and looked at me haughtily and her eyes seemed to demand, "What can the creeping creature want now?"

I said, in a low voice, "Mr. Rochester?"

He turned and made a curious grimace, threw down his cue and followed me from the room.

"Well, Jane?" he said, when we were in the corridor.

I wanted to slap away the haughty look on his face as he stared down at me and I was full of shame that I allowed myself to be used so by him.

"If you please, sir, I want leave of absence for a week or two," I said in a harsh tone.

"What to do? Where to go?"

"To see a sick lady who has sent for me."

"And what have you to do with her?"

"Mr. Reed was my uncle—my mother's brother. John Reed, my cousin, is dead, sir. He ruined himself and half-ruined his family, and is supposed to have committed suicide. The news so shocked his mother that it brought on an apoplectic attack."

"How long will you stay?"

"I do not know, sir."

"Promise me only to stay a week."

I was angered and confused by his desire to keep me here.

I barely looked or spoke to him and if he was so wrapped in the clutches of Miss Ingram, I scarcely think he should notice my absence.

"I had better not pass my word, I might be obliged to break it," I said tartly.

"At all events you will come back. You will not be induced under any pretext to take up a permanent residence with her?"

I could not see that it would be much to him if I did, but I said, "I shall return if all be well."

Mr. Rochester meditated.

"When do you wish to go?"

"Early to-morrow morning, sir."

He nodded and looked at the carpet.

"Mr. Rochester, I may as well mention another matter of business to you while I have the opportunity," I added.

"I am curious to hear it."

"You have as good as informed me, sir, that you are going shortly to be married?"

"Yes, what then?"

"In that case, sir, Adele ought to go to school. I am sure you will perceive the necessity of it."

"To get her out of my bride's way, who might otherwise walk over her rather too emphatically? There's sense in the suggestion, not a doubt of it. Adele, as you say, must go to school and you, of course, must march straight to the devil?"

"I must seek another situation somewhere."

"In course!" he exclaimed, with a twang of voice and a distortion of features equally fantastic and ludicrous. He looked at me some minutes. "Promise me one thing," he said at last.

"What is that, sir?"

"Not to advertise. Trust this quest of a situation to me and I'll find you one in time."

I thought this curious. Perhaps he wished to keep me here as long as possible, bedding me until his wedding day when he would have another to satisfy his needs. This I would not do, but I would consent to let him find me another position, he owed me that much, at least,

"I shall do if you, in your turn, will promise that I and Adele shall be both safe out of the house before your bride enters it."

"Very well! Very well! I'll pledge my word on it," he answered agitatedly, his dark eyes distant with thought. "You go to-morrow, then?" he asked.

"Yes, sir. Early."

"Then you and I must bid good-bye for a little while?"

"Yes. Farewell, Mr. Rochester, for the present."

His eyes twinkled mischievously. "Farewell, Miss Eyre . . . for the present."

He looked as though he was about to say more but the dinner-bell rang, and suddenly away he bolted, without another syllable. I saw him no more during the day, and was off before he had risen in the morning.

I reached the lodge at Gateshead about five o'clock in the afternoon of the first of May. Accompanied by Bessie who met me, I quitted the lodge for the hall. It was also accompanied by her that I had, nearly nine years ago, walked down the path I was now ascending. On a dark, misty, raw morning in January, I had left a hostile roof with a desperate and embittered heart. The same hostile roof now again rose before me and my prospects were doubtful yet. I still felt as a wanderer on the face of the earth, but I experienced firmer trust in myself and my own powers. The gaping wound of my wrongs was now quite healed, and the flame of resentment extinguished.

"You shall go into the breakfast-room first," said Bessie, as she preceded me through the hall, "the young ladies will be there."

In another moment I was within that apartment. There was every article of furniture looking just as I remembered it. Glancing at the bookcases, I remembered my loved volume of portraits with my dark-eyed lover among their collection, which Mrs. Reed had cruelly torn out. I had my own dark-eyed lover now, but he was not as I had always imagined he would be.

Two young ladies appeared before me; one very tall, almost as tall as Miss Ingram and very thin too, with a sallow face. There was something ascetic in her look, which was augmented by the extreme plainness of a straight-skirted, black dress, a starched linen collar and hair combed away from the temples. This I felt sure was Eliza, though I could trace little resemblance to her former self in that elongated and colourless visage.

The other was certainly Georgiana, but not the Georgiana I remembered—the slim and fairy-like girl of eleven. This was a full-blown, very plump damsel, fair as waxwork with handsome and regular features, languishing blue eyes and ringleted yellow hair. The hue of her dress was black too, but its fashion was much more flowing and becoming than her sister's.

Both ladies, as I advanced, rose to welcome me and both addressed me by the name of "Miss Eyre."

Eliza's greeting was delivered in a short, abrupt voice, without a smile, and then she sat down again, fixed her eyes on the fire and seemed to forget me. Georgiana added, "How d'ye do?" and asked several commonplaces about my journey, but she seemed more interested in looking me over than listening to my answers.

As I sat between my cousins, I was surprised to find how easy I felt under the total neglect of the one and the semi-sarcastic attentions of the other. The fact was, I had other things to think about. Within the last few months feelings had been stirred in me so much more potent than any they could raise—pains and pleasures so much more acute and exquisite had been excited than any it was in their power to inflict or bestow. Their airs gave me no concern either for good or bad.

"How is Mrs. Reed?" I asked soon, looking calmly at Georgiana.

"She is extremely poorly. I doubt if you can see her to-night."

No more was said and a sour silence fell. Deciding to attend to matters myself, I rose, quietly took off my bonnet and gloves uninvited, and said I would just step out to Bessie and ask her to ascertain whether Mrs. Reed was disposed to receive me to-night. Then I went and despatched Bessie on my errand.

She returned soon saying, "Missis is awake. I have told her you are here. Come and let us see if she will know you."

I did not need to be guided to the well-known room to which I had so often been summoned for chastisement or reprimand in former days. I hastened before Bessie and softly opened the door.

Well did I remember Mrs. Reed's face, and I eagerly sought the familiar image. It is a happy thing that time quells the longings of vengeance and hushes the promptings of rage and aversion. I had left this woman in bitterness and hate and I came back to her now with no other emotion than a yearning to forget and forgive all injuries.

"Is this Jane Eyre?" she said as I approached the four-poster bed.

"Yes, Aunt Reed. How are you, dear aunt?"

I had once vowed that I would never call her aunt again, but I thought it no sin to forget and break that vow now.

My fingers had fastened on her hand which lay outside the sheet, and had she pressed mine kindly, I should at that moment have experienced true pleasure. But Mrs. Reed took

her hand away and turning her face rather from me, she remarked that the night was warm. Again she regarded me so
icily, I felt at once that her feeling towards me was unchanged
and unchangeable.

"You sent for me," I said, taking a chair beside her pillow,
"and I am here. It is my intention to stay till I see how you
get on."

"Oh, of course! You have seen my daughters?"

"Yes."

"Well, you may tell them I wish you to stay till I can talk
some things over with you. To-night it is too late and I have
a difficulty in recalling them. But there was something I wished to say, let me see——"

The wandering look and changed utterance told what
wreck had taken place in her once vigorous frame. Turning
restlessly, she drew the bedclothes round her.

"Are you Jane Eyre?" she barked.

"I am Jane Eyre."

"I have had more trouble with that child than any one
would believe. Such a burden to be left on my hands. What
did they do with her at Lowood? The fever broke out there
and many of the pupils died. She did not, but I said she did—
I wish she had died!"

"A strange wish, Mrs. Reed. Why do you hate her so?"

"I had a dislike to her mother always, for she was my
husband's only sister and a great favourite with him. When
news came of her death, he wept like a simpleton. And that
child, that Jane Eyre baby—he loved it more than his own!"

She was getting much excited.

"I think I had better leave her now," said I to Bessie, who
stood on the other side of the bed.

"Perhaps you had, Miss. She often talks in this way
towards night, but in the morning she is calmer."

I rose and left.

More than ten days elapsed before I had again any conversation with her. She continued either delirious or lethargic and the doctor forbade everything which could painfully excite her. Meantime, I got on as well as I could with Georgiana and Eliza. They were very cold, indeed. Eliza would sit half the day sewing, reading, or writing, and scarcely utter a word either to me or her sister. Georgiana would chatter nonsense to her canary bird by the hour, and take no notice of me. But I was determined not to seem at a loss for occupation or amusement, I had brought my drawing materials with me, and they served me for both.

Finally, one wet and windy afternoon when Georgiana had fallen asleep on the sofa and Eliza had gone to attend a saint's-day service at the new church, I bethought myself to go upstairs and see how the dying woman sped.

I found the sick-room unwatched as I had expected, and the patient lay still and seemingly lethargic; her livid face sunk in the pillows. The fire was dying in the grate so I renewed the fuel, re-arranged the bedclothes, gazed awhile on her and then moved away to the window.

The rain beat strongly against the panes, the wind blew tempestuously and I sighed.

A feeble voice murmured, "Who is that?"

I knew Mrs. Reed had not spoken for days, was she reviving? I went up to her.

"It is I, Aunt Reed."

"Who?" was her answer. "Who are you?" looking at me with surprise and a sort of alarm, but still not wildly. "You are quite a stranger to me—where is Bessie?"

"She is at the lodge, aunt."

"Aunt?" she repeated. "Who calls me aunt? You are not one of the Gibsons and yet I know you—that face and the eyes and forehead are quiet familiar to me. You are like, why, you are like Jane Eyre!"

I said nothing, I was afraid of occasioning some shock by declaring my identity.

"Yet," said she, "I am afraid it is a mistake and my thoughts deceive me. I wished to see Jane Eyre and I fancy a likeness where none exists. Besides, in eight years she must be so changed."

I now gently assured her that I was the person she supposed and desired me to be, and seeing that I was understood and that her senses were quite collected, I explained how Bessie had sent her husband to fetch me from Thornfield.

"I am very ill, I know," she said ere long. "I was trying to turn myself a few minutes since, and find I cannot move a limb. Is the nurse here? Or is there no one in the room but you?" I assured her we were alone.

"I have twice done you a wrong which I regret now. One was in breaking the promise which I gave my husband to bring you up as my own child, the other—" she stopped. "After all, it is of no great importance, perhaps," she murmured to herself, "and then I may get better; and to humble myself so to her is painful."

She made an effort to alter her position, but failed. Her face changed and she seemed to experience some inward sensation—the precursor, perhaps, of the last pang.

"Well, I must get it over. Eternity is before me and I had better tell her. Go to my dressing-case, open it, and take out a letter you will see there."

I obeyed her directions. "Read the letter," she said.

It was short and thus conceived: "Madam, will you have the goodness to send me the address of my niece, Jane Eyre, and to tell me how she is? It is my intention to write shortly and desire her to come to me at Madeira. Providence has blessed my endeavours to secure a competency and as I am unmarried and childless, I wish to adopt her during my life,

and bequeath her at my death whatever I may have to leave.
—John Eyre."

It was dated three years back.

"Why did I never hear of this?" I asked.

"Because I disliked you too fixedly and thoroughly ever
to lend a hand in lifting you to prosperity. I wrote to him
and I said I was sorry for his disappointment, but Jane Eyre
was dead, she had died of typhus fever at Lowood. Now act
as you please: write and contradict my assertion; expose my
falsehood as soon as you like. You were born, I think, to be
my torment and my last hour is racked by the recollection of
a deed which, but for you, I should never have been tempted
to commit."

"If you could but be persuaded to think no more of it,
Aunt, and to regard me with kindness and forgiveness? I long
earnestly to be reconciled to you now: kiss me, Aunt."

I approached my cheek to her lips, but she would not
touch it. She said I oppressed her by leaning over the bed and
again demanded water.

"Love me, then, or hate me, as you will," I said at last.
"You have my full and free forgiveness. Ask now for God's
and be at peace."

Poor, suffering woman! It was too late for her to make
now the effort to change her habitual frame of mind. Living
she had ever hated me and dying she must hate me still.

The nurse now entered and Bessie followed. I yet lingered
half-an-hour longer, hoping to see some sign of amity, but she
gave none. At twelve o'clock that night she died.

CHAPTER XXII

Mr. Rochester had given me but one week's leave of absence, yet a month elapsed before I quitted Gateshead. I wished to leave immediately after the funeral, but there were matters to be seen to that neither Eliza nor Georgiana seemed capable of.

At last I saw Georgiana off to stay with her uncle in London and I was at liberty to return to Thornfield. Thus I began preparations and on my day of leaving, Eliza surprised me by saying, "I am obliged to you for your valuable services and discreet conduct, Jane. You perform your own part in life and burden no one."

I was shocked to hear this and then further shocked when I parted and she uttered the words, "Fairwell, cousin Jane."

However, I was too preoccupied with my return to Thornfield to ponder it much. I was pleased that I had made some kind of reconciliation with my cousins, but I was aware that I had left Thornfield in a storm of angry spirits and I would have some more reconciliations to make when I returned. The time away had allowed me to gain some perspective and my previous thoughts of Mr. Rochester loving me or feeling anything of the sort now seemed ridiculous. Of course he did not and would not. I wished to return and show that I was not such a fool to have thought so.

My journey was tedious—very tedious. I had heard from Mrs. Fairfax in the interim of my absence that the party at the hall was dispersed and Mr. Rochester had left for London three weeks ago, but he was then expected to return in a fortnight. Mrs. Fairfax surmised that he was gone to make arrangements for his wedding, as he had talked of purchasing a new carriage and she could no longer doubt that the event would shortly take place. I had never doubted it at all.

I had not notified to Mrs. Fairfax the exact day of my return for I did not wish either car or carriage to meet me at Millcote. I proposed to walk the distance quietly by myself and very quietly, after leaving my box in the ostler's care, did I slip away from the George Inn, about six o'clock of a June evening and take the old road to Thornfield.

As I walked, I calmed myself and tried not to remember the very first time I had met Mr. Rochester on this road, when we had laid together in the ditch. I briefly wondered whether it would have been better if that had never occurred and we had possessed the normal relationship of master and governess, but despite the heartache and pain, I would not give up my moments of pleasure with him. I had never experienced an ecstasy like it.

I was thinking this very thought when I turned a corner and there was Mr. Rochester, sitting with a book and a pencil in his hand, writing.

I started as if I had seen a ghost and looked all about me wildly. A deep blush arose in my cheeks and I felt unprepared and panicked.

"Hello!" he cried, putting his book and his pencil down. "There you are!"

I stared at him mutely as if in a stupor.

"And this is Jane Eyre?" he carried on. "Are you coming from Millcote, and on foot? Yes, just one of your tricks not to send for a carriage and come clattering over street and road like a common mortal, but to steal into the vicinage of your home along with twilight as if you were a dream or a shade. What the deuce have you done with yourself this last month?"

"I have been with my aunt, sir, who is dead," I muttered.

"A true Janian reply! She comes from the other world, from the abode of people who are dead and tells me so when she meets me alone here in the gloaming! If I dared, I'd touch you to see if you are substance or shadow!" He added, when he had paused an instant, "Absent from me a whole month and forgetting me quite, I'll be sworn!"

I could scarcely heed his words, I was so flustered. He did not leave the stile, and I hardly liked to ask to go by so I inquired soon if he had not been to London.

"Yes, I suppose you found that out by second-sight."

"Mrs. Fairfax told me in a letter."

"And did she inform you what I went to do?"

"Oh, yes, sir! Everybody knew your errand."

"You must see the carriage, Jane, and tell me if you don't think it will suit Mrs. Rochester exactly. She will look like Queen Boadicea, leaning back against those purple cushions. I wish, Jane, I were a trifle better adapted to match with her externally. Tell me now, fairy as you are, can't you give me a charm to make me a handsome man?"

He was acting in the manor of our usual, jesting conversations and I was somehow heartened by this, hoping we might return to at least being friends if we were not lovers.

"It would be past the power of magic, sir," and, in thought, I added, "A loving eye is all the charm needed. To such you are handsome enough, or rather your sternness has a power beyond beauty."

Mr. Rochester smiled at me with a certain smile he had of his own, which he used but on rare occasions. He seemed to think it too good for common purposes and it was the real sunshine of feeling, which he shed over me now.

"Pass, Jane," said he, making room for me to cross the stile. "Go up home, and stay your weary little wandering feet at a friend's threshold."

I got over the stile without a word, and meant to leave him calmly. An impulse held me fast—perhaps my wish to reconcile and I said, "Thank you, Mr. Rochester. I am strangely glad to get back again with you."

I walked on so fast that even he could hardly have overtaken me had he tried.

Little Adele was half wild with delight when she saw me. Mrs. Fairfax received me with her usual plain friendliness. Leah smiled, and even Sophie bid me "bon soir" with glee. This was very pleasant; there is no happiness like that of being loved by your fellow-creatures and feeling that your presence is an addition to their comfort.

That evening I shut my eyes resolutely against the future of Mr. Rochester's marriage to Miss Ingram and resolved to be happy. When tea was over and Mrs. Fairfax had taken her knitting, I had assumed a low seat near her and Adele, kneeling on the carpet, had nestled close up to me, a sense of mutual affection seemed to surround us with a ring of golden peace. I uttered a silent prayer that we might not be parted far or soon and when, as we thus sat, Mr. Rochester entered, he seemed to take pleasure in the spectacle of a group so amicable. He said he supposed the old lady was all right now that she had got her adopted daughter back again, and added that he saw Adele was "Prete e croquer sa petite maman Anglaise." After this, I half ventured to hope that he would, even after his marriage, keep us together somewhere under the shelter of his protection and not quite exiled from the sunshine of his presence.

A fortnight of dubious calm succeeded my return to Thornfield Hall. Nothing was said of the master's marriage and I saw no preparation going on for such an event. Almost every day I asked Mrs. Fairfax if she had yet heard anything decided and her answer was always in the negative. Once she said she had actually put the question to Mr. Rochester as to when he was going to bring his bride home, but he had answered her only by a joke and one of his queer looks, and she could not tell what to make of him.

One thing specially surprised me, and that was that there were no journeyings backward and forward and no visits to Ingram Park. To be sure it was twenty miles off, on the borders of another county, but what was that distance to an ardent lover? To so practised and indefatigable a horseman as Mr. Rochester, it would be but a morning's ride. I began to cherish hopes I had no right to conceive that the match was broken off, that rumour had been mistaken and that one or both parties had changed their minds. I used to look at my master's face to see if it were sad or fierce, but I could not remember the time when it had been so uniformly clear of clouds or evil feelings. If, in the moments I and my pupil spent with him, I lacked spirits and sank into inevitable dejection, he became even gay. Never had he called me more frequently to his presence, never been kinder to me when there and, alas, never had I loved him so well. He did not venture to touch me at all or even hint to our past laying together. He merely smiled at me sweetly and treated me as he had never treated me before—a true friend.

CHAPTER XXIII

A splendid Midsummer shone over England. It was as if a band of Italian days had come from the South like a flock of glorious passenger birds and lighted to rest on the cliffs of Albion. The hay was all got in and the fields round Thornfield were green and shorn, the roads were white and baked, and the trees were in their dark prime. On Midsummer-eve, Adele, weary with gathering wild strawberries in Hay Lane half the day, had gone to bed with the sun. I watched her drop asleep, and when I left her, I sought the garden.

I walked a while on the pavement, but a subtle, well-known scent—that of a cigar—stole from some window and I saw the library casement open a handbreadth and knew I might be watched, so I went apart into the orchard. No nook in the grounds more sheltered and more Eden-like; it was full of trees and a very high wall shut it out from the court.

I was passing across it when I saw Mr. Rochester enter and look around leisurely, smoking his cigar.

I was about to turn and walk on before he caught my eye and smiled at me. Though I had reconciled myself to our new friendship, I still preferred not to be alone with him and I had endeavored since I had been back to always be in company. I found I could more easily resist the tempting darkness of his eyes with Adele or Mrs. Fairfax beside me.

"Jane," he said, approaching me, "Thornfield is a pleasant place in summer, is it not?"

"Yes, sir."

"You must have become in some degree attached to the house?"

"I am attached to it, indeed."

"And though I don't comprehend how it is, I perceive you have acquired a degree of regard for that foolish little child Adele and even for simple dame Fairfax?"

"Yes, sir. I have an affection for both."

"And would be sorry to part with them?"

"Yes."

"Pity!" he said, and sighed. "It is always the way of events in this life," he continued presently. "No sooner have you got settled in a pleasant resting-place, than a voice calls out to you to rise and move on."

"Must I move on, sir?" I asked. "Must I leave Thornfield?"

"I believe you must, Jane. I am sorry, Jane, but I believe indeed you must."

This was a blow, but I did not let it prostrate me.

"Well, sir, I shall be ready when the order to march comes."

"It is come now, I must give it to-night."

"Then you are going to be married, sir?"

"With your usual acuteness, you have hit the nail straight on the head."

"Soon, sir?"

"Very soon. You'll remember, Jane, the first time I plainly intimated to you that it was my intention to enter into the holy estate of matrimony and take Miss Ingram to my bosom, you said that both you and little Adele had better trot forthwith. I pass over the sort of slur conveyed in this suggestion on the character of my beloved and I shall notice only its wisdom. Adele must go to school and you, Miss Eyre, must get a new situation."

I felt a deep tear of emotion and if he were not there, I should have cried out in pain. I had tried to convince myself that our new friendship was what I wished for but suddenly, his marriage to Miss Ingram, which had always seemed fanciful, was real and happening so soon. It forced me to admit that I still loved him dearly.

"Yes, sir," I answered quietly. "I will advertise immediately."

"In about a month I hope to be a bridegroom," continued Mr. Rochester, "and in the interim, I shall myself look out for employment for you. I have already heard of a place that I think will suit in Ireland. You'll like Ireland, I think, they're such warm-hearted people there."

"It is a long way off, sir."

"A girl of your sense will not object to the voyage or the distance."

"Not the voyage, but the distance, and then the sea is a barrier—"

"From what, Jane?"

"From England and from Thornfield and—"

"Well?"

"From you, sir."

I said this almost involuntarily and, with as little sanction of free will, my tears gushed out.

"It is a long way to Ireland, Jane, and I am sorry to send my little friend on such weary travels. I sometimes have a queer feeling with regard to you—especially when you are near me, as now. It is as if I had a string somewhere under my left ribs, tightly and inextricably knotted to a similar string situated in the corresponding quarter of your little frame. And if that boisterous Channel, and two hundred miles or so of land come broad between us, I am afraid that cord of communion will be snapped and then I've a nervous notion I should take to bleeding inwardly. As for you, you'd forget me."

"That I never should, sir. You know—" My words were lost in tears.

"Jane, do you hear that nightingale singing in the wood? Listen!"

In listening, I sobbed convulsively for I could repress what I endured no longer and I was shaken from head to foot with acute distress. When I did speak, it was only to express an impetuous wish that I had never been born, or never come to Thornfield.

"Because you are sorry to leave it?"

The vehemence of emotion, stirred by grief and love within me was claiming mastery and struggling for full sway. At last, I said, "I grieve to leave Thornfield. I love Thornfield. I love it because I have lived in it a full and delightful life. I have not been trampled on. I have not been petrified. I have not been buried with inferior minds and excluded from every glimpse of communion with what is bright and energetic and high. I have known you, Mr. Rochester and it strikes me with terror and anguish to feel I absolutely must be torn from you for ever. I see the necessity of departure and it is like looking on the necessity of death."

"Where do you see the necessity?" he asked suddenly.

"In the shape of Miss Ingram. A noble and beautiful woman—your bride."

"My bride! What bride? I have no bride!"

"But you will have."

"Yes. I will! I will!" He set his teeth.

"Then I must go, you have said it yourself."

"No, you must stay! I swear it and the oath shall be kept."

"I tell you, I must go!" I retorted, roused to something like passion. "Do you think I can stay to become nothing to you? Do you think I am a machine without feelings? Do you think, because I am poor, obscure, plain, and little, I am soulless and heartless? You think wrong! I have as much soul as you and full as much heart! And if God had gifted me with some beauty and much wealth, I should have made it as hard for you to leave me as it is now for me to leave you."

With a suddenness that startled me, Mr. Rochester clasped his arms around me and pressed me against his chest. I was in too excited spirits to experience any pleasure from this and I could only think of him doing the same to Miss Ingram.

"You are a married man—or as good as a married man. Let me go!" I said, pulling away.

"Jane, I ask you to pass through life at my side—to be my second self and best earthly companion."

"You mock me!"

"I do not! I summon you as my wife and it is you only I intend to marry. Come hither."

"Your bride stands between us."

"My bride is here," he said, again drawing me to him, "because my equal is here and my likeness. Jane, will you marry me?"

Still I did not answer, and still I writhed myself from his grasp for I was incredulous.

"Do you doubt me, Jane?"

"Entirely."

"I would not—I could not—marry Miss Ingram. You, you poor and obscure, small and plain as you are, I entreat to accept me as a husband. I must have you for my own—entirely my own. Will you be mine? Say yes, quickly."

I stared at him uncertainly.

"Oh, Jane, you torture me!" he exclaimed. "With that searching and yet faithful and generous look, you torture me!"

"Do you truly love me? Do you sincerely wish me to be your wife?"

"I do, and if an oath is necessary to satisfy you, I swear it."

"Then, sir . . . I will marry you."

"Come to me—come to me entirely now," said he.

With some trepidation, I closed the distance between us. Stepping into his arms, he enclosed them around me and held me tightly to his chest.

"Oh, Jane, I love you," he whispered.

I tilted my head and looked up into his sincere, dark eyes. In turn, they scrutinised mine and then began to spark with the heat of desire. I felt it too; a rippling sensation beneath my petticoat that was delicious and warm. My blood boiled with it and a torrent of passion swept through me.

He gently cupped my chin with his hands and slowly brought his lips to mine. Overhead I heard a slight breeze ruffle the branches of the chestnut tree in the duskiness of the evening and the nightingale began its song once more. His lips against mine burnt like fire and my own body answered by pressing his with a desperate, hungry fever. At first we were delicate, but all at once our craving overtook us and we grasped for each other with trembling fingers and heaving chests.

As he pulled away from me, my breath hitched in my throat and I slid my hands beneath his jacket, letting them roam eagerly across his broad chest. His dark eyes were soft and loving whilst being fierce and commanding at the same time, and all at once I realised that he did love me, for I had never seen that look on his face before, or rather, it had always been hidden.

I began sinking to my knees and pulled him down also, my hands clasped around his neck, my fingers knotting themselves in his hair.

"I want to lay with you here, right now," I whispered, a smile spreading across my face.

He gave me a devilish grin in return and took me by the waist, pushing me to the ground. The earth was cool and moist, but I did not pay it much heed as he pinned me against it.

"I will take you here, Jane, but I want you to be bare," he said.

We were alone in the grounds of Thornfield and on an evening like this, it was unlikely that we would be disturbed.

"I have wanted to do this since I met you on the causeway and you bewitched my heart," he added.

"I thought you had forgotten that time, sir."

"Oh, Jane, I never forgot."

With that, he roughly turned me over and began expertly unlacing my dress. He had it undone in seconds and my undergarments were soon off and pooled beside me. The cool breeze against my bare skin made me shiver, as did my intense anticipation.

I made to turn around but he stopped me. "Stay where you are," he said huskily.

My heart thumped in my chest and waves of yearning coursed through my body. He lightly touched his forefinger to the nape of my neck and them achingly slowly, he ran it down my spine, grazing my back with his rough nail. I shivered. Next, he placed his tongue at the base of my spine and licked up, between my shoulder-blades and to my neck. I gasped in surprised delight.

He paused for a moment and I heard a soft scuffling sound as he removed his clothes. I tried to turn to look, but he said, "Arh, no Jane."

Suddenly I could feel his warm bare skin against mine as he pressed his chest to my back. I shuddered with pleasure as he pulled my buttocks into his lap and I felt his long, hard erection between my legs.

"Oh, Jane," he grunted, as he leant down and smelt my hair.

My breathing became shallow as he nuzzled his nose against my ear, gently bit the lobe, and then trailed kisses across my neck. Meanwhile, his hands stroked my stomach, skimmed my ribs, and took each of my breasts firmly in his palms. His lips began to lick, kiss, and nip my shoulders as his hands massaged my breasts and his fingers tugged and flicked my nipples.

I leant into him, pressing myself as hard against him as I could and throwing my head over his shoulder in pleasure. He responded by gently biting my chin. My hands caressed his thick, muscled thighs and my nails dug into his skin as hot yearning raced through me.

Suddenly, he pushed me forward so that I was on my hands and knees and I gasped at the shock of it. I made to turn around but again, he stopped me. He placed each of his hands firmly on my waist and leant into me, brushing his erection against my thighs. I sighed with wanting and sank down onto my elbows, pressing my cheek to the earth.

Without warning, I heard a sharp slap and felt a sting of pain as he smacked my behind and before I could react, he slammed into me, forcing me to cry out. The feeling was deeper than anything I had experienced before and he pounded into me again and again, faster and faster. I groaned as an intense thrill coiled in my stomach and threatened to overflow. His hips thudded against my buttocks and I clenched my teeth in unbelievable pleasure.

My whole body convulsed and bowed as I climaxed. I cried aloud, collapsing against the hard, wet ground. Waves of ecstasy rocked my body and my limbs tingled with release.

A second later, Mr. Rochester pulled out of me and came. He laid down beside me as we both panted, our brows sweaty and our bodies trembling.

We stayed in companionable, blissful silence for a while, staring at the sky as stars began to appear. However, it was clear that the wind had picked up and we noticed a cluster of dark clouds moving this way.

"We must go in," said Mr. Rochester, "the weather changes. I could have lay with thee till morning, Jane."

"And so I," I whispered.

The rain began rushing down and we hurried back into our clothes. He helped me with my dress, then hurried me up the walk to the house. He was taking off my shawl in the hall and shaking the water out of my loosened hair, when Mrs. Fairfax emerged from her room. I did not observe her at first and nor did Mr. Rochester.

"Good-night, good-night, my darling!" he said, kissing me repeatedly.

When I looked up on leaving his arms, there stood the widow: pale, grave, and amazed. I only smiled at her and ran upstairs. "Explanation will do for another time," thought I. Still, when I reached my chamber, I felt a pang at the idea that she should even temporarily misconstrue what she had seen. But joy soon effaced every other feeling and loud as the wind blew, near and deep as the thunder crashed, fierce and frequent as the lightning gleamed, I experienced no fear and little awe.

Before I left my bed in the morning, little Adele came running in to tell me that the great horse-chestnut at the bottom of the orchard had been struck by lightning in the night and half of it split away.

CHAPTER XXIV

As I rose and dressed, I thought over what had happened and wondered if it were a dream. I could not be certain of the reality till I had seen Mr. Rochester again and heard him renew his words of love and promise.

While arranging my hair, I looked at my face in the glass and felt it was no longer plain; there was hope in its aspect and life in its colour. I had often been unwilling to look at my master, because I feared he could not be pleased at my look; but I was sure I might lift my face to his now, and not cool his affection by its expression. I took a plain but clean and light summer dress from my drawer and put it on: it seemed no attire had ever so well become me because none had I ever worn in so blissful a mood.

I was not surprised, when I ran down into the hall, to see that a brilliant June morning had succeeded to the tempest of the night, and to feel through the open glass door the breathing of a fresh and fragrant breeze. The rooks cawed, and blither birds sang; but nothing was so merry or so musical as my own rejoicing heart.

Mrs. Fairfax surprised me by looking out of the window with a sad countenance when I approached her and saying gravely, "Miss Eyre, will you come to breakfast?" During the meal she was quiet and cool, but I could not undeceive her then. I must wait for my master to give explanations and so must she. I ate what I could and then I hastened upstairs. I met Adele leaving the schoolroom.

"Where are you going? It is time for lessons."

"Mr. Rochester has sent me away to the nursery."

"Where is he?"

"In there," pointing to the apartment she had left.

I went in and there he stood.

"Come and bid me good-morning," said he.

I gladly advanced and it was not merely a cold word now or even a shake of the hand that I received, but an embrace and a kiss. His lips tasted sweet and succulent and I wanted to carry on kissing him and run my fingers through his combed, dark hair.

"Jane, you look blooming and smiling and pretty," said he. "Truly pretty this morning. Is this my pale, little elf?"

"It is Jane Eyre, sir."

"Soon to be Jane Rochester," he added, "in four weeks, not a day more. Do you hear that?"

I did, and I could not quite comprehend it—it made me giddy. The feeling the announcement sent through me was something stronger than was consistent with joy—something that smote and stunned. It was, I think almost fear.

"You blushed, and now you are white, Jane. What is that for?"

"Because you gave me a new name as Jane Rochester and it seems so strange."

"Yes, Mrs. Rochester," said he.

"It can never be, sir, it does not sound likely. Human beings never enjoy complete happiness in this world."

"This morning I wrote to my banker in London to send me certain jewels he has in his keeping—heirlooms for the ladies of Thornfield. In a day or two I hope to pour them into your lap."

"Oh, sir! Jewels for Jane Eyre sounds unnatural and strange. I would rather not have them."

"I will myself put the diamond chain round your neck and the circlet on your forehead. I will clasp the bracelets on these fine wrists, and load these fairy-like fingers with rings."

"No, no, sir! Don't address me as if I were a beauty for I am your plain, Quakerish governess."

"You are a beauty in my eyes."

I smiled and looked down at my hands.

"Something troubles you, Jane," he said sternly, hooking his finger beneath my chin and lifting it.

Some thought was indeed troubling me.

"Tell me."

I swallowed and said, "Why did you take such pains to make me believe you wished to marry Miss Ingram?"

"Is that all? Thank God it is no worse!" He unknit his black brows and looked down, smiling at me, before stroking my hair. "I feigned courtship of Miss Ingram, because I wished to render you as madly in love with me as I was with you and I knew jealousy would be the best ally I could call in for the furtherance of that end. Did it work?"

I nodded and turned my lips to the hand that lay on my shoulder. I loved him very much—more than I could trust myself to say—more than words had power to express, and though I knew that such behavior was wrong, I could not be angry with him when I was so happy.

"Is there anything else you should like to ask of me?"

There was and I was again ready with my request. "Communicate your intentions to Mrs. Fairfax, sir. She saw me with you last night in the hall and she was shocked. Give her some explanation before I see her again. It pains me to be misjudged by so good a woman."

"Go to your room, and put on your bonnet," he replied. "I mean you to accompany me to Millcote this morning, and while you prepare for the drive, I will enlighten the old lady's understanding. Did she think, Jane, you had given the world for love, and considered it well lost?"

"I believe she thought I had forgotten my station and yours, sir."

"Station! Station! Your station is in my heart. Now go."

I lingered and he gave me a knowing, rakish smile. "There will be plenty of time for that later, Jane. You are insatiable, my dear."

I blushed and hurried away, happy.

I was soon dressed and when I heard Mr. Rochester quit Mrs. Fairfax's parlour, I hurried down to it. The old lady, had been reading her morning portion of Scripture and her Bible lay open before her. Seeing me, she roused herself and made a sort of effort to smile but the smile expired. She shut the Bible and pushed her chair back from the table.

"I feel so astonished," she began, "I hardly know what to say to you, Miss Eyre. Now, can you tell me whether it is actually true that Mr. Rochester has asked you to marry him and you have accepted?"

"Yes."

She looked at me bewildered. "It passes me, but no doubt it is true since you say so. How it will answer, I cannot tell. Equality of position and fortune is often advisable in such cases and there are twenty years of difference in your ages. He might almost be your father."

"No, Mrs. Fairfax!" exclaimed I, nettled. "Mr. Rochester looks as young, and is as young as some men at five-and-twenty."

"Is it really for love he is going to marry you?" she asked.

I was so hurt by her coldness and scepticism, that the tears rose to my eyes.

"I am sorry to grieve you," pursued the widow, "but you are so young and I wished to put you on your guard."

"Is it impossible that Mr. Rochester should have a sincere affection for me?"

"No, you are very well, but believe me, you cannot be too careful. Gentlemen in his station are not accustomed to marry their governesses."

I was growing truly furious, but happily, Adele ran in.

"Let me go, let me go to Millcote too!" she cried. "Mr. Rochester won't, though there is so much room in the new carriage. Beg him to let me go mademoiselle."

"That I will, Adele," and I hastened away with her, glad to quit my gloomy monitress.

The rest of the day was spent in Millcote with Adele and Mr. Rochester, trying to steer them both away from picking out bright, ornate jewels for me and even brighter, fashionable dresses. I was exhausted with exclaiming that I had no use for pink silk and pearls as a governess and besides, would look odd and out of place, when we finally returned to Thornfield in the evening.

Mrs. Fairfax received me well and appeared to want to make up for her straight-talking earlier by being most attentive to my well-being. I readily forgave her, for I was fond of the old woman and we ate our dinner in companionable chatter about our day, led by Adele.

That evening, Mr. Rochester called me to his presence and I readily fulfilled his wishes, meeting him in the drawing room where he was sitting in an armchair.

"Come here, my love," he said as I entered, and I saw a warm smile stretch across his handsome, dark face that reassured me.

"It was torture to be with you all day and not be able to touch you," he said as I approached.

I perched on the arm of the chair, but he pulled me into his lap, running his hands over my waist and I giggled.

"You did touch me, sir." I said, thinking of our stolen caresses that were carried out whenever we thought and hoped no one was observing us.

He grinned. "Ah, yes. But I should like to touch you some more."

He smelt deliciously of leather and sweat and I told him so.

"I have just been riding," he said with a laugh, indicating his muddy boots and then he paused.

"What is it, sir?" I asked.

He reached down beside his chair and grasped a riding crop. He held it in both hands in front of me, his eyes glittering deviously. I did not follow what he meant and I looked confused.

"Dear Jane," he purred. "How should you like pleasure and pain?"

I still could not fathom what he meant.

"Sir, I only want you," I said truthfully.

"Yes, and I only want to please you. In any way that I can." He ran the whip through his fingers and caressed the worn leather. "I was thinking of you as I rode," he said. "And I should like to ride you now."

I swallowed and a thrill shot through my body, making the hairs on the back of my neck stand on end. I desired that too and I felt a deep blush rise to my cheeks.

"Stand, Jane," he added. "I will undress you."

I obeyed and he gently began unlacing my dress. His movements were feather-light and I could barely feel it as he dropped my bodice to the floor and began on my corset. With deliberate tenderness and the softest of touches, he removed all of my garments until I was bare. I stood naked in the drawing room, feeling bashful and wanting to cover myself.

"Jane, you look beautiful," he whispered.

I turned to him. The whip was in his hand.

"It is your turn," I said softly, stepping towards him.

With our eyes locked, I slowly removed his clothing too; his jacket, shirt, and breeches, until he was bare. He stood before me with his strong, muscled torso, chest of short black hair, and sculpted, thick legs. Then I reached out and gently ran my hands up and down his smooth, firm erection. He closed his eyes and groaned under his breath.

I went to kiss him, but he moved away. "Hold out your hand, Jane," he said.

I did as he asked, confused.

He turned it so that my palm faced upwards and then suddenly, he swiped it with the riding crop that whistled through the air. I yelped with shock, but it happened so quickly that I barely registered it. Except for a slight stinging, I felt little else.

"How was that, Jane?" he asked.

I stared at him, startled still.

"It gave me immense pleasure," he added.

"It did not hurt," I said. "Perhaps I should return the favor?"

A large smile spread across his face. "Jane, I should like that very much, but there is something else I would like to do first. Turn around."

I obeyed. This was different and thrilling and I felt my whole body tremble in apprehension.

He gently stroked the tail of the whip up and down my back, fluttering it over the contours of my spine. Lazily, he trailed it over my buttocks and down the backs of my thighs until I was gasping with longing.

Suddenly, he flicked the crop and it hit me on the right cheek of my behind.

I flinched and sighed, closing my eyes and savoring the burning throb of pain that mixed with the bubbling heat of desire pooling in my groin.

He flicked it again on my other cheek and the shock ran right through me to my core. Then he smacked it right across both cheeks and I writhed with the sweet, stinging bite. I moaned softly.

"Does it feel good, Jane?" he asked, walking around to my front so that he was facing me.

With his eyes again locked on mine, he brushed the crop against each of my breasts, circling my nipples and watching them harden. His dark eyes scorched mine with their depth and his brow was wet with sweat. Slowly, I licked my lips and watched him shudder with pleasure. He raised the crop to my mouth and I took it between my lips gently and bit down hard.

He threw the crop away and roughly pulled me to him, raking his fingers through my hair. I groaned with pain and pleasure and felt his hands grope every part of my body feverishly. Touching my breasts, my thighs, my neck, and my hips with clasping fingers. I melted under his hands and bent my body into him, wishing to be taken completely.

He began tugging on my arm and I followed him as he moved me smoothly to the opposite wall, pinning me up against it. He gathered my hips in his arms and pulled me up so that I was level with him, pushing my head hard against the wall with his fierce kisses, his tongue teasing the inside of my mouth with slow circles.

And suddenly he thrust himself inside of me and he was easing in and out slowly, rocking my body against the wall. As he pushed deeper and deeper, I cradled my legs around him and leant my head back, closing my eyes. He started to move faster and harder and then faster and harder still until I was panting and taking small, sharp breaths.

A tightly coiled throb of delight swelled inside me, before ripping through my body in a rush of ecstasy. I called out his name and fell limp in his arms as he too gently pulled himself out of me and came.

We were silent for a while, holding each other and breathing great sighs of relief as a sense of release tingled through our limbs.

"I should like to do that again tomorrow evening," said Mr. Rochester, stroking my hair. "And the next."

CHAPTER XXV

There was no putting off the day that advanced—the bridal day. After a month of courtship, its eve arrived and I at least had nothing more to do, for my packing and all else had been done for me. My trunks lay ready in my room to travel with me to London tomorrow when I became Mrs. Rochester.

Mrs. Rochester! She did not exist. It was enough that in yonder closet, opposite my dressing-table, garments said to be hers had already displaced my black stuff Lowood frock and straw bonnet. Instead there was a suit of wedding raiment; a pearl-coloured robe and a vapoury veil pendent. I shut the closet to conceal the strange, wraith-like apparel it contained, which at this evening hour of nine o'clock gave out certainly a most ghostly shimmer.

It was not only the hurry of preparation that made me feverish nor only the anticipation of the great change for though both these circumstances had their share in producing my restlessness, it was a third cause that influenced my mind more than they. I had at heart a strange and anxious thought. Something had happened which I could not comprehend the preceding night while Mr. Rochester was absent from home and I wished dearly to tell him.

I waited until he called for me at seven o'clock as was our way and went down to him. I sat as I usually did at first on his lap, beside the fire, but this time we did not begin to tear each other's garments off as was our normal routine. We had agreed to wait on the eve of our wedding until we were married the next day, although it pained us both. Instead we kissed, teased, and stroked one another like foolish, love-sick youths.

"It is near midnight," I said, caressing his cheek.

He frowned for he could see that something troubled me. "What is the matter?" he asked. "Tell me what you feel."

"Yesterday you were from home, sir and all day I was very busy and very happy in my ceaseless bustle. In the evening, I called Sophie to me upstairs to look at my wedding-dress, which they had just brought and under it in the box I found your present—the veil which, in your princely extravagance, you sent for from London, resolved, I suppose, since I would not have jewels, to cheat me into accepting something as costly."

"How well you read me, you witch!" interposed Mr. Rochester. "But what did you find in the veil besides its embroidery? Did you find poison or a dagger that you look so mournful now?"

"No, no, sir. But as it grew dark, the wind rose and blew mournfully. I wished you were at home. I came into this room and the sight of the empty chair and fireless hearth chilled me. For some time after I went to bed, I could not sleep— a sense of anxious excitement distressed me. The gale still rising, seemed to my ear to muffle a mournful under-sound; whether in the house or abroad I could not at first tell, but it recurred, doubtful yet doleful at every lull. At last I made out it must be some dog howling at a distance. I was glad when it ceased. On sleeping, I continued in dreams the idea of a dark and gusty night. I continued also the wish to be with you and experienced a strange, regretful consciousness of some barrier dividing us."

"And this dream weighs on your spirits now, Jane, when I am close to you? Little nervous subject! Forget visionary woe and think only of real happiness!"

"Let me finish my tale, sir, and hear me to the end."

"I thought, Jane, you had told me all. I thought I had found the source of your melancholy in a dream."

I shook my head.

"What! Is there more? But I will not believe it to be anything important. I warn you of incredulity beforehand. Go on."

The disquietude of his air, the somewhat apprehensive impatience of his manner, surprised me, but I proceeded.

"I dreamt another dream, sir, that Thornfield Hall was a dreary ruin. I thought that of all the stately front nothing remained but a shell-like wall, very high and very fragile-looking."

"Now, Jane, that is all."

"Just the preface, sir, the tale is yet to come. I woke and a gleam dazzled my eyes. I thought—Oh, it is daylight! But I was mistaken and it was only candlelight. Sophie, I supposed, had come in. There was a light in the dressing-table and the door of the closet, where I had hung my wedding-dress and veil, stood open. I heard a rustling there. I asked, 'Sophie, what are you doing?' No one answered, but a form emerged from the closet and it took the light and held it aloft. 'Sophie! Sophie!' I again cried and still it was silent. I had risen up in bed and I bent forward, at first surprised and then bewildered. My blood crept cold through my veins. Mr. Rochester, this was not Sophie, it was not Leah, it was not Mrs. Fairfax, it was not—no, I am sure of it—it was not even that strange woman, Grace Poole."

"It must have been one of them," interrupted my master.

"No, sir. I solemnly assure you to the contrary. The shape standing before me had never crossed my eyes within the precincts of Thornfield Hall before and the height and the contour were new to me."

"Describe it, Jane."

"It seemed, sir, a woman; tall and large, with thick, dark hair hanging long down her back."

"Did you see her face?"

"Not at first. But presently she took my veil from its place and she held it up to gaze at it long. Then she threw it over her own head and turned to the mirror. At that moment, I saw the reflection of the visage and features quite distinctly in the dark oblong glass."

"How were they?"

"Fearful and ghastly to me. Oh, sir, I never saw a face like it! It was discoloured and savage. I wish I could forget the roll of the red eyes and the fearful blackened inflation of the lineaments!"

"Ghosts are usually pale, Jane."

"This, sir, was purple and the lips were swelled and dark."

"What did it do?"

"It removed my veil from its gaunt head, rent it in two parts, and flinging both on the floor, trampled on them."

"Afterwards?"

"It drew aside the window-curtain and looked out; perhaps it saw dawn approaching, for, taking the candle, it retreated to the door. Just at my bedside, the figure stopped and the fiery eyes glared upon me. She thrust up her candle close to my face and extinguished it under my eyes. I was aware her lurid visage flamed over mine and I lost consciousness. I became insensible from terror."

"Who was with you when you revived?"

"No one, sir, but the broad day. I rose, bathed my face in water, drank a long draught and felt that though enfeebled, I was not ill. Now, sir, tell me who and what that woman was?"

"The creature of an over-stimulated brain, that is certain. I must be careful of you, my treasure. Nerves like yours were not made for rough handling."

"Sir, depend on it, my nerves were not in fault! The thing was real."

"And your previous dreams, were they real too? Is Thornfield Hall a ruin? Am I severed from you by insuperable obstacles?"

"But when I said so to myself on rising this morning, on the carpet I saw the veil torn from top to bottom in two halves!"

I felt Mr. Rochester start and shudder, and he hastily flung his arms round me. "Thank God!" he exclaimed, "that if anything malignant did come near you last night, it was only the veil that was harmed. Oh, to think what might have happened!"

He drew his breath short, and strained me so close to him, I could scarcely pant. After some minutes' silence, he continued, cheerily, "Now, Jane, I'll explain to you all about it. It was half dream, half reality. A woman did, I doubt not, enter your room and that woman was—must have been— Grace Poole. In a state between sleeping and waking, you noticed her entrance and her actions, but feverish, almost delirious as you were, you ascribed to her a goblin appearance different from her own. The spiteful tearing of the veil was real and it is like her. I see you would ask why I keep such a woman in my house and when we have been married a year and a day, I will tell you, but not now. Are you satisfied, Jane? Do you accept my solution of the mystery?"

I reflected, and in truth it appeared to me the only possible one. Satisfied I was not, but to please him I endeavoured to appear so. I answered him with a contented smile. And now, as it was long past one, I prepared to leave him.

"Does not Sophie sleep with Adele in the nursery?" he asked, as I lit my candle.

"Yes, sir."

"And there is room enough in Adele's little bed for you. You must share it with her to-night, Jane. It is no wonder that the incident you have related should make you nervous, and I would rather you did not sleep alone. Promise me to go to the nursery."

"I shall be very glad to do so, sir."

"And fasten the door securely on the inside. And now, no more sombre thoughts. How is my Jane?"

"The night is serene, sir, and so am I."

"And you will not dream of separation and sorrow to-night, but of happy love and blissful union."

This prediction was but half fulfilled for I did not indeed dream of sorrow, but as little did I dream of joy for I never slept at all. With little Adele in my arms, I waited for the coming day and as soon as the sun rose, I rose too.

CHAPTER XXVI

Sophie came at seven to dress me and she was very long indeed in accomplishing her task; so long that Mr. Rochester, grown impatient of my delay, sent up to ask why I did not come. She was just fastening my veil (the plain square of blond after all) to my hair with a brooch when I hurried from under her hands as soon as I could.

"Stop!" she cried in French. "Look at yourself in the mirror, you have not taken one peep."

So I turned at the door and I saw a robed and veiled figure, so unlike my usual self that it seemed almost the image of a stranger.

"Jane!" called a voice, and I hastened down.

I was received at the foot of the stairs by Mr. Rochester.

"Jane, are you ready?"

"Yes, sir," I replied breathlessly.

There were no groomsmen, no bridesmaids, and no relatives to wait for or marshal. None but Mr. Rochester and I and together we went.

Mrs. Fairfax stood in the hall as we passed. I would have spoken to her, but my hand was held by a grasp of iron and I was hurried along by a stride I could hardly follow; I did not know why we rushed so but to look at Mr. Rochester's face was to feel that not a second of delay would be tolerated for any purpose.

I know not whether the day was fair or foul in descending the drive, I gazed neither on sky nor earth for my heart was with my eyes and both seemed migrated into Mr. Rochester's frame.

At the churchyard wicket he stopped and discovered I was quite out of breath. "Am I cruel in my love?" he said. "Delay an instant and lean on me, Jane."

He earnestly looked at my face from which the blood had, I daresay, momentarily fled and felt my forehead. But I rallied and he walked gently with me up the path to the porch of the grey, steepled church.

We entered the quiet and humble temple where the priest waited in his white surplice at the lowly altar, a clerk beside him. All was still. We took our places at the communion rail and I happened to hear a step behind me. Glancing over my shoulder, I saw a gentleman advancing up the chancel, but the service began so I turned back. The explanation of the intent of matrimony was gone through and then the clergyman came a step further forward, and bending slightly towards Mr. Rochester, went on.

"I require and charge you both that if either of you know any impediment why ye may not lawfully be joined together in matrimony, ye do now confess it; for be ye well assured that so many as are coupled together otherwise than God's Word doth allow, are not joined together by God, neither is their matrimony lawful."

He paused, as the custom is. When is the pause after that sentence ever broken by reply? Not perhaps, once in a hundred years. And the clergyman, who had not lifted his eyes from his book and had held his breath but for a moment, was proceeding with his hand already stretched towards Mr. Rochester when a distinct and near voice said, "The marriage cannot go on! I declare the existence of an impediment."

The clergyman looked up at the speaker and stood mute, while the clerk did the same. Mr. Rochester moved slightly, as if an earthquake had rolled under his feet and taking a firmer footing and not turning his head or eyes, he said, "Proceed."

A profound silence fell.

Presently Mr. Wood said, "I cannot proceed without some investigation into what has been asserted and evidence of its truth or falsehood."

"The ceremony is quite broken off," subjoined the voice behind us. "I am in a condition to prove my allegation. An insuperable impediment to this marriage exists."

Mr. Rochester heard but heeded not, he stood stubborn and rigid making no movement but to possess himself of my hand. What a hot and strong grasp he had! How his eye shone still watchful and yet wild beneath!

Mr. Wood seemed at a loss. "What is the nature of the impediment?" he asked. "Perhaps it may be got over-explained away?"

"Hardly," was the answer. "I have called it insuperable, and I speak advisedly."

The speaker came forward and leaned on the rails. He continued, uttering each word distinctly, calmly, steadily, but not loudly, "It simply consists in the existence of a previous marriage. Mr. Rochester has a wife now living."

My nerves vibrated to those low-spoken words as they had never vibrated to thunder and my blood ran cold, but I was collected and in no danger of swooning. I looked at Mr. Rochester and I made him look at me. His whole face was a colourless rock and his eye was both spark and flint.

"Who are you?" he asked of the intruder.

"My name is Briggs, I am a solicitor."

"And you would thrust on me a wife?"

"I would remind you of your lady's existence, sir, which the law recognises, if you do not."

"Favour me with an account of her—with her name, her parentage and her place of abode."

"Certainly." Mr. Briggs calmly took a paper from his pocket, and read out in a sort of official, nasal voice, "'I affirm and can prove that on the 20th of October A.D.— (a date of fifteen years back), Edward Fairfax Rochester, of Thornfield Hall, in the county of—, and of Ferndean Manor, in -shire, England, was married to my sister, Bertha Antoinetta Mason, daughter of Jonas Mason, merchant, and of Antoinetta his wife, a Creole, at -church, Spanish Town, Jamaica. The record of the marriage will be found in the register of that church—a copy of it is now in my possession. Signed, Richard Mason.'"

"That—if a genuine document—may prove I have been married, but it does not prove that the woman mentioned therein as my wife is still living."

"She was living three months ago," returned the lawyer.

"How do you know?"

"I have a witness to the fact, whose testimony even you, sir, will scarcely controvert."

"Produce him—or go to hell."

"I will produce him first—he is on the spot. Mr. Mason, have the goodness to step forward."

Mr. Rochester, on hearing the name, set his teeth and experienced a sort of strong convulsive quiver of fury and despair. A man who had hitherto lingered in the background now drew near and a pale face looked over the solicitor's shoulder. It was Mason himself.

Mr. Rochester turned and glared at him. Contempt palpable in his eyes. "What have you to say?" he demanded.

An inaudible reply escaped Mason's white lips.

"I again demand, what have you to say?"

"Sir—sir," interrupted the clergyman, seeing his mad anger, "do not forget you are in a sacred place." Then addressing Mason, he inquired gently, "Are you aware, sir, whether or not this gentleman's wife is still living?"

"Courage," urged the lawyer beside him, "speak out."

"She is now living at Thornfield Hall," said Mason, in more articulate tones. "I saw her there last April. I am her brother."

"At Thornfield Hall!" ejaculated the clergyman. "Impossible! I am an old resident in this neighbourhood, sir, and I never heard of a Mrs. Rochester at Thornfield Hall."

I saw a grim smile contort Mr. Rochester's lips, and he muttered, "No, by God! I took care that none should hear of it." For ten minutes he held counsel with himself and forming his resolve, he announced, "Enough! Leave the church for there will be no wedding to-day."

I could not speak or swoon, I merely listened as my love went on.

"Bigamy is an ugly word! I meant, however, to be a bigamist, but fate has out-manoeuvered me. Gentlemen, my plan is broken up—what this lawyer and his client say is true. I have been married and the woman to whom I was married lives! You say you never heard of a Mrs. Rochester at Thornfield, but I daresay you have many a time inclined your ear to gossip about the mysterious lunatic kept there under watch and ward. Some have whispered to you that she is my bastard half-sister, some my cast-off mistress. I now inform you that she is my wife whom I married fifteen years ago—Bertha Mason by name and sister of this resolute personage who quivers before me. Bertha Mason is mad and she came of a mad family as I found out after I had wed the daughter, for they were silent on family secrets before. But I invite you all to come up to the house and visit my wife, Mrs. Poole's patient. You shall see what sort of a being I was cheated into espousing and judge whether or not I had a right to seek sympathy with something at least human. This girl," he continued, looking at me, "knew no more than you of the disgusting secret and she thought all was fair. But come all of you and follow!"

Still holding me fast, he left the church and the three gentlemen came after. At our entrance to Thornfield,
Mrs. Fairfax, Adele, Sophie and Leah advanced to meet and
greet us.

"Away with your congratulations!" cried the master.
"They are fifteen years too late!"

He passed on and ascended the stairs, still holding my
hand and still beckoning the gentlemen to follow him,
which they did. We mounted the first staircase, passed up
the gallery and proceeded to the third storey. Mr. Rochester
opened a low black door and admitted us to a tapestried
room.

"You know this place, Mason," said our guide, "she bit
and stabbed you here."

He lifted the hangings from the wall, uncovering the
second door and this he also opened. A room without a
window revealed itself and inside there burnt a fire guarded
by a high and strong fender and a lamp suspended from the
ceiling by a chain. Grace Poole bent over the fire, apparently
cooking something in a saucepan. In the deep shade at the
farther end of the room, a figure ran backwards and forwards.
What it was, whether beast or human being, one could not,
at first sight, tell. It grovelled seemingly on all fours and snatched and growled like some strange wild animal, but it was
covered with clothing and a quantity of dark, grizzled hair,
wild as a mane, hid its head and face.

"Good-morrow, Mrs. Poole!" said Mr. Rochester. "How
are you? And how is your charge to-day?"

"We're tolerable, sir, I thank you," replied Grace, lifting
the boiling mess carefully on to the hob. "Rather snappish,
but not 'rageous."

A fierce cry seemed to give the lie to her favourable report
and the clothed hyena rose up, and stood tall on its hind-feet.

"Ah! Sir, she sees you!" exclaimed Grace, "you'd better
not stay."

"Only a few moments, Grace. You must allow me a few moments."

"Take care then, sir! For God's sake, take care!"

The maniac bellowed and parted her shaggy locks from her visage to gaze wildly at her visitors. I recognised well that purple face and those bloated features. Mrs. Poole advanced.

"Keep out of the way," said Mr. Rochester, thrusting her aside. "She has no knife now, I suppose, and I'm on my guard."

"One never knows what she has, sir, she is so cunning. It is not in mortal discretion to fathom her craft."

"We had better leave her," whispered Mason.

"Go to the devil!" was his brother-in-law's recommendation.

"Beware!" cried Grace.

The three gentlemen retreated simultaneously and Mr. Rochester flung me behind him. The lunatic sprang and grappled his throat viciously, laid her teeth to his cheek and they struggled. She was a big woman, in stature almost equalling her husband and corpulent besides and more than once she almost throttled him, athletic as he was. He could have settled her with a well-planted blow, but he would not strike, he would only wrestle. At last he mastered her arms and Grace Poole gave him a cord, which he used to bound her to a chair. The operation was performed amidst the fiercest yells and the most convulsive plunges. Mr. Rochester then turned to the spectators and looked at them with a smile both acrid and desolate.

"That is my wife," said he. "And this is what I wished to have," he added, laying his hand on my shoulder. "This young girl who stands so grave and quiet at the mouth of hell. Compare these clear eyes with the red balls yonder and this form with that bulk, then judge me! Off with you now. I must shut up my prize."

We all withdrew silently and Mr. Rochester stayed a moment behind us to give some further order to Grace Poole. The solicitor addressed me as he descended the stair.

"You, madam," said he, "are cleared from all blame and your uncle will be glad to hear it if, indeed, he should be still living when Mr. Mason returns to Madeira."

"My uncle! What of him? Do you know him?"

"Mr. Mason does. Mr. Eyre has been the Funchal correspondent of his house for some years. When your uncle received your letter intimating the contemplated union between yourself and Mr. Rochester, Mr. Mason, who was staying at Madeira to recruit his health on his way back to Jamaica, happened to be with him. Mr. Eyre mentioned the intelligence for he knew that my client here was acquainted with a gentleman of the name of Rochester. Mr. Mason, astonished and distressed as you may suppose, revealed the real state of matters. Your uncle, I am sorry to say, is now on a sick bed from which, considering the nature of his disease, he is unlikely ever to rise. He could not then hasten to England himself to extricate you from the snare into which you had fallen, but he implored Mr. Mason to lose no time in taking steps to prevent the false marriage. He referred him to me for assistance and I am thankful I was not too late as you doubtless must be also. Were I not morally certain that your uncle will be dead ere you reach Madeira, I would advise you to accompany Mr. Mason back, but as it is, I think you had better remain in England till you can hear further, either from or of Mr. Eyre. Have we anything else to stay for?" he inquired of Mr. Mason.

"No, no. Let us be gone," was the anxious reply and without waiting to take leave of Mr. Rochester, they made their exit at the hall door. The clergyman stayed to exchange a few sentences, either of admonition or reproof with his haughty parishioner and this duty done, he too departed.

I heard him go as I stood at the half-open door of my own room, to which I had now withdrawn. I shut myself in, fastened the bolt that none might intrude and proceeded to weep mournfully.

CHAPTER XXVII

Some time in the afternoon I raised my head, and looking round and seeing the western sun gilding the sign of its decline on the wall, I asked, "What am I to do?"

But the answer my mind gave—"Leave Thornfield at once"—was so prompt and so dread, that I stopped my ears. I could not bear such words now. But then, a voice within me averred that I could do it and foretold that I should do it.

I rose up suddenly, terror-struck at the thought. My head swam as I stood erect and I perceived that I was sickening from excitement and inanition since neither meat nor drink had passed my lips that day, for I had taken no breakfast. And, with a strange pang, I now reflected that as long as I had been shut up here, no message had been sent to ask how I was or to invite me to come down. Not even little Adele had tapped at the door. Not even Mrs. Fairfax had sought me.

I undrew the bolt of my door to pass out, but stumbled over an obstacle outside. Weak as I was, I could not soon recover myself and I fell, but an outstretched arm caught me. I looked up and I saw that I was supported by Mr. Rochester, who sat in a chair across my chamber threshold.

"You come out at last," he said. "I have been waiting for you long and listening yet not one movement have I heard, nor one sob. Five minutes more of that death-like hush, and I should have forced the lock like a burglar. I would rather you had come and upbraided me with vehemence. You are passionate. I expected a scene of some kind. I was prepared for the hot rain of tears only I wanted them to be shed on my breast." he paused. "Well, Jane! Not a word of reproach? You sit quietly where I have placed you and regard me with a weary, passive look?"

Still I said nothing.

"Jane, I never meant to wound you thus. Will you ever forgive me?"

Reader, I forgave him at the moment and on the spot. There was such deep remorse in his eye, such true pity in his tone, such manly energy in his manner and besides, there was such unchanged love in his whole look and mien. I forgave him all yet not in words, not outwardly, only at my heart's core.

"You know I am a scoundrel, Jane?"

"Yes, sir."

"Then tell me so roundly and sharply—don't spare me."

"I cannot. I am tired and sick. I want some water."

He heaved a sort of shuddering sigh, and taking me in his arms, carried me downstairs. At first I did not know to what room he had borne me, but presently I felt the warmth of a fire for, summer as it was, I had become icy cold in my chamber. He put wine to my lips and it revived me, then I ate something he offered and was soon myself. I was in the library, sitting in his chair and he was quite near.

"How are you now, Jane?"

"Much better, sir. I shall be well soon."

He bent his head to kiss me, but I turned away; an act I thought that I would never perform.

"Adele must have a new governess, sir."

"Oh, Adele will go to school—I have settled that already. I was wrong ever to bring you to Thornfield Hall, knowing as I did how it was haunted. I charged them to conceal from you, before I ever saw you, all knowledge of the curse of the

place; merely because I feared Adele never would have a governess to stay if she knew with what devil inmate she was
housed. All is prepared for your prompt departure to-morrow. I only ask you to endure one more night under this roof,
Jane, and then farewell to its miseries and terrors for ever! I
have a place to repair to, which will be a secure sanctuary
from hateful reminiscences and—"

"Then take Adele with you, sir," I interrupted, "she will
be a companion for you."

He had been walking fast about the room and he stopped, as if suddenly rooted to one spot. He looked at me long
and hard and I turned my eyes from him and fixed them on
the fire instead.

"Jane! Jane!" he said, in such an accent of bitter sadness
it thrilled along every nerve I had. "You don't love me, then?
It was only my station and the rank of my wife that you va-
lued? Now that you think me disqualified to become your
husband, you recoil from my touch as if I were some toad or
ape."

These words cut me. I ought probably to have done or
said nothing, but I was so tortured by a sense of remorse at
thus hurting his feelings, I could not control the wish to drop
balm where I had wounded.

"I do love you," I said, "more than ever. But I must not
show or indulge the feeling and this is the last time I must
express it. Mr. Rochester, I must leave you."

"For how long, Jane?"

"I must leave Adele and Thornfield. I must part with
you for my whole life. I must begin a new existence among
strange faces and strange scenes."

"No, you must become Mrs. Rochester!"

"How can I, sir? You are married!"

"I am a fool!" cried Mr. Rochester suddenly. "I keep telling you I am not married and do not explain why. I forget

you know nothing of the character of that woman or of the circumstances attending my infernal union with her. I will in a few words show you the real state of the case. Can you listen to me?"

"Yes, sir," I replied, for I dearly wished what he said to be true.

"Jane, did you ever hear or know that I was not the eldest son of my house, that I had once a brother older than I?"

"I remember Mrs. Fairfax told me so once."

"Well, Jane, it was my father's resolution to keep the property together for he could not bear the idea of dividing his estate and leaving me a fair portion. All, he resolved, should go to my brother, Rowland. Yet as little could he endure that a son of his should be a poor man and he felt I must be provided for by a wealthy marriage. He sought me a partner betimes and a Mr. Mason, a West India planter and merchant, was an old acquaintance of his. Mr. Mason, he found, had a son and daughter and he learned that he could give a fortune of thirty thousand pounds for the latter. When I left college, I was sent out to Jamaica, to espouse a bride already courted for me. My father said nothing about her money, but he told me Miss Mason was the boast of Spanish Town for her beauty and this was no lie. I found her a fine woman in the style of Blanche Ingram: tall, dark, and majestic. Her family wished to secure me because I was of a good race and so did she. They showed her to me in parties, splendidly dressed. I seldom saw her alone and had very little private conversation with her. She flattered me and lavishly displayed for my pleasure her charms and accomplishments. All the men in her circle seemed to admire her and envy me. I was dazzled, stimulated, and my senses which were inexperienced, were excited. I thought I loved her. Her relatives encouraged me and a foolish marriage was achieved almost before I knew where I was. I did not even know her. Blockhead that I was, I married her.

"My bride's mother I had never seen and I understood she was dead. The honeymoon over, I learned my mistake for she was not dead but mad and shut up in a lunatic asylum. There was a younger brother, too—a complete dumb idiot. The elder one, whom you have seen, will probably be in the same state one day. My father and my brother knew all this, but they thought only of the thirty thousand pounds, and joined in the plot against me.

"I lived with that woman upstairs four years and before that time she had tried me indeed. Her character ripened and developed with frightful rapidity; her vices sprang up fast and rank and they were so strong, only cruelty could check them, but I would not use cruelty. Bertha Mason, the true daughter of an infamous mother, dragged me through all the hideous and degrading agonies which must attend a man bound to a wife at once intemperate and unchaste.

"My brother in the interval died, and at the end of the four years my father died too. I was rich enough now yet poor to hideous indigence. I could not rid myself of Bertha by any legal proceedings for the doctors now discovered that she was mad. Jane, you don't like my narrative and you look almost sick—shall I defer the rest to another day?"

"No, sir, finish it now. What did you do when you found she was mad?"

"I approached the verge of despair. At the age of twenty-six, I was hopeless. My reputation was tainted and so I took my mad wife to England with me, where no one would know of her and I placed her at Thornfield. Grace Poole and the surgeon Carter (who dressed Mason's wounds that night he was stabbed and worried), are the only two I have ever admitted to my confidence. Mrs. Fairfax may indeed have suspected something, but she could have gained no precise knowledge as to facts."

"And what next, sir? How did you proceed?"

"For ten long years I roved about, living first in various countries with a series of mistresses. Then I came back and I was bewitched by a creature on the causeway. I have thought of no one since. I am truly in love with her."

I thought of his "series" of mistresses and knew that I did not want to be one of them. I did not want to be like Adele's mama.

"Jane, promise just this—'I will be yours, Mr. Rochester.'"

"Mr. Rochester, I will not be yours."

A long silence.

"Jane, do you mean to go one way in the world, and to let me go another?" he asked in a low, dangerous voice.

"I do."

"Do you mean it now?" he asked, running his fingers down my neck.

"I do."

"And now?" He softly kissed my forehead and cheek.

"I do!" I cried, extricating myself from him completely.

"Then you snatch love and innocence from me? You fling me back to my dark, lonely world?"

"Mr. Rochester, you will forget me before I forget you."

"You make me a liar by such language and you sully my honour!"

As he said this, he released me from his clutches and only looked at me. The look was far worse to resist than the frantic strain. Only an idiot, however, would have succumbed now. I had dared and baffled his fury and I must elude his sorrow. I retired to the door.

"You are going, Jane?"

"I am going, sir."

"You are leaving me?"

"Yes."

"Withdraw then, I consent, but remember that you leave me here in anguish. Go up to your own room and think over all I have said. Jane, think of me."

He turned away.

I reached the door but, Reader, I walked back. I walked back as determinedly as I had retreated and I knelt down by him. I turned his face from the cushion to me and I kissed his cheek and I smoothed his hair with my hand.

"Farewell," I whispered, standing again. Despair added, "Farewell for ever!"

That evening I never thought to sleep, but a slumber fell on me as soon as I lay down in bed. I awoke in the night after troubled dreams and knew I must leave now. In a trance-like state, I rose, dressed, took my purse containing twenty shillings and stole from my room. Wishing a farewell to all, I crept out of Thornfield Hall and fled into the night.

CHAPTER XXVIII

Two days later on a summer evening, a coachman set me down at a place called Whitcross. He could take me no farther for the sum I had given and I was not possessed of another shilling in the world. Once I had alighted, the coach carried on and I was alone. I quickly discovered that I had forgotten to take my parcel out of the pocket of the coach, where I had placed it for safety and now I was absolutely destitute.

Whitcross was no town, nor even a hamlet, but a stone pillar set up where four roads met. Four arms sprung from its summit displaying the directions of towns and from the well-known names of these towns, I learnt in what county I had lighted. There were great moors behind and on each hand of me; waves of mountains and deep valleys. The population there must have been thin and I saw no passengers on those roads.

I began striding straight into the heath, wading knee-deep in its dark growth. What was I to do? Where to go? Oh, intolerable questions, when I could do nothing and go nowhere! A long way must yet be measured by my weary, trembling limbs before I could reach human habitation and beg for charity.

Night fell and I stopped beside a crag to sleep beneath the stars. My hunger was sharp and I tried to satisfy it with some nearby berries but they did little to alleviate the ache. My rest might have been blissful enough, only a sad heart broke it.

It plained of its gaping wounds, its inward bleeding, its riven chords. It trembled for Mr. Rochester and his doom and it bemoaned him with bitter pity.

The next day, I lay still for a long time before finally rousing myself. I felt safe in the tranquil quiet of this moor and almost did not want to return to Whitcross, but having regained it, I followed a road which led from the sun, now fervent and high. By no other circumstance had I will to decide my choice. I walked a long time and when I thought I had nearly done enough and might yield to the fatigue that almost overpowered me I heard a bell chime, a church bell.

I turned in the direction of the sound, and there, amongst the romantic hills, I saw a hamlet and a spire. Recalled by the rumbling of wheels to the road before me, I saw a heavily-laden waggon labouring up the hill and not far beyond were two cows and their drover. Human life and human labour were near. I must struggle on: strive to live and bend to toil like the rest.

About two o'clock, I entered the village. At the bottom of its one street there was a little shop with some cakes of bread in the window. I coveted a cake of bread. With that refreshment I could perhaps regain a degree of energy and without it, it would be difficult to proceed. The wish to have some strength and some vigour returned to me as soon as I was amongst my fellow-beings. I felt it would be degrading to faint with hunger on the causeway of a hamlet. Had I nothing about me I could offer in exchange for one of these rolls? No.

I was so sick, so weak, and so gnawed with nature's cravings that instinct kept me roaming around abodes where there was a chance of food all afternoon. I drew near houses, left them and then came back again, before wandering away. In crossing a field, I saw the church spire before me again and I hastened towards it. Near the churchyard, in the middle of a garden, stood a well-built though small house, which I had no doubt was the parsonage. It is the clergyman's function to help—at least with advice—those who wished to help themselves. I seemed to have something like a right to seek counsel here. Renewing my courage and gathering my feeble remains of strength, I pushed on. I reached the house and knocked at the kitchen-door. An old woman opened.

"Yes?"

"Is the clergyman in?"

"No, he is gone from home."

"To a distance?"

"Not so far—three miles. He has been called away by the sudden death of his father and he is at Marsh End now, and will very likely stay there a fortnight longer."

"Is there any lady of the house?"

"Nay, naught but me and I am the housekeeper."

Of her, Reader, I could not bear to ask the relief for want of which I was sinking. I could not yet beg and again I crawled away.

A little before dark I passed a farm-house, at the open door of which the farmer was sitting, eating his supper of bread and cheese. I stopped and said, "Will you give me a piece of bread? For I am very hungry."

He cast on me a glance of surprise, but without answering, he cut a thick slice from his loaf and gave it to me. I imagine he did not think I was a beggar, but only an eccentric sort of lady, who had taken a fancy to his brown loaf. As soon as I was out of sight of his house, I sat down and ate it.

I could not hope to get a lodging under a roof so sought it in a nearby wood. But my night was wretched and damp and no sense of safety or tranquillity befriended me. Towards morning it rained and the whole of the following day was wet. Do not ask me, Reader, to give a minute account of that day for as before, I sought work and as before, I was repulsed.

At the door of a cottage I saw a little girl about to throw a mess of cold porridge into a pig trough. "Will you give me that?" I asked.

She stared at me. "Mother!" she exclaimed. "There is a woman wants me to give her this porridge."

"Well lass," replied a voice within, "give it her if she's a beggar. T' pig doesn't want it."

The girl emptied the stiffened mould into my hand, and I devoured it ravenously.

As the wet twilight deepened, I stopped in a solitary bridle-path, which I had been pursuing an hour or more. My strength was leaving me and I felt weaker than ever before.

My glazed eye wandered over the dim and misty landscape before me and I saw I had strayed far from the village since it was quite out of sight. I had, by cross-ways and by-paths, once more drawn near the tract of moorland and now only a few fields lay between me and the dusky hill.

I sank down where I stood and hid my face against the ground, exhaustion overtaking me. I lay still a while and the night-wind swept over the hill and over me, before dying in a moan. The rain fell fast again, wetting me afresh to the skin. Could I but have stiffened to the still frost—the friendly numbness of death—it might have pelted on and I should not have felt it, but my yet living flesh shuddered at its chilling influence. I rose ere long.

Then I saw a light, shining dim but constant through the rain. At first I mistrusted it and thought I dreamt, but it blazed on. I tried to walk again and began dragging my exhausted limbs slowly towards it. It led me aslant over the hill, through a wide bog and I fell twice, but as often I rose and rallied my faculties. This light was my forlorn hope and I must gain it.

The silhouette of a house rose to view; black, low, and rather long. In seeking the door, I turned an angle and approached a very small latticed window instead. Looking in, I saw a group near the hearth, sitting still amidst the rosy peace and warmth suffusing it. Two young, graceful women— ladies in every point—sat wearing deep mourning of crape and bombazeen, which sombre garb singularly set off very fair necks and faces. A large old pointer dog rested its massive head on the knee of one girl and in the lap of the other was cushioned a black cat. A strange place was this humble kitchen for such occupants! Who were they? They could not be the daughters of the elderly person at the table for she looked like a rustic, and they were all delicacy and cultivation.

"Listen, Diana," said one, consulting one of the books before them. "Franz and old Daniel are together in the night-time, and Franz is telling a dream from which he has awakened in terror—listen!" And in a low voice she read a strange language that I later learnt was German. "That is strong," she said, when she had finished. "I relish it."

"Is there ony country where they talk i' that way?" asked the old woman, looking up from her knitting.

"Yes, Hannah—a far larger country than England."

"Well, for sure case, I knawn't how they can understand t' one t'other: and if either o' ye went there, ye could tell what they said, I guess?"

"We could probably tell something of what they said, but not all for we are not as clever as you think us, Hannah. We don't speak German, and we cannot read it without a dictionary to help us."

"And what good does it do you?"

"We mean to teach it some time and then we shall get more money than we do now."

"Varry like: but give ower studying; ye've done enough for to-night."

"I think we have," replied Diana. "At least I'm tired. Mary, are you?"

"Mortally. I wonder when St. John will come home."

"Surely he will not be long now, it is just ten. But it rains fast, Hannah, will you have the goodness to look at the fire in the parlour?"

The old woman rose and she opened a door, through which I dimly saw a passage. Soon I heard her stir a fire in an inner room and she presently came back.

"Ah, childer!" said she. "It fair troubles me to go into yond' room now since it looks so lonesome wi' the chair empty and set back in a corner."

She wiped her eyes with her apron and the two girls, grave before looked sad.

"But Father is in a better place," continued Hannah. "We shouldn't wish him here again. And then, nobody need to have a quieter death nor he had."

They were silent for a moment, till the clock struck ten.

"Ye'll want your supper, I am sure," observed Hannah. "And so will Mr. St. John when he comes in."

And she proceeded to prepare the meal. The ladies now rose and they seemed about to withdraw to the parlour. Till this moment, I had been so intent on watching them that I had half-forgotten my own wretched position, but now it recurred to me. I turned and groped out the door, knocking at it hesitatingly. Hannah opened.

"What do you want?" she inquired, in a voice of surprise, as she surveyed me by the light of the candle she held.

"May I speak to your mistresses?" I said.

"You had better tell me what you have to say to them. Where do you come from?"

"I am a stranger."

"What is your business here at this hour?"

"I want a night's shelter in an out-house or anywhere, and a morsel of bread to eat."

Distrust, the very feeling I dreaded, appeared in Hannah's face. "I'll give you a piece of bread," she said, after a pause, "but we can't take in a vagrant to lodge. It isn't likely."

"Do let me speak to your mistresses."

"No, not I. What can they do for you? You should not be roving about now for it looks very ill."

"Tell the young ladies. Let me see them—"

"Indeed, I will not."

"But I must die if I am turned away."

"Not you. I'm fear'd you have some ill plans agate that bring you about folk's houses at this time o' night."

Here, the honest but inflexible servant clapped the door to and bolted it within.

This was the climax. A pang of exquisite suffering heaved my heart and I sank on the wet doorstep. I groaned, wrung my hands and wept in utter anguish.

"I can but die," I said aloud.

"All men must die," said a voice quite close at hand, "but all are not condemned to meet a lingering and premature doom such as yours would be if you perished here of want."

"Who or what speaks?" I asked, terrified at the unexpected sound and incapable now of deriving from any occurrence a hope of aid.

A form was near but I could not distinguish it from the gloom. With a loud long knock, the new-comer appealed to the door.

"Is it you, Mr. St. John?" cried Hannah.

"Yes, yes, open quickly."

"How wet and cold you must be on such a wild night as it is! Come in—your sisters are quite uneasy about you and I believe there are bad folks about. There has been a beggar-woman—I declare she is not gone yet!—laid down there. Get up! For shame! Move off, I say!"

"Hush, Hannah! I have a word to say to the woman. You have done your duty in excluding, now let me do mine in admitting her. I was near and listened to both you and her. I think this is a peculiar case I must at least examine into it.

Young woman, rise and pass before me into the house."

With difficulty I obeyed him. Presently I stood within that clean, bright kitchen, trembling, sickening, and conscious of my disgusting appearance. The two ladies, their brother, Mr. St. John, and the old servant, were all gazing at me.

"St. John, who is it?" I heard one ask.

"I cannot tell. I found her at the door," was the reply.

"She does look white," said Hannah.

"As white as clay or death," was responded. "She will fall, let her sit."

And indeed my head swam. I dropped, but a chair received me. I still possessed my senses but just now I could not speak.

"Perhaps a little water would restore her. Hannah, fetch some. How very thin, and how very bloodless she is!"

"A mere spectre!"

"Is she ill, or only famished?"

"Famished, I think. Hannah, is that milk? Give it me, and a piece of bread."

Diana (I knew her by the long curls which I saw drooping between me and the fire as she bent over me) broke some bread, dipped it in milk, and put it to my lips. Her face was near mine and I saw there was pity in it, I felt sympathy in her hurried breathing. In her simple words, too, the same balm-like emotion spoke. "Try to eat," she whispered.

"Yes—try," repeated Mary gently.

Mary's hand removed my sodden bonnet and lifted my head. I tasted what they offered me, feebly at first, but eagerly soon.

"Try if she can speak now," said St. John. "Ask her her name."

I felt I could speak and I answered, "My name is Jane Elliott."

"And where do you live? Where are your friends?"

I was silent.

"Can we send for any one you know?"

I shook my head.

"But what, then," said he. "Do you expect me to do for you?"

"Nothing," I replied.

All three were silent.

"Hannah," said Mr. St. John, at last, "let her sit there at present, and ask her no questions. In ten minutes more, give her the remainder of that milk and bread. Mary and Diana, let us go into the parlour and talk the matter over."

They withdrew, but very soon one of the ladies returned although I could not tell which. A kind of pleasant stupor was stealing over me as I sat by the genial fire. In an undertone she gave some directions to Hannah and ere long, with the servant's aid, I contrived to mount a staircase. My dripping clothes were removed; soon a warm, dry bed received me and I slept.

CHAPTER XXIX

The more I knew of the inmates of Moor House, the better I liked them. In a few days I had so far recovered my health that I could sit up all day and walk out sometimes. I could join with Diana and Mary in all their occupations, converse with them as much as they wished and aid them when and where they would allow me.

I liked to read what they liked to read. What they enjoyed, delighted me and what they approved, I reverenced. They were both more accomplished and better read than I was, but with eagerness I followed in the path of knowledge they had trodden before me and as they saw I had learned skills, they no longer thought me a beggar-woman. I devoured the books they lent me and it was with full satisfaction that I discussed with them in the evening what I had perused during the day.

If in our trio there was a superior and a leader, it was Diana. Physically she far excelled me: she was handsome and vigorous. In an evening I was fain to sit on a stool at her feet, to rest my head on her knee and listen alternately to her and Mary, while they sounded thoroughly on a topic. Diana offered to teach me German, which I readily accepted, and Mary helped also with her kind, gentle manner.

As to Mr. St John, the intimacy which had arisen so naturally and rapidly between me and his sisters did not extend to him. One reason of the distance yet observed between us was that he was comparatively seldom at home since a large proportion of his time appeared devoted to visiting the sick and poor among the scattered population of his parish. No weather seemed to hinder him in these pastoral excursions: rain or fair, he would go out on his mission of love and duty.

But besides his frequent absences, there was another barrier to friendship with him: he seemed of a reserved, an abstracted, and even of a brooding nature. Zealous in his ministerial labours and blameless in his life and habits, he yet did not appear to enjoy that mental serenity which should be the reward of every sincere Christian and practical philanthropist. Incommunicative as he was, some time elapsed before I had an opportunity of gauging his mind. I first got an idea of its calibre when I heard him preach in his own church at Morton. I wish I could describe that sermon, but it is past my power. I cannot even render faithfully the effect it produced on me, but he was bitter, frustrated, and troubled. It was not the speech of a calm spirit.

Meantime, a month was gone. Diana and Mary were soon to leave Moor House, and return to the far different life and scene which awaited them as governesses in a large, fashionable, south-of-England city, where each held a situation in families by whose wealthy and haughty members they were regarded only as humble dependants. It became urgent that I too should have a vocation of some kind again, though I had told no one of my past life at Thornfield Hall and when asked, had merely replied that I did not remember. They all supposed that I had fallen somewhere on the moor and lost my memory and at first, had asked around to discover a family that may be missing me, but none came forward. In the end, they stopped asking me if I remembered from where I was borne and instead accepted me for what I was.

One morning, being left alone with St. John a few minutes in the parlour, I approached his desk, hoping to ask a favor of him.

"You have a question to ask of me?" he said before I could speak.

"Yes, I wish to know whether you have heard of any service I can offer myself to undertake?"

"Indeed, I found or devised something for you. I did not want to cast you out of this house onto the moor once again and since we still do not know from whence you came, I took the liberty of securing a place for you to go."

I waited a few moments, expecting he would go on with the subject first broached, but he seemed to have entered another train of reflection. His look denoted abstraction from me and my business. I was obliged to recall him to a theme which was of necessity one of close and anxious interest to me.

"What is the employment you had in view, Mr. Rivers?"

"Let me frankly tell you, I have nothing eligible or profitable to suggest. Since I am myself poor and obscure, I can offer you but a service of poverty and obscurity. You may even think it degrading—for I see now your habits have been what the world calls refined; your tastes lean to the ideal and your society has at least been amongst the educated."

He looked at me before he proceeded and he seemed leisurely to read my face, as if its features and lines were characters on a page. The conclusions drawn from this scrutiny he partially expressed in his succeeding observations.

"I believe you will accept the post I offer you," said he, "and hold it for a while, but not permanently, for I think you shall eventually depart from whence you came."

"Do explain," I urged, when he halted once more.

"I shall not stay long at Morton now that my father is dead. I shall leave the place probably in the course of a twelve-month, but while I do stay, I will exert myself to the utmost for its improvement. Morton, when I came to it two years ago, had no school and the children of the poor were excluded from every hope of progress. I established one for boys and I mean now to open a second school for girls. I have hired a building for the purpose with a cottage of two rooms attached to it for the mistress's house. Her salary will be thirty pounds a year and her house is already furnished very simply, but sufficiently. Will you be this mistress?"

In truth it was humble, but then it was sheltered and I wanted a safe asylum. It was plodding, but then compared with that of a governess in a rich house, it was independent. It was not unworthy, not mentally degrading and I made my decision.

"I thank you for the proposal, Mr. Rivers, and I accept it with all my heart."

"But you comprehend me?" he said. "It is a village school and your scholars will be only poor girls—cottagers' children and at the best, farmers' daughters. Knitting, sewing, reading, writing, ciphering, will be all you will have to teach. What will you do with your accomplishments?"

"Save them till they are wanted. They will keep."

I now smiled; not a bitter or a sad smile, but one well pleased and deeply gratified.

"And when will you commence the exercise of your function?" he asked.

"I will go to my house to-morrow, and open the school, if you like, next week."

"Very well, so be it."

He rose and walked through the room. He still puzzled me.

Diana and Mary Rivers became more sad and silent as the day approached for leaving their brother and their home. They both tried to appear as usual, but the sorrow they had to struggle against was one that could not be entirely conquered or concealed.

One evening we were sitting in the kitchen, sewing when St. John entered abruptly.

"Our uncle John is dead," said he.

Both the sisters seemed struck, but not shocked or appalled.

"Dead?" repeated Diana.

"Yes."

She riveted a searching gaze on her brother's face. "And what then?" she demanded, in a low voice.

He threw a letter into her lap and she glanced over it before handing it to Mary. Mary perused it in silence and returned it to her brother. All three looked at each other and all three smiled—a dreary, pensive smile enough.

"Amen! We can yet live," said Diana at last.

"At any rate, it makes us no worse off than we were before," remarked Mary.

For some minutes no one spoke. Diana then turned to me.

"Jane, you will wonder at us and our mysteries," she said, "and think us hard-hearted beings not to be more moved at the death of so near a relation as an uncle, but we have never seen him or known him. He was my mother's brother and my father and he quarrelled long ago. It was by his advice that my father risked most of his property in the speculation that ruined him. Mutual recrimination passed between them, they parted in anger and were never reconciled. My uncle engaged afterwards in more prosperous undertakings and it appears he realised a fortune of twenty thousand pounds. He was never married, and had no near kindred but ourselves and one other person not more closely related than we. My father always cherished the idea that he would atone for his error by leaving his possessions to us and that letter informs us that he has bequeathed every penny to the other relation with the exception of thirty guineas which is to be divided between St. John, Diana, and Mary Rivers, for the purchase of three mourning rings. He had a right, of course, to do as he pleased and yet a momentary damp is cast on the spirits by the receipt of such news. Mary and I would have esteemed ourselves rich with a thousand pounds each, and to St. John such a sum would have been valuable, for the good it would have enabled him to do."

This explanation given, the subject was dropped, and no further reference made to it by either Mr. Rivers or his sisters. The next day, I left Marsh End for Morton. The day after, Diana and Mary quitted it for distant B-. In a week, Mr. Rivers and Hannah repaired to the parsonage and so the old grange was abandoned.

CHAPTER XXX

My new home then was a cottage; a little room with whitewashed walls and a sanded floor containing four painted chairs and a table, a clock, and a cupboard. Above, there was a chamber of the same dimensions as the kitchen with a deal bedstead and chest of drawers. I settled in there immediately and was pleased to have a place, however small, to call my own. I soon too settled into my new life and position as a teacher at the school. I grew to love my students and I believe they were fond of me also.

One evening, after dismissing the little orphan who served me as a handmaid, I sat alone on the hearth. As was usual, my thoughts wandered painfully to Mr. Rochester.

You may have supposed, Reader, that since I have not mentioned him, I did not think of my lover, but in truth, he was with me every moment of every day. I tried hard as I might to push him from my mind, but he sprang back to it more often than not, his dark, beautiful eyes searing into my heart. I wept every night, remembering his hot, feverish hands over me, remembering the pleasure of having him inside me and the comfort that I received in his arms. I could not bear to wonder what had become of him and I spent many a sleepless night tossing and turning in my bed, disturbed by dreams of a lover I could not touch. He was lost to me and I did not know if I would ever be whole again.

In the meantime, I continued the labours of the village-school as actively and faithfully as I could. It was truly hard work at first and some time elapsed before, with all my efforts, I could comprehend my scholars and their nature. The rapidity of their progress, in some instances, was even surprising and an honest and happy pride I took in it.

I felt I became a favourite in the neighbourhood. Whenever I went out, I heard on all sides cordial salutations and was welcomed with friendly smiles. Time began to pass me by and although my sufferings and heart never healed, I relaxed into routine. I liked my little cottage and the solitude it allowed me.

One snowy night in November, Mr. St. John came to visit as he was wont to do. I had just closed my shutter, laid a mat to the door to prevent the snow from blowing in under it and was sitting by the hearth listening to the muffled fury of the tempest, when he came in out of the frozen hurricane—the howling darkness—and stood before me. I was almost in consternation, so little had I expected any guest from the blocked-up vale that night.

"Any ill news?" I demanded. "Has anything happened?"

"No. How very easily alarmed you are!" he answered, removing his cloak and hanging it up against the door, towards which he again coolly pushed the mat which his entrance had deranged. He stamped the snow from his boots.

"But why are you come?" I could not forbear saying.

He sat down. I had never seen that handsome-featured face of his look more like chiselled marble than it did just now, as he put aside his snow-wet hair from his forehead and let the firelight shine free on his pale brow and cheek. I waited, but his hand was now at his chin, his finger on his lip and he was thinking deeply.

I was about to give up hope of his speaking when he said, "I have a story to tell."

I was puzzled but I said, "Then I should like to hear it."

"Twenty years ago, a poor curate fell in love with a rich man's daughter and they married against the advice of all her friends, who consequently disowned her immediately after the wedding. Before two years passed, the rash pair were both dead and laid quietly side by side under one slab. They left a daughter, a friendless thing, which was sent to the house of its rich maternal relations and reared by an aunt-in-law, called Mrs. Reed of Gateshead."

I gasped slightly, but tried to control myself.

"You start—did you hear a noise?" said St. John. "I daresay it is only a rat scrambling along the rafters of the adjoining schoolroom. To proceed, Mrs. Reed kept the orphan ten years, but at the end of that time she transferred it to a place called Lowood School. I remember you telling Diana once that you believe you went there yourself, although you said your memory was uncertain. Well it seems her career there was very honourable since from a pupil she became a teacher like yourself—it really it strikes me there are parallel points in her history and yours—and she left it to be a governess. She undertook the education of the ward of a certain Mr. Rochester."

"Mr. Rivers!" I interrupted.

"I can guess your feelings," he said, "but restrain them for a while for I have nearly finished. Of Mr. Rochester's character I know nothing, but the one fact that he professed to offer honourable marriage to this young girl and that at the very altar she discovered he had a wife yet alive, though a lunatic. The next day, the governess, it was discovered, had gone. No one could tell when, where, or how. She had left Thornfield Hall in the night and every research after her course had been vain. Yet that she should be found has become a matter of serious urgency and advertisements have been put in all the papers. I myself have received a letter from one Mr. Briggs, a solicitor, communicating the details I have just imparted. Is it not an odd tale?"

"Just tell me this," said I. "Since you know so much, you

surely can tell it me what of Mr. Rochester? How and where is he? What is he doing? Is he well?"

"I am ignorant of all concerning Mr. Rochester. You should rather ask the name of the governess and the nature of the event which requires her appearance."

"Did no one go to Thornfield Hall, then? Did no one see Mr. Rochester?"

"I suppose not."

"But they wrote to him?"

"Of course."

"And what did he say? Who has his letters?"

"Mr. Briggs intimates that the answer to his application was not from Mr. Rochester, but from a lady, it is signed 'Alice Fairfax.'"

I felt cold and dismayed for my worst fears then were probably true—he had in all probability left England and rushed in reckless desperation to some former haunt on the Continent. And what opiate for his severe sufferings had he sought there? I dared not answer the question. Oh, my poor master.

"He must have been a bad man," observed Mr. Rivers.

"You don't know him—don't pronounce an opinion upon him," I said, with warmth.

"Very well," he answered quietly. "Since you won't ask the governess's name, I must tell it of my own accord. Briggs wrote to me of a Jane Eyre and the advertisements demanded a Jane Eyre. I knew a Jane Elliott and I confess I had my suspicions, but it was only yesterday afternoon they were at once resolved into certainty. You own the name and renounce the alias?"

"Yes, yes, but where is Mr. Briggs? He perhaps knows more of Mr. Rochester than you do."

"Briggs is in London. I should doubt his knowing anything at all about Mr. Rochester for it is not in Mr. Rochester he is interested. Meantime, you forget essential points in pursuing trifles—you do not inquire why Mr. Briggs sought after you and what he wanted with you."

"Well, what did he want?"

"Merely to tell you that your uncle, Mr. Eyre of Madeira, is dead and that he has left you all his property. You are now rich."

"I! Rich?"

"Yes, you. Rich and quite an heiress."

Silence succeeded and I thought this over, my heart racing. I was neither overjoyed nor sad. I was merely shocked.

"You unbend your forehead at last," said Mr. Rivers. "Perhaps now you will ask how much you are worth?"

"How much am I worth?"

"Twenty thousand pounds."

Here was a new stunner for I had been calculating on four or five thousand. This news actually took my breath for a moment and Mr. St. John, whom I had never heard laugh before, laughed now.

"It is a large sum—don't you think there is a mistake?"

"No mistake at all."

"Perhaps you have read the figures wrong, it may be two thousand!"

"It is written in letters, not figures, and it says twenty thousand."

I again felt rather like an individual of but average gastronomical powers sitting down to feast alone at a table spread with provisions for a hundred.

"It puzzles me to know why Mr. Briggs wrote to you about me," I said suddenly.

"Oh! I am a clergyman," he said, "and the clergy are often appealed to about odd matters."

"No, that does not satisfy me!" I exclaimed. There was something in his hasty and unexplanatory reply which, instead of allaying, piqued my curiosity more than ever.

He looked as though he held a secret and he said, "I would rather Diana or Mary informed you."

Of course this objection wrought my eagerness to a climax and gratified it must be. Without delay, I told him so.

He was silent for a moment before saying, "Your name is Jane Eyre?"

"Of course, that was all settled before."

"You are not, perhaps, aware that I am your namesake? That I was christened St. John Eyre Rivers?"

"No, indeed! But what then? Surely—"

I stopped for I could not trust myself to entertain, much less to express, the thought that rushed upon me. I knew by instinct how the matter stood before St. John had said another word, but I cannot expect the reader to have the same intuitive perception, so I must repeat his explanation.

"My mother's name was Eyre and she had two brothers—one a clergyman, who married Miss Jane Reed, of Gateshead and the other, John Eyre, Esq., merchant, late of Funchal, Madeira. Mr. Briggs, being Mr. Eyre's solicitor, wrote to us last August to inform us of our uncle's death and to say that he had left his property to his brother the clergyman's orphan daughter, overlooking us in consequence of a quarrel never forgiven between him and my father. He wrote again a few weeks since to intimate that the heiress was lost and asking if we knew anything of her. A name casually written on a slip of paper has enabled me to find her out. You know the rest."

"Your mother was my father's sister?" I gasped.

"Yes."

"You three, then, are my cousins; half our blood on each side flows from the same source?"

"We are cousins; yes."

I surveyed him. It seemed I had found a family and one I could be proud of. The two girls, who I had watched through the latticed window of Moor House kitchen, were my near kinswomen, and the young and stately gentleman who had found me almost dying at his threshold was my blood relation. Glorious discovery to a lonely wretch! This was wealth indeed! This was a blessing, bright, vivid, and exhilarating. I now clapped my hands in sudden joy and my pulse bounded, my veins thrilled.

"Oh, I am glad! I am glad!" I exclaimed.

St. John smiled. "You were serious when I told you you had got a fortune; and now, for a matter of no moment, you are excited."

"What can you mean? It may be of no moment to you for you have sisters and don't care for a cousin, but I had nobody and now three relations. I say again, I am glad!"

I paced across my little room, a plan forming in my mind.

"Jane, are you all well?" asked St. John, looking concerned.

"I wish to divide my fortune," I said suddenly. "Twenty thousand pounds between the nephew and three nieces of our uncle will give five thousand to each."

"We cannot accept—"

"It would please and benefit me to have five thousand pounds but it would torment and oppress me to have twenty thousand, which could never be mine in justice, though it might in law. Let there be no opposition and no discussion about it, let us agree amongst each other, and decide the point at once."

"This is acting on first impulses; you must take days to consider such a matter."

"You cannot at all imagine the craving I have for fraternal and sisterly love," I cried. "I never had a home, I never had brothers or sisters and I must and will have them now."

"Jane, I will be your brother and my sisters will be your sisters without stipulating for this sacrifice of your just rights."

"Accept it, I beg of you! Nothing would please me more and it is yours to do with what you wish."

St. John looked as though he was battling inwardly with himself. "I will come and speak to you tomorrow, when the news is not so fresh to you."

"My answer will be no more."

He smiled. "What of the school, Miss Eyre? It must now be shut up, I suppose?"

"No. I will retain my post of mistress till you get a substitute."

He smiled again and we shook hands before he took leave.

I need not narrate in detail the further struggles I had, and arguments I used, to get matters regarding the legacy settled as I wished. My task was a very hard one, but as I was absolutely resolved and as my cousins saw at length that my mind was really and immutably fixed, they finally yielded to my wishes. The instruments of transfer were eventually drawn out and St. John, Diana, Mary, and I each became possessed of a competency.

CHAPTER XXXI

It was near Christmas by the time all was settled and the season of general holiday approached. I now closed Morton school and gave my lessons for the last time. I was sad to leave it and my cottage, but happy to retire again to Moor House and live there with my family.

Sweet was the evening that I was reunited with Diana and Mary. We were full of exhilaration and wildly joyful to be together again. I felt something akin to happiness and a little of my dark past that had been clutching at me since I left Thornfield, faded. Thus our lives became a pleasant routine of reading and learning together; sharing our knowledge and delighting in each other's company. St. John, of course, did not join in with this comfort, there was something cold and hard about his character that I had always noticed, but he appeared content all the same.

Perhaps you think I forgot Mr. Rochester, Reader, amidst these changes of place and fortune. Not for a moment. I still thought of him every night before I slept and every moment of the day that was not filled with another pastime. In the course of my necessary correspondence with Mr. Briggs about the will, I had inquired if he knew anything of Mr. Rochester's present residence and state of health; but he was quite ignorant of all concerning him. I then wrote to Mrs. Fairfax, entreating information on the subject. I had calculated with certainty on this step answering my end, but I was astonished when a fortnight passed without reply. Two months wore away, and day after day the post arrived and brought nothing for me. I fell a prey to the keenest anxiety.

I wrote again since there was a chance of my first letter having missed. Renewed hope followed renewed effort and it shone like the former for some weeks. But not a line, not a word reached me. When half a year wasted in vain expectancy, my hope died out, and I felt dark indeed.

One evening at bedtime, St. John's sisters and I stood round him bidding him good-night and he kissed each of them, as was his custom. Diana, who chanced to be in a frolicsome humour, exclaimed, "St. John! You call Jane your third sister, but you don't treat her as such—you should kiss her too."

She pushed me towards him and for the first time, I was angry with her. While I was thus thinking and feeling, St. John bent his head, brought his handsome face level with mine, and kissed me. There are no such things as marble kisses or ice kisses, but there may be experiment kisses and his was an experiment kiss. When given, he viewed me to learn the result and I am sure I did not blush; perhaps I might have turned a little pale. He never did it again.

Springtime came and went and then summer approached. One day I happened to be alone in the parlor with St. John when he surprised me by saying, "Jane, you shall take a walk with me."

"I will call Diana and Mary."

"No, I want only one companion this morning, and that must be you. Put on your things, go out by the kitchen-door and take the road towards the head of Marsh Glen. I will join you in a moment."

I was struck by his harsh directions, but I obeyed and in ten minutes I was treading the wild track of the glen, side by side with him.

"Let us rest here," said St. John, as we reached the first stragglers of a battalion of rocks.

We were completely alone on the moor and all around us was silence. We sat and stared at the wild, reckless landscape.

"Jane, I go in six weeks," he said suddenly. "I have taken my berth in an East Indiaman which sails on the 20th of June. There I hope to bring God to the masses."

I was not surprised, I had expected he would do as much.

"I am sure you will be successful," I said.

"Jane, I believe God intended you for a missionary's wife."

I was struck cold and I looked at him in shock. Did he mean me to be his wife? I knew it was so by his expression and I recoiled from the idea. It was not that St. John was repulsive, for he was indeed very handsome, but he was also cold and hard and I had forever pledged my heart to another. I could not marry anyone else.

"I regard you as a brother," I said levelly, knowing that he did not love for me or care for me as a husband and wife should do. "So let us continue."

"I seek a wife."

I shuddered as he spoke and I felt his influence in my marrow. He seemed resolute in this and I knew that he was not one to be denied but deny him I must.

"Seek one elsewhere than in me, St. John, seek one fitted to you."

"You would be perfect, Jane. You possess all of the qualities that I am looking for. It would be wrong for you to turn me down. Besides, what life awaits you here? Come to India with me and put your talents to good use."

"St. John!" I exclaimed.

"Well?" he answered icily.

"I freely consent to go with you as your fellow-missionary to India for I should like to see more of the world and there is nothing for me here as you have rightly said, but I cannot go as your wife. I cannot marry you and become part of you."

"A part of me you must become," he answered steadily, "otherwise the whole bargain is void. How can I, a man not yet thirty, take out with me to India a girl of nineteen unless she be married to me? How can we be for ever together—sometimes in solitudes, sometimes amidst savage tribes—and unwed?"

"But I am your sister."

"Not in the eyes of others! You must marry me!"

"I cannot and I will not. I will never, St. John. You are wasting your time attempting to reason with me. I will not marry you."

And with that answer he left me; he stormed back across the moor, evidently furious.

CHAPTER XXXII

St. John and I were wary of each other in the weeks leading to his departure. We ensured we were never alone together and always in the bright, chatter of Diana and Mary so that they might see that nothing was amiss. The night before he left home, happening to see him walking in the garden about sunset, I was moved to make a last attempt to regain the friendship of this man who had once saved me. I went out and approached him as he stood leaning over the little gate.

"St. John, I am unhappy because you are still angry with me. Let us be friends."

"I hope we are friends," was the unmoved reply.

"No, St. John, we are not friends as we were. You know that."

"Are we not? That is wrong. For my part, I wish you no ill and all good."

"I believe you, St. John, for I am sure you are incapable of wishing any one ill; but, as I am your kinswoman, I should desire somewhat more of affection than that sort of general philanthropy you extend to mere strangers."

"Of course," he said. "Your wish is reasonable, and I am far from regarding you as a stranger. I have given you ample time to think, do you say again that you will not come to India with me?"

"Not as your wife."

He sighed. "I know where your heart turns and to what it clings. The interest you cherish is lawless and unconsecrated. Long since you ought to have crushed it and now you should blush to allude to it. You think of Mr. Rochester?"

It was true. I confessed it by silence.

"Are you going to seek Mr. Rochester?"

"I must find out what is become of him."

"It remains for me, then," he said, "to remember you in my prayers, and to entreat God for you, in all earnestness, that you may not indeed become a castaway."

He opened the gate, passed through it and strayed away down the glen, soon out of sight.

On re-entering the parlour, I found Diana standing at the window, looking very thoughtful. Diana was a great deal taller than I and she put her hand on my shoulder, stooping to examine my face.

"Jane," she said, "you are always agitated and pale now. I am sure there is something the matter."

She paused but I did not speak.

"That brother of mine cherishes peculiar views of some sort respecting you," she carried on. "I am sure he has long distinguished you by a notice and interest he never showed to any one else. I wish he loved you—does he, Jane?"

"No, not one whit."

"Then why does he follow you so with his eyes, and get you so frequently alone with him, and keep you so continually at his side? Mary and I had both concluded he wished you to marry him."

"He does—he has asked me to be his wife."

Diana clapped her hands. "That is just what we hoped and thought! And you will marry him, Jane, won't you? And then he will stay in England and give up this notion of India."

"Far from that. His sole idea in proposing to me is to procure a fitting fellow-labourer in his Indian toils."

"What! He wishes you to go to India?"

"Yes."

"Madness!" she exclaimed. "You never shall go! You have not consented, have you, Jane?"

"I have refused to marry him—"

"And have consequently displeased him?" she suggested.

"Deeply and he will never forgive me, yet I offered to accompany him as his sister."

"It was frantic folly to do so, Jane. Think of the task you undertook—one of incessant fatigue, where fatigue kills even the strong, and you are weak. St. John—you know him—would urge you to impossibilities: with him there would be no permission to rest during the hot hours; and unfortunately, I have noticed, whatever he exacts, you force yourself to perform. I am astonished you found courage to refuse his hand. You do not love him then, Jane?"

"Not as a husband."

"Yet he is a handsome fellow."

"And I am so plain, you see. We should never suit."

"Plain! You? Not at all. You are much too pretty as well as too good to be grilled alive in Calcutta." And again she earnestly conjured me to give up all thoughts of going out with her brother.

"I must indeed," I said, "for when just now I repeated the offer of serving him for a deacon, he expressed himself shocked at my want of decency. He seemed to think I had committed an impropriety in proposing to accompany him unmarried, as if I had not from the first hoped to find in him a brother, and habitually regarded him as such."

"What makes you say he does not love you, Jane?"

"You should hear himself on the subject. He has again and again explained that it is not himself, but his office he wishes to mate. He has told me I am formed for labour, not for love, which is true, no doubt. But in my opinion, if I am not formed for love, it follows that I am not formed for marriage. Would it not be strange to be chained for life to a man who regarded one but as a useful tool?"

"Insupportable! Unnatural! Out of the question!"

"He is a good and a great man; but he forgets, pitilessly, the feelings and claims of little people, in pursuing his own large views. It is better, therefore, for the insignificant to keep out of his way, lest in his progress he should trample them down. Here he comes! I will leave you, Diana."

And I hastened upstairs as I saw him entering the garden.

"Jane! Jane! Jane!"

The cry awoke me in the middle of the night and I sat up in bed.

"O God! what is it?" I gasped.

I might have said, "Where is it?" for it did not seem in the room—nor in the house—nor in the garden. It did not come out of the air—nor from under the earth—nor from overhead. It was the voice of a human being; a known, loved, well-remembered voice—that of Edward Fairfax Rochester, and it spoke in pain and woe, wildly, eerily, urgently.

"I am coming!" I cried to my empty room. "Wait for me! Oh, I will come!"

Silence answered me.

I did not sleep again but lay in my bed for the rest of the night unscared and enlightened—waiting for the daylight.

CHAPTER XXXIII

The daylight came and I rose at dawn. I busied myself for an hour or two with arranging my things in my chamber, putting my drawers and wardrobe in the order wherein I should wish to leave them during a brief absence. Meantime, I heard St. John quit his room. He stopped at my door and I feared he would knock for today he was also leaving, but he walked on.

It was the first of June; yet the morning was overcast and chilly and rain beat fast on my casement. I heard the front-door open, and St. John pass out. Looking through the window, I saw him traverse the garden. He took the way over the misty moors in the direction of Whitcross where he would meet the coach.

"In a few more hours I shall succeed you in that track, cousin," thought I. "I too have a coach to meet at Whitcross."

It wanted yet two hours of breakfast-time. I filled the interval in walking softly about my room and pondering the visitation which had given my plans their present bent. I recalled the voice I had heard; again I questioned whence it came as vainly as before and it seemed in me—not in the external world. I asked was it a mere nervous impression—a delusion? I could not conceive or believe for it was more like an inspiration.

At breakfast I announced to Diana and Mary that I was going on a journey and should be absent at least four days.

"Alone, Jane?" they asked.

I answered yes, I was going to see or hear news of a friend about whom I had for some time been uneasy. They might have said, as I have no doubt they thought, that they had believed me to be without any friends save them for I had often said so, but with their true natural delicacy, they abstained from comment.

I left Moor House at three o'clock and soon after four, I stood at the foot of the sign-post of Whitcross, awaiting the arrival of the coach which was to take me to distant Thornfield. Amidst the silence of those solitary roads and desert hills, I heard it approach from a great distance. It was the same vehicle whence, a year ago, I had alighted one summer evening on this very spot. It stopped as I beckoned and I entered. Once more on the road to Thornfield, I felt like a messenger-pigeon flying home.

It was a journey of six-and-thirty hours. I had set out from Whitcross on a Tuesday afternoon, and early on the succeeding Thursday morning the coach stopped to water the horses at a wayside inn, situated in the midst of scenery whose green hedges and large fields and low pastoral hills met my eye like the lineaments of a once familiar face. Yes, I knew the character of this landscape: I was sure we were near my bourne.

"How far is Thornfield Hall from here?" I asked of the ostler.

"Just two miles, ma'am, across the fields."

"My journey is closed," I thought to myself. I got out of the coach, gave a box I had into the ostler's charge to be kept till I called for it and paid my fare.

Then I began to walk across the very fields through which I had last fled from Thornfield. How fast I walked! How I ran sometimes! How I looked forward to catch the first view of the well-known woods! With what feelings I welcomed single trees I knew, and familiar glimpses of meadow and hill between them! I was aware that Mr. Rochester might not be at Thornfield—I told myself this rationally for he might well have returned to traveling about the Continent, but an inner sense told me that this was not so and I was desperate to see him.

At last I reached the orchard, turned its angle and assumed to look with timorous joy towards a stately house. Instead I saw a blackened ruin.

The lawn and grounds were trodden and waste—the portal yawned void. The front was, as I had once seen it in a dream, very fragile-looking, perforated with paneless windows: no roof, no battlements, no chimneys—all had crashed in.

And there was the silence of death about it: the solitude of a lonesome wild. No wonder that letters addressed to people here had never received an answer. The grim blackness of the stones told by what fate the Hall had fallen—by fire. But what story belonged to this disaster? What loss, besides mortar and marble and wood-work had followed upon it? Had life been wrecked as well as property? There was no one here to answer it.

In wandering round the shattered walls and through the devastated interior, I gathered evidence that the calamity was not of late occurrence. Winter snows, I thought, had drifted through that void arch, winter rains beaten in at those hollow casements; for amidst the drenched piles of rubbish, spring had cherished vegetation.

Saddened and distraught, I returned to the town and an inn to gather my wits.

"You know Thornfield Hall, of course?" I asked the inn keeper, a middle-aged man.

"Yes, ma'am, I lived there once."

"Did you?"

Not in my time, I thought, for you are a stranger to me.

"I was the late Mr. Rochester's butler," he added.

The late! I seem to have received, with full force, the blow I had been trying to evade.

"The late!" I gasped. "Is he dead?"

"I mean the present gentleman, Mr. Edward's father," he explained.

I breathed again and my blood resumed its flow.

"Is Mr. Rochester living at Thornfield Hall now?" I asked, knowing, of course, what the answer would be, but yet desirous of deferring the direct question as to where he really was.

"No, ma'am—oh, no! No one is living there. I suppose you are a stranger in these parts or you would have heard what happened last autumn. Thornfield Hall is quite a ruin and it was burnt down just about harvest-time. A dreadful calamity! Such an immense quantity of valuable property destroyed and hardly any of the furniture could be saved. The fire broke out at dead of night and before the engines arrived from Millcote, the building was one mass of flame. It was a terrible spectacle, I witnessed it myself."

"Was it known how it originated?" I demanded.

He began speaking low, "There was a lady—a lunatic kept in the house and when all occupants were fast asleep, she set fire to the place. She was Mr. Rochester's mad wife would you believe? He had been hiding her in the attic ere long! Alas, he woke that night to the smell of fire and saved all of the servants before returning to get his mad wife out of her cell. But she was on the roof, standing and waving her arms above the battlements. Mr. Rochester tried to call her, but she yelled, gave a spring and the next minute she lay smashed on the pavement!"

"Dead?"

"Dead! Ay, dead as the stones on which her brains and blood were scattered."

He shuddered.

"And afterwards?" I urged.

"Well, ma'am, afterwards the house was burnt to the ground."

"Were any other lives lost?"

"No, but perhaps it would have been better if there had."

"What do you mean?"

"Poor Mr. Edward!" he ejaculated, "He is stone-blind."

I had dreaded worse. I had dreaded he was mad. I summoned strength to ask what had caused this calamity.

"It was all his own courage: he wouldn't leave the house till every one else was out. As he came down the great staircase at last, after Mrs. Rochester had flung herself from the battlements, there was a great crash and all fell. He was taken out from under the ruins alive but one eye was knocked out and one hand so crushed that Mr. Carter, the surgeon, had to amputate it directly. The other eye inflamed and he lost the sight of that also. He is now helpless—blind and a cripple."

"Where is he? Where does he now live?"

"At Ferndean, a manor-house on a farm he has, about thirty miles off."

"Who is with him?"

"Old John and his wife: he would have none else. He is quite broken down, they say."

"Have you any sort of conveyance?"

"We have a chaise, ma'am, a very handsome chaise."

"Let it be got ready instantly, I'll pay you twice the hire you usually demand."

CHAPTER XXXIV

The manor-house of Ferndean was a building of considerable antiquity, moderate size, and no architectural preten-
sions, deep buried in a wood. To this house I came just ere dark
on an evening marked by the characteristics of a sad sky. The
last mile I performed on foot, having dismissed the chaise and
driver and I hurried as fast as I could.

As I approached it, I heard a movement—the narrow
front-door opened slowly and a figure came out. It was my
master, Edward Fairfax Rochester.

I held my breath and stood watching him. His form was
of the same strong and stalwart contour as ever, his hair was
still raven black, his features were not altered or sunk, but
in his countenance I saw a change. It reminded me of some
wronged and fettered wild beast or bird, dangerous to approach in his sullen woe.

He descended the one step and advanced slowly and gro-
pingly towards the grass-plat.

At this moment, John approached him from some quarter. "Will you take my arm, sir?" he said. "There is a heavy
shower coming on, has you not better go in?"

"Let me alone," was the answer.

John withdrew without having observed me and
Mr. Rochester now groped his way back to the house too
and closed the door.

I now drew near and knocked. John's wife opened for me
and she started as if she had seen a ghost.

"Mary," I said. "How are you?"

"Is it really you, miss, come at this late hour to this lonely place?"

I answered by taking her hand and then I followed her into the kitchen, where John now sat by a good fire. I explained to them in few words that I had heard all which had happened since I left Thornfield, and that I was come to see Mr. Rochester. Just as I had finished my tale, the parlour-bell rang.

"When you go in," I said to Mary, "tell your master that a person wishes to speak to him, but do not give my name."

"I don't think he will see you," she answered. "He refuses everybody."

When she returned, I inquired what he had said. "You are to send in your name and your business," she replied. She then proceeded to fill a glass with water, and place it on a tray, together with candles.

"Is that what he rang for?" I asked.

"Yes, he always has candles brought in at dark, though he is blind."

"Give the tray to me; I will carry it in."

I took it from her hand and she pointed me out the parlour door. The tray shook as I held it and the water spilt from the glass. My heart struck my ribs loud and fast. Mary opened the door for me and shut it behind me.

This parlour looked gloomy and a neglected handful of fire burnt low in the grate. Pilot lay nearby and pricked his ears when I came in. Then he jumped up with a yelp and a whine, and bounded towards me, almost knocking the tray from my hands. I set it on the table and then patted him, and said softly, "Lie down!"

Mr. Rochester turned mechanically to see what the commotion was, but as he saw nothing, he returned and sighed.

"Give me the water, Mary," he said.

I approached him with the now only half-filled glass, but

Pilot followed me, still excited.

"What is the matter?" he inquired.

"Down, Pilot!" I again said.

Mr. Rochester drank, and put the glass down. "This is you, Mary, is it not?" he asked tentatively.

"Mary is in the kitchen," I answered.

He put out his hand with a quick gesture, but not seeing where I stood, he did not touch me. "Who is this? Who is this?" he demanded. "Answer me!"

"Pilot knows me, and John and Mary know I am here. I came only this evening."

"What delusion has come over me? What sweet madness has seized me?"

He groped and I arrested his wandering hand, imprisoning it in both of mine.

"Her very fingers!" he cried. "Her small, slight fingers! If so there must be more of her."

The muscular hand broke from my custody and my arm was seized, then my shoulder, my neck, my waist, and I was gathered to him.

"Is it Jane? This is her shape—this is her size—"

"And this her voice," I added. "She is all here—her heart too."

"Jane Eyre! Jane Eyre," was all he said.

"I am Jane Eyre and I have found you out. I am come back to you."

I pressed my lips to his once brilliant and now ray-less eyes, and swept his hair from his brow, kissing that too. He suddenly seemed to arouse himself; the conviction of the reality of all this seized him.

"It is you—is it, Jane? You are come back to me then?"

"I am."

"And you do not lie dead in some ditch under some stream? And you are not a pining outcast amongst strangers?"

"No, sir! I am an independent woman now of fortune."

But he was too overcome to answer me. "My Jane," was all he uttered, touching every part of me that he could. "My Jane . . ."

"I am here and I shall never leave again."

"You would want to stay here?" he asked, his voice dripping in hope. "With a cripple—a disgusting, vile creature as this?"

"You are not disgusting and vile, sir. I shall show you."

I alighted from him and he would scarce have let me go, but I promised to come back. Quickly, I ushered Pilot out of the room and locked the door from the inside.

"I have dreamt of lying with you once more," I whispered, coming back to his open arms.

"Jane, you cannot mean it."

"I do. I love you and I always have."

I gently ran my finger down his cheek, along the edge of his sideburn to his dark, stubbly chin. Then I carried on—down his neck, tickling his chest.

"Hush," I whispered, ignoring his protests.

I began running the fingers of my other hand through his hair and heard him moan softly as a gentle wave of desire rolled through him. I too was experiencing the old sensation of thrills that I thought I would never feel again. Leaning forward, I lightly pressed my lips to his and felt him return my sweet kiss. A bank of yearning welled up inside me and over-flowed. I began to kiss him more fervently and forced my tongue between his teeth, tasting him. He was exactly as I remembered and I kissed him harder and harder, hungry for him.

In return, he kissed me back and ran his hand expertly over my body for he evidently remembered it well, cupping my breasts and stroking them over the fabric of my dress. I pulled off his jacket and tugged at his shirt.

"But, Jane—"

"I do not care," I interrupted feverishly. "I want you now."

"I want you too."

I tore off his shirt and saw that his chest was still broad, strong, and muscular as I remembered it. I saw not his missing, wounded arm or the scars. I saw only him. Then I pulled off his breeches and his other garments and gently guided him down to the rug before the burning embers of the fire.

"Jane," he breathed, as I kissed him again and again.

I let my hands glide up and down his body, relishing the feel of him. I took his erection within my grasp and teased and tugged it mischievously. He grunted and sighed in delight and, emboldened, I ran my tongue down the length of it before delicately sucking the tip.

Leaving him gasping for more, I stood and quickly unlaced my dress, throwing off my clothing with haste. Then I sat astride him and waited as his hand searched my whole body; stroking my thighs, my hips, my stomach, and my behind tenderly. He caressed each of my breasts and thumbed my nipples until they stood hard and erect.

Then I leant forward and whilst I kissed him lightly, I tilted my hips so that he was pushed inside me.

He grunted and writhed as I thrust, and throwing my head back, I moaned quietly. I angled him to the deepest, furthest point of pleasure inside of me and rode him harder and faster, harder and faster until my whole body was throbbing with hot, delicious indulgence.

"Oh, Jane," he panted and I knotted my fingers with his and pounded onto him.

I thrust once more and then melted into him as an intense thrill of ecstasy overtook my body and left me raw and gasping. I collapsed over him in a hazy daze of pleasure and he came inside me.

We both lay still, recovering from the release.

"Jane, you should have pulled off of me," he chided, stroking my hair as I laid my head on his chest.

"I suppose you will have to marry me now," I said with a grin.

"Would you marry me, Jane?"

"Of course."

"I would not sentence you to a life with this monster."

"You do not have a choice."

He curled his arm around me and held me tightly.

"I love you, Jane."

"I love you too."

And, Reader, I married him.

FIFTY SHADES OF DORIAN GRAY
Oscar Wilde and Nicole Audrey Spector

Night after night she awoke in a feverish sweat, her hips writhing on their own accord, the bed sheet balled in a coil and clenched between her legs. It was so . . . real. Like he'd really been there.

First published to sensational scandal amidst accusations that the novel was hedonist, unclean and depicted distorted views of morality, *The Picture of Dorian Gray* was a hit back in the day. In 1890, the *Daily Chronicle* wrote that Wilde's novel 'will taint every young mind that comes in contact with it.' Well, Victorian critics, gird your loins and prepare to meet Nicole Audrey Spector's *Fifty Shades of Dorian Gray*: hotter, lewder, sexier, steamier and more morally corrupt than Oscar Wilde's original story!

Rediscover this celebrated novel as it traces the moral degeneration of a beautiful young Londoner seduced by art and beauty into a cruel and reckless pursuer of pleasure. Meet artist Rosemary Hall and follow her inevitable downfall brought by her lust for the famous Dorian Gray – a tale both familiar and new in this brilliant erotic mash-up of one of the world's most beloved novels. With a mix of old fashioned Victorian debauchery and erotic 21st-century lust, this cleverly sexed-up classic will leave you wanting more!

It's a tale both familiar and new in this brilliant erotic mash-up of one of Oscar Wilde's most talked-about and cautionary tales: *Fifty Shades of Grey* meets *The Picture of Dorian Gray*.

978-0-7499-5943-2